light as a
FEATHER

By

CAMERON JAMES

	Alcohol, body shaming, eating disorder, starvation, vomiting, mental illness.

Published in 2021

A CIP catalogue record for this title is available from the British Library.

For Ellie

Stay Strong. Keep Fighting.
Stay Hydrated.

Chapter 1

"Off your phone prodigy." Frankie said from behind me, I just about managed to move my phone out of the way before he grabbed it. "We're going on." He added, so I looked up at him. "Tie your ribbons." He stated, I laughed lifting my foot onto the chair in front of me and tied my ribbons up my ankle,

"This is weird." I said as Max sat on the chair I'd just lowered my foot from. I lifted my other foot onto his knee, he smiled at me as he began to tie my shoe for me.

"I can imagine it is weird." He whispered, I hummed.

"This, *this* show was the first time I ever saw you. I hadn't even done ballet beforehand. This is mad." I stated, he nodded as he tapped my foot so I lowered it, then held his hands out to me, I stood and walked with him to the side of the stage.

"Nervous?" he whispered as we stood opposite Cory and Frankie.

"About this? No." I said, he laughed quietly.

"*No*, about your audition for the National Ballet School. *Tomorrow*." He stressed, I looked at him. "Don't act chill, it's the National Ballet School Jacob." He said, I smiled.

"Not the Royal Ballet." I said,

"Yet." He replied, "two years, then you'll be there Jacob, all because of National Ballet School."

"Great. Now I'm nervous." I said, he laughed hugging my shoulders, placing a kiss on the side of my head.

"Go get 'em kid." He said, I nodded taking a deep breath before following him onto the stage taking hold of Frankie's waiting hand. He smiled at me as Max held my other. I nodded to him, he squeezed my hand back then the curtain rose, and I could look around my old school hall.

The school hall that hadn't changed at all, but given that I only left two years ago it was unlikely the school would've changed too much. I squeezed Max's hand back as the music began. My solo within the compilation was *Dancing* by Kylie. I took over from Max, who winked at me as he left the stage.

I am stood on stage. The lights were not as bright as they could be, I could see every face that was looking back at me, each of them sat watching in silence. I wear my performance leotard, white with black shorts, which are accompanied by a *slightly* padded ballet belt, and on my feet are my black strong pointes, the ribbons of them not tied too perfectly around my ankles although the ones Max had tied were.. I *probably* needed to replace sometime in the near future, as they were beginning to look a bit worn.

I take my bow.

▾▾▾

"I got in." I said, as I reread the letter, two, three, four times. "Oh my god. I got in."

"You got in." Max repeated, then lifted me up as he hugged me, I laughed hugging him back but not dropping the letter.

"You got in? To the National Ballet School? You got in?" Cameron said, I nodded to him once Max put me down, then went in for another hug. "We knew you'd do it." Cameron said into my ear. "Congratulations." He added, "we should go out tonight. Have a celebratory meal?" he asked Max, he got a very happy nod back, I smiled at them both as I refolded my letter.

It had been one thousand, five hundred and twenty-one days since Max and Cameron had officially adopted me. Since the three of us had stood in that court room and had been overjoyed to hear the judge say that Max and Cameron now had full parental rights of me. Training for the National Ballet School started a year later, when I was almost sixteen, as I'd always been under Max's guidance when it came to ballet, he had always been my ballet teacher, and sometimes that came before everything else.

He had suggested the National Ballet School to me when we were sat in the studio after a lesson of pointe, he suggested if I wanted to be in the Royal Ballet by the time I was twenty it was where I needed to go, and I had accepted that.

Training began the next week. I went to school, then I went to the studio, every night after school. If Max was teaching I trained alone, or I taught alongside him, and if he wasn't, he danced alongside me. We spent hours, and hours in the studio, using Cameron's role on the West End as an excuse not to go home. Until of course, Cameron's contract came to an end and he requested his husband and son were home of a reasonable time to eat our evening meal. We didn't always make it home to eat, but it was always in the microwave to be reheated when we got home.

"A toast." Cameron said lifting up his glass of wine, Max copied, so I lifted up my coke. "To Jacob."

"For getting into The National Ballet School." Max said, his smile almost splitting his face in half. I laughed, looking down only slightly embarrassed as I could feel the pride radiating off him, it made me feel oddly warm but mostly embarrassed.

"I can't even gush enough to justify how I feel." Cameron said, I laughed as I looked up. "Look, we raised a ballet genius." He said, Max almost scoffed.

"I will not be satisfied until we've raised a Prima Ballerina." He said, then he winked at me, I laughed picking up my burger to start an attempt at eating it. "Have you told Connor?"

"Not yet, I think I'll go and see him tomorrow." I said nodding to the both of them, to confirm it, they both nodded back. "I'm sure he'll be pretty excited." I added smiling at my burger, they both laughed, then started a conversation between themselves, so I continued to eat my burger.

I went to visit Connor's garage the next day, after promising Max I'd be back in enough time for my individual session with him this afternoon. He'd given me a hug and smiled so wide that I left in a hurry so I wouldn't get embarrassed again.

Connor was under the hood of a car when I got to the garage. I'd taken a detour to get a frappe and was still sucking on the straw as I walked towards him. I sat on his workbench, crossing my knees and swinging my legs until he re-emerged from the hood of the car.

"Alright?" Connor asked as he pulled the rag off his shoulder and began to wipe his hands, I laughed as he turned to look at me.

"You knew I was here?"

"I always know when you're here." he replied I smiled at him as he came to me, I passed him my frappe, he took a sip from it. "So, why are you here?" he asked,

"I like to watch you being a rugged man, working hard on a car."

"Shut up." He said laughing, I smiled at him then lifted my hips so I could get my letter out of my back pocket. I waved it at him, he tried to grab it. I lifted it above his head. He still attempted to grab it, then he tickled me. I gasped lowering my arm instantly, he snatched it out of my hand, walking away from me as he began to unfold it. He turned to me from the other side of the car. "You got in."

"I got in." I said, he laughed running back to me, then picking me up off the work bench as he hugged me.

Connor and I have been friends since we were four, when we'd both been moved to the residential home we lived together in. Connor had always been a *massive* part of my life, and I'd promised him, when I had been adopted that he still would be, and I had kept it up.

Initially it had been easy, we were in the same class in school, so saw each other every day, but since we'd left two years ago, and Connor had gone into a mechanical apprenticeship and my life had begun to *completely* revolve around ballet, I ensured I saw him at least once a week.

In the end, when it had come to Connor's eighteenth birthday earlier this year he hadn't been adopted, he'd had two 'almosts', but not a lot of people liked to adopt teenagers, and once Connor had turned fifteen, he'd told me that he'd accepted that fact *and* figured he was probably not going to be adopted.

Instead, he began to focus on his life following leaving the house, and he had. Having gotten a job in the garage he'd been an apprentice at, and now happily lived in a flat that wasn't too far away. He still visited the home sometimes, he went back to see our social workers and I promised I'd go with him. Every single time I promised I'd go with him.

I still hadn't.

"How the hell do you plan on celebrating?" Connor asked as he put me back down on the floor, I laughed taking back the letter and reading it again myself.

"I don't know." I admitted, "Max and Cameron took me out for a meal last night, and Max is so proud he might burst." I said,

"I *am* so proud I might burst." Connor agreed, "I'm so happy for you, you wouldn't believe it." he said, "you need to tell Ste." He added, I looked at him. "You *need* to, he'd be over the *fucking* moon for you." He stated, I began to nod, because Ste, the man who was more like father to me for ten years of my life, than a social worker would be over the moon for me.

"There's a lot of people I need to tell." I said nodding, "Ste is one of them." I added before Connor could argue. "But I felt you needed to know first."

12

"We should do something." He said nodding then he frowned at him, "I have a date tonight, tomorrow?" he asked, I lay my hand on his chest.

"Excuse me, you have a date?" I asked, he began to nod. "With a real life boy?"

"With a real life boy." He repeated amused, "I'll let you know *all* the details when we meet up tomorrow to celebrate."

"I should think so." I said, he laughed as I grinned at him.

"Cutting it a bit fine." Cameron commented as I ran through the house, picking up the sandwich he'd made for me then straight back up to my bedroom to change into my leotard. I came back down the stairs as I pulled my t-shirt over my head.

"Connor wanted to congratulate me." I said as I leant on the kitchen door and ate the sandwich, Cameron turned his head to look at me. "We're meeting tomorrow to celebrate properly, but you know how old friends talk."

"You're far too young to have 'old' friends." Cameron replied amused, then threw the dish cloth he was drying his hands on over the back of the chair nearest to him. "I'll give you a lift to the studio." He said, I nodded to him, picking up my dance bag and stepping back to let him pass.

"You know as I'm now in big ballet school." I said as we got into the car, Cameron laughed but nodded all the same. "When can I learnt to drive?" I asked, Cameron smiled as he started the car,

"Max taught me how to drive." He said, I looked at him, "he's a good teacher. Weirdly." He said tilting his head at me, I smirked at him.

"No really, I wouldn't have thought." I replied,

"If you ask him, he might teach you to drive, but I don't know if you'd feel like he's *always* teaching you." He said,

"Well, it might make the transition from him no longer teaching me ballet easier?" I said, Cameron chewed on his bottom lip.

"You *know* he's so proud of you, so pleased for you?" he said, I nodded,

"I do, but I also know he's devastated." I said, Cameron smiled.

"Not quite devastated. Yes, he's sad that he will no longer be your teacher but he *knows* what opportunities this'll open up for you." He said then he smiled, "he truly believes you deserve this, and *I* truly believe you deserve this."

"I'm scared." I said, Cameron nodded as he parked outside of Max's studio. He put the handbrake on, then he took my hand.

"If you weren't scared I'd be worried Jacob." He said, I exhaled. "This is big, and it'll probably make the top five of big things that have happened in your life, so being scared is right."

"Right." I said, he nodded, then he winked at me.

"Go to your lesson. Enjoy it." he said, I nodded, smiling at him then getting out of his car. I let myself into the studio, smiling pleasantly at the receptionist as I walked past her, she smiled back as I made my way up to the studio.

The Grade Six class Max had taught before I arrived ran past me on the stairs, smiling at me and waving as I passed them. I didn't knock when I reached the studio, letting myself in and sitting under the nearest barre to put my pointes on. Max turned to me as I tied and tucked in my ribbons.

"Pointe then?" He asked, I nodded to him, so he nodded back coming to sit opposite me to put his own pointes on.

"Well, at School I will be doing mostly flat ballet pump, no?" I asked, he nodded in agreement as he tied his pointes. "So, I figure I will dance on pointe as much as I can, that way I don't get withdrawal."

"Fair." Max agreed, then he knocked the block of his shoe against mine. "You need new pointes." He said as he looked up at me, I nodded. "Especially if you'll be teaching my Saturday afternoon pointe class with me?"

"For real?" I asked, he smiled at me,

"For real." He replied, I fist pumped, making him laugh then he stood, reaching his hands out to me, so I stood with him. "Let's dance." He said, then stood central, I stood beside him, watching him as he searched through his watch until he chose a song, I began to laugh when it started.

"Oh we haven't danced to this in a while." I said, Max nodded to me, then raised onto his pointes as I did. I grinned at him in the mirror, making him laugh as we began to dance

"Are you ready?" Max asked as we approached the chorus, I nodded to him as I began to prepare. "Three,"

"Two." I said, then bit my lip so I wouldn't begin to laugh, as that would most certainly not help my pirouettes.

"One." Max said, he sounded amused then we began to turn, I got to four turns before I had to stop, Max laughed happily as he turned an extra two times then stopped with a flourish lifting his arms into the air, then he winked at me so I began to laugh, he soon did too, *but* we continued to dance not going a foot wrong as we laughed and taunted each other, it got worse as we approached the chorus again, going into the second pirouette section. I was laughing so hard I didn't get pass two turns; Max didn't pass three. I sat myself on the floor letting myself calm down, Max grinned at me as the music played out.

Chapter 2

I looked up shocked when I heard a knock on the doorframe, my eyes met Max's quickly as he leant in the doorway.

"It's half five Jacob?" He said, then he smiled at me. "You're never up this early. Even if I promise you can train." He added, I smiled then folded my legs on the seat, "what's up?" he asked as he crossed his jacket over his front, the zips not quite meeting as he folded his arms, then he came to sit opposite me.

"I don't know." I said, shaking my head. "I don't know." I whispered, he nudged his knee against mine under the table,

"Scared?" he asked, I nodded. "So am I." he said, I frowned at him. "I'm terrified. You're representing my teaching in this school, what if I'm crap?" He said, I laughed as he smiled at me. "You know, the night before I started in my boarding school. I didn't sleep." He said, I nodded to him, asking him to continue. "I was scared out of my wits. I was an eleven year old, who had always been the best in my class. I was so excited, don't get me wrong, it had been my lifelong dream. Which you know at eleven is a pretty huge deal, but I was scared because I thought what if I'm not as good as everyone else? What if everyone hates me, what if they fail me?"

"What if I don't like it?" I said, he nodded,

"Exactly. What if my dream is not all it's cracked up to be?" he said, I nodded.

"Was it?" I asked, he smiled at me.

"Hell yes." He replied, so I laughed. "I loved every second of school, and you know what I think you will too." He said, then he sighed. "I get it. I promise. I do but you love ballet Jacob. You always have, and I know that, *and* you know what, if you don't like your roommates, you can move back home. You don't have to board." He said, "and with you helping in Immediate Pointe, you'll come home Saturday afternoons, you can then stay, and we'll have our Sunday dinner."

"I like the sound of that." I said, he smiled at me as he stroked the back of my hand with his thumb. "I think I'm slightly nervous of the fact that it'd be like going back to the home." I said, then I bit my lip because I'd been thinking that for *weeks* but I hadn't wanted to say it, Max sighed.

"You're eighteen Jacob." He said, I nodded.

"I know, I know that means I'm off the social system, I know all this, but it might feel like it."

"Boarding was the best experience of my life, and I believe if you ask Cameron, he'll agree that boarding was

18

the best time of his life as well. It's normal to be scared, it's not worth doing it if it doesn't scare you." He said, I nodded, then looked at the doorway again as Cameron stood in it, he looked moderately confused.

"Why is everyone up so early?" he asked, Max laughed as he turned his head to look at Cameron.

"We're dancing."

"Ugh." Cameron moaned, "I'm going back to bed." He said, I laughed more as Max nodded and pulled his phone out of his pocket.

"We're not taking you until ten. Go back to bed, get some more sleep." He said nodding to me, I began to nod with him. "It'll be fine."

"It'll be fine." I repeated then I stood from the table, I walked around the table to the door, then went back, wrapping my arms around Max's shoulders, he laughed and rubbed my hands as I hugged him.

The drive to school really wasn't that long. My case had been packed for a number of days, it had been stood in the corner of my room, just there.

It wasn't too full, Max had pointed out with me returning on Saturday's I only really needed a week worth of clothes at a time, so I had packed all my dance wear and training gear and some clothes to wear out of hours. We'd packed every pair of flat ballet pump I had that still fit, and Max had taken me to Cory's shop to buy another pair, and a new leotard. Cory had given me them for free, as he was so proud of me for getting into the National Ballet School.

"Are you ready for this?" Max asked, as he parked up the car, I took a deep breath in, then I began to nod.

"Let's do this." I said,

"You heard him, let's do this." Cameron said, opening the passenger door. Max looked at me over his shoulder as Cameron got out of the car.

"You sure?"

"As sure as I can be right now." I said, then opened my own door. I saw Max smile at me as he also got out. I took my suitcase out of the boot, then walked in front of them towards the reception. The receptionist seemed happy as I stepped through the automatic doors, she seemed to prepare herself, poising her hands above the box with multiple folders in.

"Good morning. Welcome to your first year." She said her voice light and cheerful, I laughed softly as I walked closer to the reception desk. "Name please?" she asked, I swallowed.

"Jacob Kennedy." I replied, she nodded flicking through the folders until she smiled.

"Kennedy, Jacob. Fantastic." She said then lifted the folder out, she handed it to me then didn't let it go. "Inside is your code of conduct, your uniform, correct attire, and rules and regulations. Your room number is on the front and your key is inside. Any questions?" she asked, I shook my head then looked at Cameron and Max over my shoulder.

"I don't think so." I said, they both agreed.

"If you need anything just ask." She said happily then released the folder, I took it from her reading the little sticky note that had my name and room number on. I waited at the second set of automatic doors. Reaching in my folder for my key, I tapped it against the door and it opened.

I took a deep breath as Max and Cameron came to stand beside me. We walked together down the corridor and towards the number I had on my sticky note. The corridor looked almost bare, with royal red carpets and cream-coloured walls. I'd expected there to be more students with suitcases but the hallways were deserted. I couldn't quite work out if I was early, or if I was so late that everything had started without me.

"Relax." Max whispered squeezing my shoulder, I nodded to him then tapped my card against the door with my number on. I pushed it open then let out a deep breath.

It was a reasonably sized room, with two beds on the walls. The room itself was white, with light wooden floors. There was a cream-coloured shag rug in-between the two beds, and every piece of furniture was a light wooden colour.

"It's nice." Max said, Cameron scoffed.

"Nice. It's amazing. We had five beds stuffed into a room half the size of this." Cameron stated as he walked towards the window, he moved the light curtains to look out at the view.

"Cameron you sound a bit bitter, my love." Max said, I laughed as I sat on the bed closest to the window Cameron was looking out of.

"I will be bitter. I got to know every inch of those boys in those seven years." He said, turning to look at Max.

"I haven't heard you complain about that before." He teased, Cameron winked at him then began to laugh as Max did, then they both looked at me.

"Well?"

"I like it." I said nodding, "it'll do." I added amused, I watched as they smiled at each other.

"You call us if ever you need to, even if it's just to talk to us, yeah?" Cameron said, I nodded to him as I took another deep breath in.

"And of course. I'll see you Saturday."

"Of course." I agreed grinning at Max then I stood, I hugged Cameron first. I felt as it surprised him, but he hugged me back.

I was as tall as him now, *but* I'd been gaining on him since I was fifteen. He laughed into my ear as we hugged, it sounded slightly sad but I decided not to look at him, at risk of him making me cry. He squeezed me again then turned me by the shoulder, so I looked at Max. I saw him wiping his eyes as I turned, I pretended to ignore it.

"We got you something. As a home warming gift." He said then held a bag to me, it was a paper bag but big and square, I took it frowning at both of them. "I thought we'd get you something you need, and can use. Even if you can't use it in school." He said, so I took the box out of the bag, I stroked my hand over the top because I recognised the name, I lifted the lid off then covered my mouth as I smiled.

"Thank you." I said, then looked at Cameron and nodded, "thank you." I repeated then ran my finger down the black pointe shoes that sat in the box.

"Now, come here and give me a hug." Max said, I smiled putting the box back on my bed and walking towards Max, he cuddled me tight almost lifting me off the floor as he did. I didn't want to let him go. When he kissed my cheek, I let him go. I took a sharp intake of breath.

"Don't cry." Cameron said pointing at me, I laughed instead. "We're really not that far away. Not at all. Okay you need us; you call and we'll be here." Max said, I nodded then I smiled at them both.

"I know." I said, they smiled back at me.

"Now, we better go. Let you get settled in." Max said, I nodded because if I hugged them again, I most definitely was not letting them go.

"Have fun." Cameron said, "I'm sure you will." He added, I nodded to him almost laughing then I sat back on my bed stroking over the duvet as they left my bedroom.

My roommate appeared as I unpacked my case.

I was in the wardrobe when the door opened. I closed the wardrobe door over, as the boy that had walked in closed the bedroom door. We smiled at each other. He was cute, definitely cute. He was about my height, maybe a bit taller, with black hair, which was shaved at the side and curly on the top, he had brown eyes, and his face was covered in freckles. Apparently, I *liked* freckles. He had big button earrings in both ears, and simply wore a hoodie and jeans. I finished looking him up and down, when he finished looking me up and down. I awkwardly pulled my t-shirt closer to my jeans as his eyes travelled back up my body.

"Kian." He said letting go of his suitcase and holding his hand out to me, I smiled taking his hand.

"Jacob." I replied, he nodded then came further into the room.

"So, what's your story Jacob?" he asked as he lifted his suitcase onto the other bed, and he began to unpack.

"My story?" I asked, he nodded then waved his hand in a circular motion at me, "age, ballet history. You know."

"Oh I'm eighteen." I said, he nodded. "I've been doing ballet since I was fourteen." I added, only his head turned towards me. "My…" I said, "my ballet teacher adopted me." I said, he smiled.

"Cute." He said nodding,

"Yourself?"

"I am also eighteen." He said, then smirked at me. "Obviously." He added, I laughed as I continued to fill my wardrobe, "I've been doing ballet since I was about four. I

23

still don't know fully why I started, but I'm good at it, and well I guess I enjoy it." he said nodding, I nodded back to him. "Only four years ay?" he said, I nodded again but slower as I looked at him. "You must be a natural." He added then winked at me, I looked down then closed the wardrobe and opened the drawers.

Kian decided he wanted to have a shower once we were fully unpacked, so had opened the en-suite door and stated that I had to see it. It was worth it when I had, then he laughed and went in.

I decided to use the time to sew the ribbons onto the pointes Max had given me, so I sat on my bed, after sending a text to Cameron, Max and my group to tell them I was officially unpacked. I spent most of Kian's shower trying to thread the needle, he reappeared, his boxers on and drying his hair as I finished the first shoe. He ruffled his hair as he walked towards me, little droplets of water splattering against the mirror he walked past, then he frowned at me, I tilted my head back at him.

"Pointes?" he asked, I nodded as he sat on his bed. "Explanation, maybe?"

"I dance…" I said then waved my hand towards the pointes. "On pointe." I added, he smirked at me so I shrugged. "Max, my ballet teacher slash father taught me how to, he's been dancing on pointes since he was sixteen."

"Cool." He said nodding, as I lifted the second shoe to begin sewing the ribbon on. "Must hurt." He said thoughtfully, then he began to get dressed.

"It does." I replied, then I shrugged. "Or it did. Now it doesn't hurt as much." I said, "and my ankles are very strong." I added, he smiled.

24

"Impressive." He said nodding then dropped a checked shirt over his head, it fell nicely over him until it stopped around the top of his thighs, he sat back on his bed to put some socks on. "We should go out."

"Out, where?" I asked, he shrugged at me obviously in thought as he reached for his shoes.

"For a drink."

"A drink?"

"You drink right?" he asked, I looked back at my shoe as I tied off the thread. I had drank, a couple of times with Connor, and I'd had wine with celebratory meals before today. I looked back at Kian.

"Yeah." I said, he nodded.

"Well come on then, let's go out, have some fun." He said as he stood, he smirked at me as he held his hand out to me. "Get to know each other a little better." He added, I laughed putting the pointes back into their box then taking his hand.

"Hello Ladies." Kian stated as we walked down our corridor. We'd crossed through another door that required our key card, which apparently meant that we'd crossed through to the girl's end of the corridor. He'd said hello to every girl we'd walked past, only two had responded.

The girl nearest to me had long blonde hair that was currently resting over her shoulder in what looked like an overly complex braid, she wore a summer dress with vertical stripes across the bust, and horizontal stripes down the skirt. She was smiling at me, when I felt like she should have been smiling at Kian. The second girl had long black hair which she was wearing down, she wore ripped jeans, with a vest top and a grey checked shirt open on top. The sleeves were rolled up to her elbows, her arms full of braided bracelets.

"Margo." She said, offering her hand to me, I looked at her face as she smirked at me, I took her hand shaking it once.

"Abi." Her blonde friend said quietly, I nodded to her as Kian grinned at them both.

"We're going out. For a drink. Would you lovely ladies like to join us?" he asked, Margo nodded without a moment's thought, then she looked at Abi who looked a little more apprehensive.

"Oh, come on Abs." Margo said, "we need some fun before lessons start."

"Exactly." Kian stated, "my thoughts exactly." He said happily to me. I nodded back to him because that seemed to prove that he'd thought this. Margo grinned at him, as she closed their bedroom door behind them, then she began to walk with Kian who had started to walk ahead. "Well, Margo love, age and ballet history please." Kian said, I laughed as I began to follow them as I now figured he was going to ask everyone that.

"Eighteen." She replied, then looked at me over her shoulder. "Of course." She added, I laughed. "And I've been dancing since I was seven." She added, Kian began to nod back to her.

"You don't look like the run of the mill Ballet Girl." Kian teased, they both turned, so I also did we seemed to be looking at Abi.

"No." Margo said, "but I dance better than them." she added as I turned back to look at her, she winked at me so I laughed.

There was, conveniently a pub a few doors down from the school, *which* we had managed to leave without too much trouble. We took a seat in the booth with a little round table between us.

"Now, it's your turn" Kian said as Abi slipped into the booth, she looked at him, she appeared to be very confused.

"For what?" she asked, Margo and Kian laughed together,

"Age, ballet history." Kian said happily, it made me smile.

"Eighteen." She said, then she frowned, "isn't everyone in first year eighteen?" She added, I nodded as Kian waved his hand at her,

"Yes, yes but it's better to ask two questions, than just one. Gets us talking." He added, Abi nodded back to him, then she looked at me, she smiled at me, so I smiled back at her.

"I've been doing ballet since I could walk." She said. "My Mum was a part of the Royal Ballet." She said,

"Wow." I whispered, she grinned at me.

"Jacob's Dad is a ballet dancer." Kian said helpfully, I nodded to him,

"Really? Where did he perform?" Abi asked, I stuttered lightly,

"He was a competition dancer. World Champion." I said, I heard as Kian and Margo both gasped, Abi instead frowned at me,

"So not a real ballet dancer then?" she said, I frowned straight back at her.

"No, I think you'll find Max is a real ballet dancer." I replied, "he trained in a ballet school for seven years. He competed and won gold. He performs in musicals, like Billy Elliot, like Cats, and he also teaches." I stated, Abi's eyes narrowed at me.

"Drinks." Kian stated, I looked away from her and at him. "Let's get some drinks. What do you feel like Jacob?" he asked, I didn't quite want to shrug at him.

I didn't like beer. A party when I was fourteen had proven that to me, at that same party I discovered I had a liking for WKD, but I didn't want to ask for that. I remembered Jack, a boy from the home Connor and I lived in telling us we could only drink WKD until we were sixteen, otherwise people would judge us hard for not drinking proper alcohol.

"Coke." Abi said simply, I looked at her then turned back to Kian.

"Vodka in it?" He asked, I began to nod to him. "One shot or two?" he asked amused, so I smiled.

"One." I replied, he nodded leaving the table and going to the bar.

"Your Dad taught you?" Margo asked me, I nodded to her. "That sounds both horrendous and amazing." He said, I laughed.

"He was my ballet teacher first, so it was just amazing." I said, she frowned at me, I glanced at Abi as she was also frowning at me.

"He adopted me." I cleared up, Margo laughed, but it definitely wasn't a mean laugh.

"That's so cool." She said nodding to me. "Did he adopt you because you were a ballet prodigy and he felt it necessary to keep you close?" She teased, I laughed but nodded.

"I was a threat." I replied, as Kian returned placing a little round tray on the table then sliding the drinks to each of us.

We were back before midnight, not because we tried to be but because it fell that way. We left Margo and Abi at their bedroom on our way back down to our own. We got ready for bed quietly, working around the bathroom without a problem or a word. He was sat on his bed in bed shorts and a bed shirt when I came out of the bedroom in my pyjamas. I sat myself on my bed, looking briefly at my phone then taking off my glasses and resting them on the bedside cabinet.

"I don't agree with Abi." Kian said as I pulled my duvet up and got into my bed, I frowned in his general direction as he was now a fuzzy shape. "I think it's far more fun to be a competition dancer and do musicals, and everything else. If I don't get into a company, that's where I want to go, that's what I want to do."

"When he talks about it, it sounds like it was the best time." I said, then lay on my back looking up at the ceiling. I covered my eyes.

"Margo said she was well out of order for saying he wasn't a real ballet dancer." He said, I nodded.

"Do you like Margo?" I asked,

"She's cool." He replied, I turned my head to look at him again, I tried to focus in on him it didn't really work.

"No, I mean. Do you like her?" I asked, he laughed.

"Jacob." He said, I nodded. "I'm gay." He said, I covered my eyes again as I smiled. "Do you like her?" he asked, I shrugged, I heard him laugh. "Goodnight Jacob." He said, I sighed.

"Goodnight."

"Welcome First Years." Our technique teacher Madame Rose said as we stood in lines against the barres. The boys were on the middle two barres, whilst the girls were on the barres near the mirrors, all of them in raspberry coloured leotards and skirts, their hair all perfectly placed into a bun.

I'd spent a lot of Madame Rose's opening speech looking around the room at everybody in my class. I'd just about started listening again as she began the warm-up. My eyes followed her as she walked around the room whilst we warmed up. She fixed people as she walked past them, arm placement, leg placement, turnout.

Everyone had something to fix, then she started up the boy's barre. I didn't dare turn around as we moved through the positions of the feet and the arms. I felt my heart quicken as she stopped next to me.

"Jacob." She read off her clipboard, I turned my head to look at her, as I figured since she'd addressed me, I could look at her. "Can you wear contacts?" she asked, I felt my eyes drop then I began to nod, even though I'd never thought about it beforehand. "Okay. From next week I will expect you not to be wearing your glasses during dance lessons." She said, I nodded again. "And, I feel you should spend any frees, or spare time in the gym." She said, I met her eyes.

"Yes Madame." I replied, she nodded back then walked on as I sighed.

Madame Rose split us into groups following our barre work. She asked us onto the floor into our groups, and shouted out a sequence for us all to follow. I stood beside Kian on the barre as we watched the first girl group dance their way through the sequence.

"No earrings from tomorrow's class." Kian said as he crossed his arms against his chest and leant on the barre, I sighed.

"No glasses from next week." I replied, he looked at me he was almost frowning.

"Okay, I get no earrings but how can she tell you, you can't wear your glasses. You need them to see." He stated, I nodded.

"No bracelets from tomorrow's class." Margo said, I turned my head to look at her, as she came to lean next to us on the barre.

"She wants me to wear contacts." I said, Kian shook his head as Margo frowned at me. "And of course, sometime in the gym." I said then leant my head back, I felt as it connected with the mirror behind me.

"I'll go with you." Kian said, "apparently the facilities are amazing here." he said nodding to me.

"Group one, boys." Madame Rose said, Kian grinned at us both as he walked to stand on the front line of his group. He stood tall, his arms in demi-bra his right toe pointed in front of him, he began to move almost instantly when Madame Rose started the music. I was pulled out of watching as Kian's group danced by Abi coming to stand beside Margo.

"What aren't you allowed to have from next lesson?" She asked amused as she played with her bracelets. Abi frowned back at her. "Bracelets." She said,

"Glasses." I added,

"Earrings." Margo and I said together as we nodded towards Kian,

"Oh. Nothing." she said, I rolled my eyes by instinct, then looked away before she realised I had.

"Perfect then?" Margo asked, I laughed because I could hear the teasing in her voice.

"Group two girls." Madame Rose requested, Margo winked at me as she walked away, then stood where Kian had, her arms beautiful, her lines were equally as beautiful.

31

"Wow." I muttered; Kian practically sniggered as he came back to lean next to me.

"Figured it out yet?" he asked, I looked at him as he smirked back at me. "That you like her." He whispered; I shook my head at him.

"No. I…" I said, then I frowned at him, "no I don't." I said, he laughed,

"I don't blame you. If I was straight, I'd be all over her." He said, then whistled quietly, "I mean, that personality, that body. She's everything." He said, then he met my eyes, I didn't drop my gaze, until he smiled and I laughed and looked away.

"Yeah, I like her." I muttered,

"Awesome." He said laughing,

"Group two boys." Madame Rose said, I raised my eyebrow at Kian, walking away from him and taking the spot Margo had been stood in.

I took a deep breath before standing up straight, I held my arms out in demi-bra, then extended my leg and pointed my toe. I could hear Max's voice in my head, all he was saying was strong, *strong*, strong.

My stance had to be strong.

My arms strong.

My feet strong.

He'd spent the last four years shouting the word strong at me from across the dance studio, he usually accompanied the words with a clap, up until last year when it became a laugh because I'd started repeating it back to him. I thought away the smile that had formed on my face and then I began to dance.

I stood trying to control my breathing as Madame Rose critiqued us one by one. Most of her critiques where simple, and fair, and on a whole about extension.

"Lovely Jacob." She said, I relaxed, "let's work on building up your core strength now. Okay." She said nodding to me, I nodded back slowly then dropped my end position.

"So, day one of six hundred and sixty-eight. How is ballet school for you guys?" Margo asked as we sat on a round table out on the patio area that was attached to the canteen.

Margo and I had been almost too over the moon when we discovered the canteen had a sandwich bar. We'd both worked out way through it, coming out with stacked high sandwiches and chips. Kian had laughed loudly when we sat back at the table, and had proceeded to steal numerous chips off both of our plate's in-between eating his own chicken and rice. Abi just had a salad, and tutted at us in regular intervals.

"Day one has been, eye opening." Kian said thoughtfully as seemed to conduct his thoughts with the piece of chicken on the end of his fork. "How do you adapt from being the favourite?" he said, Margo laughed.

"She didn't even touch you." Margo said shaking her head at him.

"Well, I've already succeeded in doing one thing by day one that I didn't think I'd have." I said, Margo nodded to me.

"And it is?" Kian asked, I grinned then looked down as I ate the individual fillings out of my sandwiches.

"I made friends." I said, they both moaned at me, a few of Margo's chips flying towards me, as Kian's napkin did, so I began to laugh, which soon made them.

"Welcome to your first Pas De Deux lesson." Miss Olivia said from the front of the studio, she seemed happy, it really made me smile. "Ladies I will expect you all to be wearing your pointes during our Pas De Deux lessons, and I will also have expected everyone to have warmed up before the class begins." She said, we all nodded to her as we stood scattered around the studio.

"So, we'll start with gentlemen on the floor. Ladies once you have your shoes on, please warm up." She said, all the girls moved to the sides. "We're going to do a simple exercise gentleman." She said, then she smiled at us. "This will warm up your shoulders, and your back. Whilst also helping me determent around what level we're all at." she said, then she smiled again and started the music. Miss Olivia seemed happy with our warmup, so sent us to the barre, beckoning the girls to the middle. I did every step of their pointe warm up with them, until Kian touched my shoulder.

"Withdrawal?" he asked, I smiled at him, then looked towards Miss Olivia as she began to pair us off.

"Kian, and Margo." She said, I looked towards Margo as she pulled her tongue at Kian whilst he walked towards her. "Jacob, and Abi." She said, then she smiled at me as I walked towards Abi. She stood just a bit in front of me, her hands on her hips "We will be beginning with balance, and touch. Ladies, you need to allow our gentlemen to guide you whilst remaining independent. Gentlemen, you will learn how to be able to tell if your lady is off centre, and will be able to guide them into the correct positions." She said, whilst talking with her arms, "so, we will start simple. Ladies, stand in front, and gentlemen, place your hands on your lady's waist." She said, I saw Abi look over her shoulder at me, I got from that look that she was not going to help me at all, as I hovered my hands over the middle of her body. I heard Miss Olivia laugh so I looked up. It appeared I

34

wasn't the only boy who was struggling to find their ladies waist.

"Well done Kian." She said as she walked down the line, lifting the boy's hands and placing them on their waists. She smiled warmly at me when she stood in front of us, she took my hands in hers then placed them where Abi's skirt met her leotard. I could feel as Abi squirmed under my touch. "Ladies raise onto pointe." Miss Olivia said, I tightened my grip as Abi rose onto her pointe, her hands touched mine, she mustn't have trusted me not to drop her. "Gentlemen, can you feel the ladies centre." She said, there was a holler from the back, it made me laugh, I felt as Abi hit my hands. "Into an arabesque." Miss Olivia requested as she walked back and forth at the front of the class. I could hear Abi's unhappiness with me, as a whole as she raised herself into an arabesque.

"You're unbalanced." I said, she glared at me. "You need to balance yourself before going up onto pointe, otherwise your arabesque will be off." I said, she turned to look at me, I'm sure if she had a ponytail it'd have whipped me across the face.

"What do you know?" she snapped back at me.

"I know that your balance was completely off, and if I wasn't holding you, you'd have fell and possibly broken your ankle." I snapped back.

"Now, now…" Miss Olivia began, as Abi scoffed.

"Well go on, do it better then." She stated, I rolled my eyes at her.

"No."

"Because you don't know what you're talking about." She stated. I scowled her, as she scowled right back.

"Now, now calm down. Pas De Deux work is difficult but you have to learn how to communicate with each other. Talk through your problems."

"I think you'll find they are talking through their problem." Kian said, Miss Olivia looked at him briefly, he beamed back at her, I'm pretty sure she rolled her eyes at him.

"Jacob, although I appreciate your assistance with teaching, but let's leave it to the teachers to teach the technique." She said, I sighed. "Now, arabesque, please." She said,

"I am not working with him, until he does an arabesque." Abi stated,

"Abi." Miss Olivia said, she didn't seem to have the end of the sentence.

"If he feels the need to correct me." she added more to Miss Olivia, so Miss Olivia sighed, then waved her hand at me.

"Do so Jacob, but do it quick. I'd like to continue with this lesson." She said, I looked down at my feet, then I sighed, pointing my right toe out in front of me, and stepping onto it. Lifting my left into the arabesque and holding my arms in fourth. I saw as Miss Olivia smiled, along with Kian and Margo who both looked amused. Abi however, did not look happy. "Is everyone happy now?" Miss Olivia asked, Abi sighed at her as I relaxed then I stood in first position waiting for Abi to stand in front of me again. She did so unhappily, and then didn't look at me for the rest of the lesson.

"She knows it isn't Princess school, right?" Margo said, as she sat leaning on Kian's bed, she had multiple bobby pins in her mouth as she unwound her bun. She thought about it for a few minutes, then took her bobble out, running her fingers through her hair to fluff it out. I sighed as I lay back on my bed.

"She hates me." I said as I closed my eyes, Margo laughed.

"On the contrary. It's quite the opposite." She said, I turned my head to look at her.

"Shut up." I said, she laughed as Kian reappeared from the en-suite, I smiled at him as he went to sit back on his bed, he'd changed out of his leotard and now sat in baby blue jogging bottoms that were covered in stars and simply a grey t-shirt.

"Are you antagonising Jacob?" Kian said, Margo began to laugh then shook her head.

"We were talking about Abi." She said, Kian rolled his eyes as he reached for his phone.

"I'm going to get changed." I said as I stood from my bed. I searched through my wardrobe until I found some jogging bottoms and a t-shirt. I took them both into the en-suite with me.

Kian's leotard, shorts and ballet belt were hung up on the back of the door, once I closed it over, so I stood frowning at them as I peed, because his ballet belt was massive. I held mine up to it once I'd stepped out of it. I frowned for a few minutes as I ran my thumb over the cup of my own ballet belt, until I sighed and threw it to the floor. I stepped into a pair of boxers, then pulled my jogging bottoms up to my hips, and pulled my t-shirt down. I picked up my leotard, shorts and belt, taking them back into the bedroom smiling as I watched Kian twirling Margo's hair around, and around as if creating a bun.

"Oh, don't we look good in yellow." Margo cooed at me; I turned my head to look at her then I began to laugh.

"Spongebob Squarepants?" Kian said raising his eyebrow at me as I sat back on my bed, I looked down at my chest. "The musical." He added, I laughed.

"My Dad was in it." I said, they both frowned at me, "My other dad. The ballet dancers' husband."

"Oh, two penis parenting. My favourite." Kian said grinning down at Margo as she shook her head, it almost looked shocked. "You have two dads?" he asked, I nodded.

"Max, is the ballet dancer. My teacher. Cameron, does musicals. He did Spongebob when I was fifteen. I loved it; I think it was my favourite musical he's been in."

"Ugh, I want to live with your family." Margo said, I laughed.

"Tell us all about your family please." Kian said, I shook my head amused.

"Tell me a bit about yours. I feel like I'm the only one talking about my parents." I said, they both laughed, Margo looked up at Kian, he sighed and shrugged.

"Run of the mill. Mum, Dad. Overachieving football playing brother, underachieving twin sister." He said amused, "I don't know why I started ballet. I don't know what actually went through my Mum's head to enrol me into ballet, but it happened, a year later I was in the same class as my sister." He said.

"So, where is your sister?"

"Ballet is my life, whereas ballet is her hobby."

"Really?" I asked, he nodded.

"She found it fun, and it didn't really bother her if she didn't pass her grades, or if she didn't move to pointe class. She just enjoyed doing it. Whereas I focused more on my Grade Six than my GCSE's."

"Ditto." I said, he laughed, I smiled back at him.

"Your turn female."

"Mum." Margo said, then shrugged. "Step-Dad I suppose. Only child." She said, "boring." She added,

"Do you guys think…" I began then tilted my head at them, "do you think if your parents hadn't put you into ballet, that you'd have chosen to go?" I asked, Kian nodded to me.

"I'm about ninety percent positive that I would because I just love it, and I think I always have." He said, it made me grin.

"I use ballet to show my Mum I can do something. It might not be useful, but I can, so, if I hadn't started ballet, I'd probably do something else and try and over achieve at it." Margo said then she grinned up at Kian as he shook his head amused.

"Now, my question." Kian said, as he finished playing with Margo's hair. "Where does our sexuality lie?" he asked, I snorted lightly as Margo smirked up at him. "Your Dad's are gay… so?" Kian asked, I laughed openly at him,

"What so that makes me gay?" I asked, he shook his head dramatically.

"Course not. I know you like girls." He said wiggling his eyebrows at me,

"Not Abi?" Margo declared, we both scoffed at her.

"I'm bi." I said, Kian's eyebrow raised.

"Oh, we have a bisexual in our midst. Do we have a story of how we know?" he asked leaning his elbows on his knees, I laughed rolling my eyes.

"Yes. Actually." I said amused, he grinned. "I kissed my best friend when I was fourteen. He's gay, he's known that since he was thirteen. We kissed and I sort of. I didn't think about it for a long time. Like you said before, with focusing on ballet over exams. I was kind of focusing on

39

ballet over everything, until I was about sixteen and Max was just talking to me, just casually, asking about boyfriends or girlfriends and it occurred to me that I'd never actually had either.

I began to think about it for real, and yeah, I've always had a thing for boys. I mean, I'm pretty certain I spent about thirty percent of the ballet videos watching for the men, than the dancing." I said, they both laughed. *Jack* had caught me watching a ballet video at one point before I was adopted. He had laughed practically into my ear and asked me in a whisper if I was just watching it for the hot guys. I'd blushed, all flustered and scared and exited the video before he could ask me any further questions about attractive men.

"And... did you sleep with this best friend?" Kian asked, I shook my head amused.

"No, no not at all. Connor and I never will either. He's my friend and just that." I said, Kian smiled at me. "I'm a virgin."

"Oh." He said, "I can change that for you." He purred at me, winking at me. I laughed.

"No thanks." I replied, then hummed. "Not tonight anyway." I added, Kian beamed. "Margo?" I asked, she raised her hands.

"I'm straight." She said then looked up at Kian,

"Full blooded homosexual." He replied, then he looked at me. "Have you ever gotten hard in your leotard?" he asked, I shook my head as I laughed, because I hadn't every lesson I'd had was with Max, and that'd have been beyond weird.

There as one lesson, when I was fifteen where I'd sat in on Immediate Pointe and the multiple older girls in leotards had certainly grabbed my attention. "Well, that's

40

how I figured out I was gay." He replied, Margo and I both began to laugh as he grinned and began to tell us the story.

Chapter 3

I had tossed and turned for what felt like *hours* but when I lifted my phone to confirm that, it had only been twenty-five minutes.

I figured Kian was well asleep, he hadn't spoken, or moved for a while, but I still looked towards the darkened area where his bed was. I was trying to figure out if I could get away with touching myself.

I knew, *or* at least after living with Kian for coming on five days I thought I knew that he wouldn't care as a whole, but he probably didn't wish to wake up to it. I groaned quietly then rubbed my eyes, taking off my glasses and placing them on my bedside cabinet. I gave up in the end reaching under my quilt, but not pushing it down.

I made sure I was still fully covered as I slipped my hand underneath my pyjama waistband. Covering my mouth the moment I groaned, biting my bottom lip to stop the sound escaping, then I gasped when the room suddenly filled with light. I heard Kian's laugh as the bathroom door close. I sat myself up, covering my face until the light came through my fingers so I looked up.

"I woke up to pee." He said as he turned the light out. "I swear." He added, I decided not replying was the way to go. "Jacob." He said, I turned my head to look at him. "I guess we didn't cover this in room inductions." He said, I shook my head at him. "My standing on the subject is. Masturbate all you like." He said, I'm sure he winked so I laughed.

"Well, noted." I said, he laughed as I heard him get back into bed.

"Feel free to finish off." He said, "and if I've made you awkward. I can make it more awkward and join you."

"Kian." I said, he laughed happily as I shook my head, then I lay back down, rolling onto my stomach and burying my face into my pillow.

Connor grinned at me as two crepes that were heavily smothered with chocolate were placed on the table in front of us. I examined Connor's before I began to eat mine.

"So, so let me get this clear. Kian's gay, but Margo likes Kian."

"I believe." I said as I wrapped some loose chocolate around my fork.

"And Abi likes you."

43

"I refuse to believe." I stated pointing my chocolatey fork at him.

"And you like?" Connor asked, I looked away from his face.

"What makes you think I like someone?"

"You have that look on your face Jacob." He said all swoony, "can I guess? Like twenty question style?" he said, I laughed.

"No." I replied,

"Okay. That was question one. Question two, male or female?"

"Yes." I replied, he narrowed his eyes at me. "I can only answer yes or no to questions. Why don't you remember the rules to this game?" I said, he laughed.

"Jack used to play it, yes, no or *fuck knows*." He said nodding to me, I laughed.

"Well ask me another."

"Do you love them?" he cooed,

"Fuck knows." I replied, he began to laugh. "I like Margo." I said nodding, he nodded back to me a slight smirk on his face. "*You* would like Kian." I said, he hummed sounding intrigued.

"I have a…" he said, then shrugged, "I have someone I like having sex with, but noted." He said, I narrowed my eyes at him, he waved his hand at me. "And Kian is who caught you touching yourself?" he asked, I laughed then groaned.

"Yes! And he was so understanding oh my god. It made it worse." I said, Connor began to laugh shaking his head at me, so I ate a too big piece of my crepe.

"If he's okay with it, you might as well just do it. Don't you think?" he said, "I'm sure Kian also masturbates." He said, I snorted.

"Alright Ste." I replied, Connor laughed.

"Have you told Ste yet?" he asked, I must have blushed. "How haven't you told Ste yet? Ste would be *over* the moon." He stated, I shrugged. "I told Jack." he said, "and Hallie, the twins, Adam, Emma, and of course…"

"Baby Willow." I said, Connor smiled back.

"Not quite a baby anymore. She started school last September." He said, I shook my head slowly.

I'd been present at Baby Willow's christening, everyone from the home had been regardless of adoption status, and as Willow had been born to Adam and Emma, both of who we'd lived with for years it had felt important to return for her christening, and her first birthday. After that, my involvement in their life sort of dwindled.

"They are all over the moon for you Jacob, they all know how hard you worked. You're a success story." He said amused, then he sighed. "I'm visiting in a few weeks, I told Ste I'd go before Christmas, so I can gage what the kid's want."

"Want?" I asked, he shrugged.

"For Christmas." He said, I frowned at him. "I'm buying them all a Christmas present. Ste somehow managed to persuade me to dress up as Santa for them." he said as he laughed quietly.

"Why are you buying them all presents?" I asked, I tried not to frown at him.

"Because I remember what it was like… do you?" he said, I looked down. "I know I was there longer than you. I know I've only been out for six months, but you *must* remember." He said, I did remember, birthdays and Christmases were very alike. On birthdays we'd all put some money in to buy whoever was celebrating a present, usually to do with something they liked. Christmas, kind of worked the same way, but it was more Ste and Diane who worked their asses off to ensure we all got something for Christmas.

"But that was normal for us." I said, Connor hummed, it was agreement.

"Yeah, but I don't want it to be normal for them, besides, I can afford it." he said shrugging. "Come visit with me Jacob."

"I will." I said, "But it depends on school." I added, then looked at my phone, I had half an hour before I had to leave to get home.

"Let me know." he said sighing, I nudged my fork against his, the metal clanged, then he smiled at me.

"Tell me more about this Kian."

I opened the doors that led into the living room, throwing my bag down behind them as I did. I folded my arms the moment I got through them. I knew I'd find Max and Cameron in the living room; I hadn't expected to find them wrapped up in each other on the couch, their mouths connected as if they needed each other to breathe. I cleared my throat. Max began laughing almost instantly as Cameron turned his head to look at me. I tilted my head at him as Max continued to kiss his neck.

"You're early?" Cameron said, I shook my head,

"I'm really not." I replied, "it was the deal. Come home, go to immediate pointe with Max then spend the weekend here." I said, "and immediate pointe begins in an hour." I said, Cameron turned his head to look at Max, I rolled my eyes as he continued on Cameron's neck.

"Back down Ballet boy." Cameron said, pushing Max down by his chest. Max laughed as he leant his forehead on Cameron's shoulder.

"Aren't you supposed to be at work?" I said, Cameron laughed.

"Not during rehearsal period. No." He replied, Max laughed, I tilted my head at him, then sighed and put my head back.

"I'm going to go practice. I'll be ready for the class." I said,

"Ah, ah no." Max said, so I looked at him as he raised his head. "This is our house. Not your studio and you know that." He stated, I met his eyes. "The deal is what it has always been Jacob. You want to rehearse you do so in the studio." He said, I sighed.

"But I presumed you want a quick fuck before class, so."

"No exceptions." Max said, I rolled my eyes.

"And no quick fucks thank you very much." Cameron said, I laughed. "*You*, go and get ready to teach." He said to Max, he sighed. "You put your stuff away." He said, I picked up my backpack. "I'll make you both something to eat before you go. Okay?" He said, I nodded sighing as I did then went up the stairs.

Max must have followed. I changed into my leotard. I pulled my purple t-shirt on over the top then stepped into my jogging bottoms and went back down the stairs, and into the kitchen where Cameron was making sandwiches.

"He's in a bad mood." I said, Cameron almost laughed.

"On the contrary, he's in a really good mood." He said, I sat on the dining room table, my feet on the nearest chair.

"I beg to differ." I said, he turned to me.

"You know the rules." He said, I scoffed. "Jacob, they apply to us all. You know that, you've always known

47

that. Home is where you relax, it's where you're with your family and you don't have to worry about anything. Home is not where you work."

"You run lines all the time." I said, he pointed at me.

"Don't be pedantic." He said, I laughed as Max came into the kitchen, he was dressed almost identical to me.

"I can run the class. If you and Cameron want some alone time." I said, wiggling my eyebrows at him, Max laughed as he ruffled my hair, then pulled me towards him so he could hug mostly my head.

"No." He said simply then pushed my head away, Cameron passed me a sandwich.

"I guess I'm wearing my headphones to bed then." I said more to Cameron, he smirked.

"It's advisable."

"Thank you girls. We'll see you next week." Max said, as I stood beside him my hands together in front of me, as I alternated from toe to toe on pointe. The girls all curtseyed, then grabbed their bags and ran to the changing room. Max turned his head to look at me then he began to nod. I smiled back at him.

"So, are you enjoying school?"

"Small talk?" I asked, he laughed as he went to the sound system.

"Yes. I'm your parent it's allowed." He said, I smiled as I turned to the mirror, watching as I rose onto pointe.

"It's hard." I said, he looked at me. "But worth it."

"Good." He said softly, then came to stand beside me.

"Missing dancing en pointe?" he asked, I nodded to him. "Frankie and I were left alone this week, and we began to choreograph. I figure you'd enjoy it." he said, then pressed play.

I began to laugh as the Mission Impossible theme tune began. "Ready?" he asked, I nodded to him as he began to show me the dance. It involved a lot of pirouettes and high kicks, *then*, we spent twenty minutes with Max trying to teach me how to do a split jump. I managed to do it once, before we sat on the floor of the studio as Max told me how he had been the one who did the Fame jump in the production he'd met Cameron.

"Speaking of…" he said as his phone vibrated against the floor. "We better get home, before Cameron goes full housewife on us." He said, I laughed as I stood then went to the barre to take my pointes off.

It was raining as we left the studio, so we both ran around the building to his car.

"Are you happy to be there?" Max asked as we put our seatbelts on, we both sat looking out of the windscreen as the rain ran down it like a waterfall.

"At school?" I asked, he nodded to me. "Yeah. I *am*. We're just worked hard, but I presume that's what I should expect right?"

"Yeah." Max said as he started the car, "Ballet school is difficult. I presume you'll start to gather I was insanely easy on you." He said, I smiled at him.

"Yes, you most certainly were." I said, he laughed. "I need contacts." I said, he frowned at me then looked in the direction he was turning.

"And you chose to tell me this on Saturday night."

"Of course." I replied, he laughed. "I'm your child. It's allowed." I stated, he scoffed at me.

"We won't be able to get you contacts by Monday, maybe by Friday?" he said, I nodded to him.

"Can you write me a letter for Madame Rose?" I asked, he looked at me then began to nod.

"Madame Rose." He repeated, I nodded.

"But I think I prefer Miss Olivia. We meet our male teacher this week." I added, he smiled so I looked at him. "He's going to teach us as an all-male group. I'm not really sure what that entails."

"Allegro. It's not too different. You just do all male numbers, or learn particular technique. It's usually whilst the girls learn pointe." He said, I began to nod to him as he reversed into our driveway.

"Can I go to that class instead?" I said, he laughed as he turned off the car, getting out of the car. I followed. We both threw our dance bags at the bottom of the stairs then went straight into the kitchen where Cameron was laying plates onto the table.

"Good timing boys." He said amused as I sat myself at the table, Max grinned at him walking around the table to kiss him, then took his own seat.

"Oh what is this?" Max asked as he picked up his fork, he began to move the pieces of salad around the plate.

"Salad." Cameron replied, as he took his own seat between us. "Tandoori chicken, and salad." He said to me, I nodded to him and began to eat it as Max laughed.

"And for dessert?" he asked, Cameron grinned lightly.

"I brought cake, and some strawberries." He said, Max nodded.

"That is most certainly more like it." Max said, I began to laugh as Cameron shook his head amused.

"Strawberries are an aphrodisiac." I said, then looked up as Cameron raised his eyebrow at Max. I groaned lightly making them both laugh. "Actually, I was going too."

I said, then tilted my head lightly. "Ask you guys something…"

"Well, strawberries help blood flow, so…"

"Max." Cameron said laughing, "what's up Jacob?"

"Two questions." I said holding up two fingers to them, they both nodded. "First… you both boarded, so I know you get it, and judge me all you like, but how do you get around the whole touching yourself and having a roommate thing?" I said, Cameron smirked as Max shook his head, a smile on his face.

"Have you spoken to your roommate about it?" Max asked, I nodded.

"Kian said he didn't mind, but I *do*."

"Do you have an en-suite?" Cameron asked, I nodded to him. "Shower." He said,

"Oh." I said laughing, Cameron smiled at me as I shook my head.

"You half board Jacob." Max said, I looked at him. "Why don't you just do it when you come home of a weekend?" He said, I pointed at him as Cameron did. He began to laugh.

"That might be better than just randomly starting the shower at like three am." I said, Cameron shook his head.

"We just used to do it during our morning shower. One of my roommates was renowned for getting a shower after our day of lessons, we *all* knew that he was doing it then." He said, I laughed. "Until I got with Max, of course." He added turning to grin at Max, who laughed.

"Of course." He repeated back, "we were usually too shattered to even consider it." he said, Cameron laughed.

"In other words. Max had a boyfriend throughout school, so didn't actually need to relieve the need." Cameron

51

said, I laughed shaking my head at him, he winked at me. "But he's right, you do half board."

"That's all well and good, if I'm not *highly* aware that you guys are humping like bunnies all night."

"Oh." Max said, as Cameron began to laugh.

"Well, how about we make a deal?" Cameron said, I nodded to him curious of what on earth he could say. "We'll start having sex during the week, and will leave the weekend open for if you want to touch yourself."

"I appreciate that." I said amused, it made him laugh too.

"And of course, you can ask us questions like this whenever." Max said, I nodded.

"I know. I figured that out through your openness about your own sex lives." I said, Max smiled at me.

"We only share what is a need to know." Max said, "we never overshare." He said, I nodded to him because I did agree. "You had a part two?" Max said, I nodded a bit warily as I used the lettuce leaf to wipe up the coleslaw and beetroot from my plate.

"It was actually about sex." I said, then looked up. "I'm not thinking about having it. Honestly. I've been there a week, I'm still single, and a virgin don't *worry*... but if the opportunity were to arise." I said, Cameron frowned at me as Max did, both were as thoughtful as each other's.

"What exactly are you asking?" Max said, I shook my head.

"I don't know." I admitted, "but I began to think about it, and I genuinely thought that I'm so not prepared for sex, it's actually frightening for an eighteen year old."

"I was like that." Cameron said, I looked back at him. "Honestly. Leading up to when I lost my virginity, I genuinely thought I know nothing about sex, about condoms, about… even kissing. It's not as scary as you think."

"If you love who you're doing it with." Max said, we both looked at him. "I mean sure, sex without love exists but your first time, you remember it. Everyone can say, what else happened on the day their lost their virginity." He said, I frowned, "it was the first day back at school. Fifth year, two days after my sixteenth birthday." Max said, I laughed.

"The day before I went home for Christmas in my seventh year." Cameron said, "but if you're not ready, or if *you* feel like you're not ready. Don't do it."

"Wait." Max said nodding,

"Do you wish you'd have waited?" I asked, Cameron shook his head, it made me smile.

"I have to say that. I married him." He added I began to laugh. "But no. I think *for me,* it was perfect. Perfectly timed, and the perfect guy."

"Ew." I said, they both laughed. "Max?" I asked, he hummed.

"It's complicated." He said, "at the time, I loved him, so at the time it was perfect and it was right. I think, now looking back that I was too young. It was too soon for me, but not too soon in our relationship."

"That makes sense." I said nodding, they both nodded back to me.

"Want some cake?" Cameron asked, I laughed but nodded to him as he stood from the table, taking the plates away.

"Knock, knock." I heard Max say, so I looked up as he came into my bedroom, he came to sit on my bed.

"In case you feel ready." Max said then went into the bag he'd brought in with him, he passed me a box of condoms. I read them, then looked at him as he nodded to me. "I'm not going to make you be celibate, or make your take an oath, or anything. I know better than most, better than Cameron that ballet school is weirdly a hot bed." He said, I frowned at him.

"You've started Pas De Deux?" he asked, I rolled my eyes but nodded. "You will see how intimidate it can get. Dancing together can be orgasmic which can ultimately lead to… searching for that orgasm." He said, it made me smile. "So, *just* use a condom. With everyone, boys, girls whatever. Make sure you're always safe. You don't want to be in the middle of a pregnancy scandal." He said, I nodded to him because I agreed. "And, use lubricate with guys." He said, passing me a bottle, he leant a little closer to me. "Also good for when you want to go at it alone." He said, I laughed. "Don't be afraid to call me, or Cameron if you need to talk though. If it's urgent don't wait until the weekend."

"What like needing contacts?" I asked, he smiled at me.

"Like needing contacts." He said, so I began to laugh as he did.

▼▼▼

Kian almost looked lost when he came out of the bathroom. It made me laugh as I pulled my shorts up over my leotard, then sat back on my bed to put my socks on. Kian looked at me then sat back on his own bed, rubbing his eyes and shaking his head at me.

"I'm too tired for today to progress." He said, then he groaned. "How long do I have?"

"Ten minutes until breakfast." I said, he sighed and nodded standing from his bed, keeping his hand on the knot in his towel around his waist. He threw his leotard behind him from the wardrobe, followed by his shorts and his ballet belt. "Why are you so tired?" I asked, he laughed and shrugged at me. "Well, I taught a class and had an hour's session myself and I'm not that tired."

"Well, aren't you fabulous." He replied, I whistled at him, "Margo's very energetic on a Saturday. I don't know why I wasn't expecting it." He added he sounded confused as he picked up his clothes, dropping them back onto his bed then dropping his towel. I trained my eyes on his face, he began to laugh almost instantly. "You know this is so padded it's ridiculous." He said, my eyes jumped to his feet as he stepped into his ballet belt, then I looked back at his face.

"Padded?" I repeated, he nodded.

"Because my brother plays football... Right?" He said, I nodded even though I did not see the connection, he smiled as he slipped his hand into his ballet belt to rearrange himself, I smirked then looked away as I figured I was blushing. "He has a jockstrap, and a cup. The whole *wham bam*. Mum got paranoid.

I was like thirteen when my ballet teacher stated I need to get a ballet belt. I couldn't wear my boxers anymore. Mum associated it with my brother's jockstrap and got all motherly. She asked the lady in the ballet shop if you could buy padded straps, whether they'd be more protective, she said they would and..." He said, I looked back at him as he stepped into his leotard, pulling it up over his shoulders.

"Oh." I said, he looked at me as he sat on his bed. "So, you don't just have a big dick then?" I said, he laughed as he pulled up his shorts then put his socks on.

"Wow." He said shaking his head at me, "way to hurt a guy's ego." He added, I laughed.

"I was concerned." I said thoughtfully, "I was fourteen when I got my ballet belt. Max said it didn't need to be padded. I followed his advice. When I got a new one last year, Corinthian, the guy who runs the ballet shop I buy stuff from, and one of Max's friends whispered to me that if I wanted it to be padded I could. I thought why not, but my cup is not as big as yours." I said, he frowned at me so I laughed. "You hang it on the bathroom door. I've noticed." I said, he smiled.

"Don't compare that." He said, I looked down. "We're in so much competition, for everything. Height, weight, technique, stamina, muscle. We're in competition for roles, for grades for everything. Don't be worried about how your cup size compares to someone else's." He said, I met his eyes.

"My ballet teacher, when I was thirteen and overly conscious about buying a ballet belt, because I thought it'd make that area more obvious in my leotard. My ballet teacher literally turned to me and said anyone watching me, whether it be a teacher, an assessor, a judge or even just an audience member are going to be far more interested in my dancing, than my penis."

"That makes sense." I said, he smiled as he stood coming to me then he kissed my forehead.

"And if you want." He said leaning a little closer to my ear. "You can borrow one of my ballet belts. If it makes you feel better." He said, I laughed shaking my head at him.

"No, I'm good." I said, he winked at me then turned back to his wardrobe, putting his zip up jacket on then nodding his head to me, so I stood, putting my own jacket on then picking up my ballet shoes and following him out of our room.

"Hello boys." Our Allegro teacher said as he stood at the front of the class. He was wearing a tank top, and joggers.

56

He wore ballet shoes with no socks, and he was *actually* beautiful. "My name is Arlo, and I will be your individual tutor. We will explore many different dances in this class, some classical, such as the mice from the Nutcracker, or numbers from Robin Hood." He said then he smiled, a dimpled smile, I looked across the group to Kian as he let out a deep breath, he nodded to me so I laughed quietly.

"We will also explore Peter Pan, Sweeney Todd. We will dance solo pieces and group numbers. Whilst also working on your core strength and your technique. We will go on a journey in this class boys."

"I'm sure." Kian whispered, I laughed again.

"So please spread yourselves out on the barres. We will complete our warm-up then start simple." He said, then clapped his hands so we scattered to the barre.

We stood in first position, then began moving through the arm positions. Arlo walked amongst us, fixing us where we needed to be fixed, smiling at those of us, like me, who didn't need to be fixed.

"Soubresaut." Arlo requested, "gain some height boys." He spoke. "Point your toes." He stated to a boy on the next barre over, his voice full of dismay, everyone else laughed quietly as we continued to jump.

Sousbresaut, a sudden straight-legged jump with toes pointed, Max had told me as we practiced over and over, he made me repeat it as I jumped.

Soo-bruh-soh, soo-bruh-soh, soo-bruh-soh.

"Beautiful Jacob." Arlo said, I grinned at him, then turned my head to look at Kian as he gasped at me. "To the floor." He requested, "into pairs please." He added, so we stood in twos at the corner of the room. "Chassé across." He requested; the first pair began to.

57

"Oh, I would." Kian said as he slotted his water bottle into the little holder on the treadmill. He stood on either side of the treadmill as he pressed a few buttons.

"That pretty?" Margo asked, we both nodded back to her, she laughed as she sat on the windowsill of the window in front of the treadmills.

"He was beautiful." Kian said as he began to walk on the treadmill. I tried to copy him, placing my own water bottle in the holder, then stepping onto the treadmill. I just stood and stared at the controls. "Here." Kian said, stepping across the belt and leant on the barrier, he pressed a few buttons then my belt began to move. "Good?" he asked, I hummed at him.

"I'll let you know." I said, he laughed as he began walking on his own machine again, so I also did. I watched as Kian's got quicker.

"So, why Jacob are you battling with a treadmill?" Margo asked, I glanced down at her then back out the window as my belt began to move quicker.

"Because Madame Rose insisted, I work on my weight."

"She didn't tell you to work on your weight." Kian said, I shook my head.

"She said I needed to spend my spare time in the gym. Therefore."

"Therefore." Margo and Kian mocked at the same time, as my treadmill quickened again, I was now doing more of a jog.

"I used to do this every day." Kian said, I looked at him momentarily. "Wake up, have breakfast…"

"Most important meal of the day." Margo interjected; Kian laughed.

"Then I'd go the gym for an hour." He said nodding, "Then school."

"The hell? What time did you wake up?" I asked, Kian smiled slightly as his became more of a run, I dreaded when mine hit that point as I was already out of breath.

"Five." He said nodding, "breakfast by half five, at *latest*. The gym by six, work out until seven, shower, changed and in school by eight fifteen, no problems."

"Oh my god. I don't envy you." Margo said, I shook my head.

"Then, I'd go straight to ballet after school. Four to seven, sometimes eight." He said, I shook my head.

"I thought I did a lot, obviously not." I said, Margo laughed as Kian did.

"I bet you calorie count." Margo said, Kian began to laugh. "You calorie count, don't you?" She said, he looked down without losing balance,

"Not every day." He replied as he looked back up, "the weekends are a free for all."

"Five, two?" I said, he nodded to me. "Can you slow this down please?" I added, he smiled as he stepped off his belt again and pressed a few buttons. My treadmill became a slow jog, I nodded to him relieved as he grinned.

"So, theoretically you could have the biggest damn pizza, *ever* on a Saturday?" Margo asked, Kian groaned.

"That sounds so good, but yes I could." He added, I smirked at him.

"Max always said to me that we should eat high energy food because we burn off so much energy." I said, Kian nodded.

"I do eat high energy food. Just not fatty food." He said, I nodded to him.

"Like chicken and rice." I asked, he nodded to me.

59

"That sounds unbelievably boring." Margo stated, I laughed as Kian did.

"We used to eat crap on a Saturday, but equally we trained for hours. From about nine in the morning to five, six in the evening. We'd have fast food for lunch and all kinds."

"We?" Margo asked as she stood, she leant on Kian's treadmill.

"My sister and I." He said nodding, "we'd have individual training, then we'd do Pas De Deux training." he said nodding, Margo looked at me she seemed mildly impressed.

"My question." Margo said raising her hand, Kian nodded to her as his treadmill slowed down. "When did you find time to touch yourself lovely?" She asked, Kian laughed shaking his head.

"That is none of your business." He replied, then began to walk again. He took a swig out of his water bottle. "I'm going to take a shower." He said as his treadmill stopped. He jumped off it.

"Don't leave me on this." I almost squeaked at him, "I don't know how to work this." I said, he laughed walking around my treadmill and turned it off. I managed to get off without falling.

"Shower then tea? Does that sound like a plan?" He asked, Margo nodded to him.

"An hour?" She asked, he nodded back then they kissed each other's cheeks. I stuttered when she also did it to me.

I was lying back on my bed when Kian came out from the shower, he smiled at me as he dried his hair with the towel. I let my eyes travel down his body, he was just wearing his boxers.

"Shouldn't have lay down, I'm guessing?" He said, I nodded to him. "Come on, get a shower. It'll relax you," he said holding his hands out to me. I took them and let him help me stand.

"Then food because I'm starving." He said, I nodded going into the bathroom and stripping, I turned the shower on and stood awkwardly naked in the middle of the bathroom waiting for the shower to reach a good temperature.

I glanced at myself in the mirror, letting my eyes jump over my body. I couldn't see past my hips because of the sink but I was more grateful for that than anything. I ran my hand from my chest to my stomach feeling as my hand rose then I held it out under the shower stream, feeling the water hitting my fingers, so I stepped into the shower.

It didn't take me long before I was taking Cameron's advice.

▾▾▾

"Gentlemen you must lift with your knees not your backs." Miss Olivia said as she walked through the lines of our Pas De Deux class.

Abi was *still* not speaking to me, but to her credit she still danced with me and let me lift her, even though her centre threw my balance off and she still squirmed whenever I touched her. Miss Olivia appreciated our attempts and smiled sympathetically at me whenever she walked past. The third time she walked past me she stopped and stood behind me. Placing her hands on my waist and holding my back straight as I lifted Abi up,

"Relevé in fifth Abi." Olivia requested, so Abi did, raising onto fifth, whilst also raising her arms into fifth, "and lift Jacob." She said, so I attempted to, bending my knees as

I lifted her by the waist. It didn't work too well. We both sighed at the same time, as I looked over my shoulder at Miss Olivia.

"Build up some muscle Jacob." She said, I nodded to her, "and Abi you have to help your partner." She said, "Pas De Deux's translation is a dance of two." She said raising her voice. "This means both dancers must give and take. It is both of your jobs to create a balance, to make yourselves look beautiful." She said, then she smiled at Kian and Margo, who in-between laughing with each other and tickling each other actually managed to do the lifts Miss Olivia was requesting we do.

"Watch as Kian lifts Margo. It is effortless." She said, we all did, and it *was* effortless. "Margo's lines are beautiful. Her extension, remains strong as Kian lifts her." She said, I heard Abi sigh. "Very good." She said, then began to walk around again. "Ladies, keep your core strong as you relevé. Gentlemen use your stomach muscles." She said. "You will have an assessment on Pas De Deux before Christmas. I encourage you to get to know your partners, to bond and to talk. This will strengthen your Pas De Deux work." She said, then she looked at her watch. "Okay." She said clapping her hands. "Thank you ladies and gentlemen." She said, the girls curtseyed as we all bowed.

"I'm thinking we should go out." Kian said as we walked towards the barre. He drank from his water bottle as I let myself slide to the floor.

"Go out, where?" Margo asked as she also sat on the floor to remove her pointes.

"For fun. Just to *get* to know each other." he teased, I looked up at him as he smiled down at me.

"Does that mean Abi comes?" I asked, he laughed softly.

"Anyone can come." He said nodding, I began to nod back to him. "I'm thinking Friday night, a few drinks, some food." He said nodding, Margo nodded back to him as I did.

"Now, though. Lunch?" he said, Margo smiled at him as she stood, she threw her pointes into her bag, so the ribbons hung out the zip. I shook my head at her slowly then stood putting a pair of joggers on over my shorts. "Come on let's get some food." Kian said as he began to leave the studio.

We followed after him. I followed Kian through the dinner queue, Margo behind me as we walked down the salad bar. He picked up a salad made mainly of onions and beetroot, with pieces of shredded chicken on top. He looked at me as he placed it on his tray, I smiled at him then pushed my tray to where his had been. I picked up the same salad.

Chapter 4

"Nice to finally see some contacts Jacob." Madame Rose commented as we all went into our plié on the barre. I nodded to her as she walked past.

They had been a nightmare to put in, and Kian hadn't helped at all. They'd arrived during breakfast yesterday in a little box, with a note from Max and Cameron, but I wasn't confident enough to try them straight after breakfast, so I waited.

Kian had spent the entire time I was in the bathroom laughing. Somehow, I'd managed to put them on, but I still had my glasses into my duffle bag because I completely expected something to go very wrong and either end up having to wear an eye patch, or be forever resigned to wearing my glasses.

"Beautiful pliés." Madame Rose said as she walked down the barres again. "We will be working on two jumps today, the flying pas de chat, and the grand jeté." She said, "Can anyone please tell me what they are?" she asked,

"The step of the cat." Abi said, I looked at her as she didn't meet anyones eyes.

"Brilliant, and how do we do a flying pas de chat?"

"Sideways jump, with first leg extended and the second in retiré." Abi said, Madame Rose nodded to her, I figured if we were in proper school, *and* much littler school she'd have gotten a well done sticker.

"Grand jeté, is a split jump." Kian said, Madame Rose nodded more towards him now.

"We will start with the flying pas de chat, please form pairs to the right." She said, so we did.

We all stood and watched as Madame Rose demonstrated the jump multiple times, then she stood and barked instructions at us as we attempted it ourselves.

Kian *of course* did it perfectly, as did Abi.

Madame Rose however didn't actually seem all too impressed by that as she was too focused on those of us who couldn't even lift ourselves from the floor.

I was use to jumping from pointe, Max had taught me pretty much every jump whilst I was dancing en pointe, so gaining the strength I needed to actually physically lift me from the floor was proving difficult.

"Come on Jacob." Madame shouted at me as I walked the rest of the way across the studio. I nodded to her as an acknowledgement as the next pair went behind me. "Extend." Madame Rose shouted, shaking her head in dismay. "Point your toes. You are ballet dancers." She barked as everyone stood in the corner breathing deeply. "Onto the barres." She ordered, so we did, "Jump." She

65

snapped, clapping her hands in time so we jumped on the beat.

We didn't speak to each other as we left Madame Rose's class, I think everyone *like* myself was still trying to regain their breath. We walked straight to the canteen, claiming a table then just sitting there.

"Oh my god." Kian moaned, "I think my thighs are on fire." He said, then shook his head and twirled himself around on the bench he was sat on. "I'm going to get some food, through my burning thighs." He said as he stood and joined the queue.

"Me too." Margo said leaving the table. I watched her go as I seriously considered having a nap on the table top. My phone vibrating stopped me. Kian returned as I picked it up and read the text from Connor.

"Not getting anything?" Kian asked, I looked at him then waved my hand.

"Will in a minute." I said replying to Connor's text. "Are we still going out tonight?" I asked, Kian nodded to me as he began to cut up his pieces of chicken.

"Definitely, especially after that lesson, that was pure torture." He said shaking his head at me, I nodded to him. "Why?"

"Can I kill two birds with one stone and invite Connor?" I said, Kian grinned.

"Will I like Connor?"

"Oh, it's highly likely." I said nodding to him,

"And is Connor gay?"

"Extremely." I replied, he laughed happily.

"Bring him." He said as Margo came back with a burger and half a plate of chips. "I'm very excited to meet

66

him." He said, as I laughed and told Connor he could come. "Now go get something to eat." Kian said, I met his eyes.

"We have Arlo this afternoon, and I'm pretty certain he's going to put us through our paces. You need food to do that." He said, I looked down at his plate, then at Margo's, *then* I stood going towards the food counters.

I picked up an apple, placing it on my tray, sliding it down to the meals. I picked up a salad that had salmon in it, then a bottle of water.

"Not bad." Kian said when I sat back opposite him, I rolled my eyes at him as I picked up my fork.

"Battement." Arlo said once we were stationed on the barres. It made me smile how we all rose our leg in front of us in perfect time. "Let's make it a grand battement." He said, "ensure this is done with ease." He said as he stood on the top barre facing us, he lifted his leg to the height of his hip and extended it straight without even a flinch.

"It must look effortless. Ensure your supporting leg is straight." He said, it sounded amused as he looked at the boy stood at the front of the barre. "Don't force your leg higher if you can't do it.

We are only in week two, we don't want anyone injuring themselves this soon into the programme, do we." He said smiling at us, it made most of us laugh. "Raise your leg as high as you feel it can go. I will come around to each of you and see if you can raise it any higher." He said, "Grand Battement." He said, I prepared.

Grand Battements and other leg extending moves were Max's speciality, after of course his signature pirouette section, he had told me he'd always been extremely flexible and could extend almost vertical to his body.

67

Once every few months we'd spend an entire lesson of mine on extension, on grand battement, on arabesque, on the splits and I had weirdly enjoyed them. Max had told me simply, if you didn't feel the burn in the back of your legs that meant you weren't doing it right. He'd made me touch the floor with my legs straight multiple times to show me what the burn should feel like. I could feel the burn in the back of my legs as I rose my leg to the height of my hip, I didn't push further because I didn't need to.

"Very good Jacob." Arlo said as he got to me, he fixed my fingers then nodded to me. "You must have an extension mad teacher." He said, I laughed.

"I do." I said, he smiled as he moved on.

▾▾▾

"Kian, this is Connor." I said, using my hands to wave to each of them. "Connor, Kian." I added, Connor smiled at me before looking at Kian, he seemed pleased with what stood before him. I nodded to him making him laugh as Kian waved then turned to where Margo was shouting.

"Wow." Connor said, I hummed at him,

"He made me realise I think freckles are cute. Did *you* know that freckles are cute?" I said, Connor began to laugh,

"And he does ballet."

"He does." I said nodding, I heard Connor as he clicked his tongue.

"Have you seen him naked?" He asked, I laughed as I nodded.

"I have." I replied, then began to walk away from him, he soon caught up to me.

"Excuse me?"

"Amazing." I said, "he can tell you all about his workout schedule and his calorie counting."

"Oh, he's not boring, is he?" He asked, I shook my head laughing softly as I led Connor to the low couches Kian and Margo had taken a seat at.

"Not at all." I said, Connor looked at me a bit warily,

"I genuinely believe today has destroyed my thighs *completely*." Kian said as he looked from the giant laminated menu towards me, "I mean Madame Rose destroyed them initially, then Arlo was all about the extension." He said, I laughed.

"You should've been in our pointe class. It was actual torture today." She said, Connor raised an eyebrow at me, I shook my head,

"I'm not allowed in the pointe class." I said,

"Well, that's the saddest thing I think I've heard in a while." Connor said, I nodded to him until Margo held her hand up in front of Connor.

"No, no don't move on, excuse me?" She said, Connor laughed.

"Jacob might be the best Ballerina I've ever seen."

"Jacob is a Cavalier." Margo said, then she looked at me, "unless of course you're informing me that you don't have a penis." She said,

"That was a rather outdated comment Margo." Kian said, I looked at him. "My best friend at home, Elijah, is the best Cavalier I think I've ever seen." He said, then he raised his eyebrows at Margo, "and he most certainly does not have a penis." He added,

"He's trans?" I asked, Kian nodded to me. "Cool." I added,

"Elijah can dance en pointe, because obviously he trained as a female, until his transition when he was

69

fourteen, and *by* then he was pretty good en pointe. He still dances on them sometimes, he enjoys it, but I also think that's why he's such a good Cavalier because he gets it."

"So, why are you so shit then?" Margo asked, I gasped at her over dramatically,

"Because I was born to be a Prima Ballerina." I replied, Connor nodded to her

"I think Jacob should meet Elijah; they'd enjoy each other's company far too much." Connor said, I laughed as Kian smiled at me.

"I'm thinking of ordering the biggest pizza on the menu, and I'll spend the extra pound to make my drink alcoholic." He said, I nodded to him as Margo did.

"I thought your two day was Saturday, Sunday." Margo teased; Kian laughed shaking his head at her in very pronounced shakes.

"I choose when I eat crap. So, Heaven forbid I might have a salad on Sunday."

"That is actual sacrilege." Connor said, we all looked at him at the same time, he laughed. "Proper roast dinner on a Sunday or nothing." He said, then smiled at me. "The hot dog."

"Always, the burger." I replied, he laughed as I grinned at him. "And I will join in you in paying the extra pound to make it alcoholic." I said, Kian whooped at me, making me laugh as I stood from the couch and took the menu with me to the bar. I returned with the pint that was pulled.

"Oh brave decision." Kian said as I retook my seat, I looked at him as I took a sip out of the pint. "The draught?" He asked, I nodded to him as Connor returned with his own pint. "There is up to two hundred and eight calories, which is just below ten percent of our daily intake." He said nodding, Connor tutted at me, I laughed.

"Drink your pint, enjoy it." I said, Kian nodded,

"I concur. Drink it. Enjoy it." He said as he stood himself with his menu, "I will be having vodka." He said, he sounded quite happy about it.

"And I will be having wine." Margo said as she also stood. "Just eighty-three calories." She said winking at me, I laughed as she walked to the bar herself,

"They didn't know you do pointe?"

"Kian did, we share a room obviously. Margo did not, and I planned on keeping it secret for as long as I could."

"Why?"

"Because boys don't dance en pointe." I said shrugging at him,

"I thought Max taught you better than that." He said, I looked away from him then drank more of the pint.

"So, let me learn more about you." Kian said as he sat back down, a small glass that looked just like coke in his hand,

"Me?" Connor said, Kian nodded as Margo retook her seat, with a glass of red wine.

"Yes you. Age, ballet experience?" He said, Margo and I both began to laugh.

"Eighteen." He replied lifting his pint, "and, all second-hand from Jacob, but I'm totally a Balletomane." He said, then he frowned at me, "right?"

"Right." I said laughing,

"What *the* hell is a Balletomane?" Margo said, I waved my hand in Connor's direction.

"A fan of ballet. I believe it was created in Russia, in the early nineteenth century."

"Wow he's well trained." Kian said, I nodded to him.

"I know." I replied, he laughed.

"So how did you guys meet?" Margo asked, Connor looked at me briefly, I figure he was trying to gage whether it was okay to tell them, so I nodded.

"We met when we were four." He said, "because we were placed in the same care home. He got the better room because he's older than me." He added, I laughed.

"He's still bitter about this, even though I literally gave my bedroom to him when I was adopted. You lived in it for four years."

"Yeah, but you got ten out of it." He replied, Kian laughed out loud.

"Brothers." He said, I looked at him. "You told me you guys would never sleep together. I now understand, because you two are literally brothers."

"Exactly." I said, Kian smiled at me as Connor laughed.

"Wait..." Margo said, Connor looked at him, "you were never adopted?" She asked, Connor shook his head,

"If you don't mind me asking, why?" Kian said, I looked at him as Connor did,

"Why wasn't I adopted?" Connor asked, "or why was I in care?"

"The latter?" Kian said, Connor looked down,

"My parents died when I was three. Car crash. I have no immediate family, or at least I've been told so I went into care."

"That's so sad." Margo said, Connor shrugged slightly.

"Don't know, means I have seven brothers and sisters that I'd have never had." He said, I smiled at him, "and I'd have probably never met him." He added nodding to me,

"Why where you?" Kian asked, I looked at him.

"My mum didn't want me." I said. "Simple. I was put straight into the system once I was born."

"Then you were adopted by your ballet teacher?" Kian said, I nodded to him,

"And his husband." Connor said, so I laughed.

"I think I got a better al- round deal. I figure if I'd been kept the likelihood of me doing ballet and ending up where I am now, was insanely slim." I said, they both nodded as a waiter appeared.

"Pizza." He said, we all pointed at Kian who began to laugh as the massive pizza was placed in front of him, "and I have a burger." He said, I raised my hand, then gawped at the two patty tall burger. "The hot dog." He said then placed it down in front of Connor, "and for the lovely lady chicken tenders." He said, then winked at her as he placed it down, we all watched him walk away.

"You all like boys..." Margo said, I began to laugh as Connor and Kian nodded back to her.

"Yes, he was totally hitting on you." Kian said, Margo smirked.

"How likely do you think it is that I have a chance with him tonight?" She asked, I looked behind the bar, as our waiter stood cleaning the same spot over and over whilst looking at her,

"Pretty high." I said, then looked back at her as she bit her lip.

"Eat your food, you can't have sex on an empty stomach." Kian said,

"Sound advice." Connor replied.

73

"Malibu." Kian said, holding the glass that looked like coke to me, I took it warily. "I think you'd like Malibu." He added grinning at me, I decided to trust him. I took a sip out of the glass. I also decided that I liked Malibu.

"Coconutty." I said, Connor laughed as he took the bottle of beer off Kian, who had a second vodka and coke.

"I didn't think she'd just go for it." Connor said, Kian began to nod as sat beside Connor on the couch.

"Last weekend." He said, I turned to look at him. "She found a guy, probably about twenty, and went through every stage of a relationship in like twenty minutes. I was bloody impressed." He said, we all laughed. "I also totally appreciated how relaxed she was about sex."

"Yeah?" Connor said, so I looked at him I almost smiled.

"Yeah. I mean I've had sex, and I think I'm good at it." Kian said, I bit my lip so I wouldn't laugh because I truly couldn't work out who was flirting with who more. Margo with the bartender, or Kian with Connor. "But I can't be that casual. At all."

"No, I totally agree." Connor said, I raised an eyebrow at him, he shushed me before looking back at Kian.

"You've?"

"Yeah." He said, I rolled my eyes and drank more out of my glass. I finished it in two gulps. "But like you said, I cannot be casual."

"Right." Kian said, then looked at Connor. "Good."

"Good?" Connor replied, they both awkwardly sipped from their drinks.

"My god." I muttered, it made Connor laugh, and he did until he looked at me. I looked up and back at him as my hand went to my stomach, because something was definitely not right in there.

"Alright?" he said, I frowned at him then shook my head and stood walking away from the little couches and into the men's room.

I threw up as soon as I got into a stall.

Both, Kian and Connor turned to look at me when I returned to them, I sat back down meekly then turned to look in the direction of the bar.

"Oh I take it she got him then." I said, Connor laughed so I looked at him.

"Feeling okay?" Connor said, I sighed.

"Likes Malibu but can't handle it I guess." Kian said, I looked down. "Don't be embarrassed, be happy you aren't drunk." He said amused, it made me smile.

"Yeah, she got him. She didn't even have to try hard. I don't know if I'm impressed or ashamed."

"Ashamed?" Connor said laughing, Kian began to laugh back.

"Ashamed that I do not have those skills." He said, they both began to laugh as I did too, it faltered when a waiter appeared, he placed a jug of water on the table. I looked up at him as he nodded to me, smiling as he did. I frowned at the jug, then frowned at Kian and Connor.

"Figured you might want some water." Kian said, then he smiled at me, I smiled back then lifted the jug and poured it into the glass.

It felt extra nice to fall into my bed, so I lay there my hands on my head as I yawned, turning my head towards the bathroom when the light clicked off. I put my glasses back on watching as Kian walked across the room to his bed, he looked at me as he got in. We seemed to have a stare off for a while.

"How do you feel?" he asked, I shrugged. "Good. No getting up to throw up during the night." he said, I laughed into my arms then shook my head.

"I don't know what it was, just felt funny. I'm not drunk."

"Nah, you're not drunk." He said, I laughed, then took my glasses back off, so I could lie comfortably on my pillow. "I want to be honest with you." He said, I hummed back at him because sleep was beginning to sound like the best decision right now. "I thought about having sex with your best friend, multiple times tonight." He said, I laughed, *I knew it.* "So, were do we stand on this?"

"Stand on it?" I asked, he hummed but I figured his nod was highly animated.

"Do you care if I actively seek out sex with your best friend?" he asked, I laughed.

"It depends." I said, then I opened my eyes and looked in his general direction. "Break his heart and you die."

"Of course." He agreed,

"I take it, it wouldn't be... casual." I said, Kian laughed softly.

"No course not. He'd have to like me back that'd be a good starting point." He said, then he sighed.

"You have my blessing." I said, he laughed.

"Thank you." He replied, "you didn't tell me he was gorgeous."

"It's not a word I think of when I talk about Connor. To be honest."

"Start thinking it." he said, I laughed.

Max smiled amused at me as I danced step by step with the immediate pointe class. I'd stood behind them as they worked through an ensemble piece Max liked to teach from Swan Lake.

"Beautiful work girls. Next week we're going to look at the solo of the Sugar Plum Fairy." He said, then he laughed. "Following we'll do a song from this century." He added, all the girls whispered '*yes*' in front of me, I laughed, then bowed as the girls curtseyed. Max nodded to them letting them go as he went to the sound system.

"So, how's the big ballet school then?" Maisie asked as she walked towards me, I laughed.

"Big." I replied, she grinned at me.

Maisie had been in the home with Connor and I, she was three or so years younger than me and had been adopted a year after I had. From what I could tell, she adored her adoptive parents, and they loved her. They had enrolled her into Max's ballet school a few months after the adoption was confirmed, it was a complete coincidence that she had been enrolled into Max's class. I only found this out when she moved up to immediate pointe last year, and we'd both exclaimed loudly and shocked that we knew each other.

"Just… big?" she replied raising her eyebrow at me, I laughed,

"Amazing." I said nodding, "every minute of every day is just ballet."

"I thought your life was like that anyway." She said amused, I smiled back at her.

"Yeah. It kind of is." I said, she laughed, then turned as the little group of girls I usually saw her spending break with called her over. "Go on. I'll tell you all about ballet school another time." I said, she grinned then she hugged me, and ran off.

"You're very good at the ballerina part of Swan Lake." Max said as I stood beside him, I leant against the barre to take my pointes off.

"Is that a compliment?" I asked, Max laughed.

"I'd say so." He said, then he smiled at me, I looked down as I smiled back. "Frankie and Cory are coming for tea. Just to warn you in advance." Max said as he packed up his bag and put it over his shoulder, I looked up at him.

"Thanks. I'll prepare myself appropriately" I said, he laughed as we left the studio.

Frankie and Cory were loud. Together with Max, I figured it made them louder. They were all school friends. Frankie and Max having been in the same class, and roommates for the seven years of school, and Cory being in the year above them.

The story was as old as time, Frankie and Cory had started dating when Frankie was sixteen, and Cory seventeen, they'd been together ever since.

Whenever Max spoke about their relationship, he always did it with a smile on his face. Cory had gotten a role in the Australian Ballet Company when he left the National Ballet School, and according to Max, had to be away up to six months at a time for his contracts, whilst Frankie stayed in London and danced in multiple ballet productions. Cory finished his contract almost ten years ago, after doing it for five years, and he opened up his ballet shop, they were married a few years later.

"It's the prodigy." Frankie said after Max had let them into the house, he was the first into the living room where I was sat on the couch beside Cameron. "How's school?" he asked, I began to nod to him. "Has it changed at all?" he asked amused then came to sit beside me, I frowned at him as he hummed, "still have Madame Rose?" he asked, I nodded to him my eyes widening as I did.

"She scares me."

"She still scares me." Cory said, I turned my head to look at him, "I can still hear her snap when she said my name." he said shivering lightly. "Corinthian." He said, then shook his head it made me laugh.

"She took a liking to calling me Francis." Frankie said, so I looked back at him. "And it was even better when she used to say it with such dismay."

"How could she have possibly said your names with dismay?" I asked, as Cory took the arm chair next to the couch.

"Madame Rose was never happy." Cory said, "you get a slight acknowledge if you do something right, but she will still find at least six things wrong with it." he said, Frankie nodded to him.

"But if it's only six that's when you know you dance well." Frankie said, I hummed at him. "The first lesson of the year was my favourite, or should I say the first lesson of second year was my favourite. She made us all stand before her and she basically stood and called us out and things she didn't want to see again." He said laughing, I nodded.

"She did that with us. Now apparently I wear contacts." I said, Cory nodded.

"We had a few people in our class who had to invest in contacts. They were too scared to defy her." He said amused as Max reappeared.

"What did you have to get rid of?" I asked, Frankie looked at Cory as he laughed.

"Bracelets, and my watch." He said, "Corinthian there is no need for you to know the time during my lesson.

It ends when I say it ends." He said, I began to laugh covering my mouth when I did.

"I had to get rid of my clingy boyfriend." Frankie said grinning at Cory, he pulled his tongue back at him. "She wasn't amused by his presence outside of our class." He said, I laughed as I turned to look at Max.

"I was thinking of ordering take away." He said, "partly because Cameron hasn't cooked anything." He said, Cameron scoffed as he reached into his pocket for his phone, he scrolled through it until he found the take away he and Max frequented at.

"Tell me about this musical you're in." Frankie said as he brought the knives and forks into the living room with him, Cameron followed with plates whilst Max brought in some glasses,

"*Pippin*." Cameron said, as Frankie sat back beside me on the couch. "Opens in December."

"And you're dancing in it?" Cory asked, Max nodded.

"En pointe too. The director liked that I could, and decided that I must do all dancing en pointe."

"And who are you playing?" Cory asked, Cameron looked up at him.

"I'm the Narrator, probably one of the only none dancing parts." He said amused,

"Who's the lead then?" Frankie asked, Max laughed it seemed happy, Frankie thought this too if his amused frown was anything to go by.

"Funny that actually." He said, Frankie nodded as if to say 'well tell us', "Because obviously Cameron got the role through auditioning about a year ago, but I got a call in the summer asking if I wanted to dance in the chorus."

"Right." Frankie said,

"Bear with, the story does have a happy ending." I said, Frankie laughed.

"Basically, the person playing the lead suggested me when they were discussing the dancers. His suggestion was so shining they didn't even feel the need to put me through the audition process."

"Sam."

"Sam." Max agreed, Frankie nodded.

"Keeping it in the family and all." Cameron said then stood to the sound of the doorbell.

"Sam… was your choreographer?" I asked, Max nodded it wasn't a complete nod, it kind of said 'ish'.

"Old friend." Frankie said, I looked towards him. "We've known Sam for years."

"Since I did *Billy Elliot*." Max added,

"Sam and Max got quite close." Frankie teased, I laughed as Max shook his head.

"He is amazing. Always has been."

"He's a celebrity in Australia, it's quite weird." Cory said, "when I was there, they loved him. Musical's he was in sold out in hours, ballet's he'd choreographed anything, they were massive."

"And of course, Cameron was a huge fan." Max said, as Cameron walked back in and placed the bags on the table top.

"Who?" Cameron asked, Max smiled at him.

"Samuel Bing." He said, Cameron laughed as he looked at me,

"Oh god yes. He was my inspiration and teenage crush all in one." He said happily, "he's on my list." He added, as the bags were ripped open and spread out amongst the plates.

81

"Your list?" I said, Cameron turned to look at Max who rolled his eyes.

"It's not fair, because he's actually a viable choice." He said, then sat on the floor behind the coffee table. "His list of people he can sleep with and I can't get annoyed about it." he said, I gasped as Cameron laughed.

"Another is Ashton Kutcher." He said, as he passed me the fork.

"Fair." I said nodding to him.

I went to bed before Frankie and Cory left, leaving them downstairs talking about everything, and *anything*. I lay back on my bed feeling as the takeaway sat heavily in my stomach.

Every time I moved, I felt as everything moved around in my stomach. Until I sat up and my stomach dropped. I rubbed my hand over it a few times then I stood out of bed and walked into the bathroom. I looked up at the ceiling as I stood by the toilet, then sighed before I threw up. I didn't sleep when I got back into my bed, I just lay back looking at my ceiling, until there was a knock on my door, I looked towards it.

"Yes?" I asked, Cameron opened it, he held a glass of water up to me, so I sat up.

"You okay?" he asked, coming to sit on my bed, he passed me the water then rested the back of his hand on my forehead. I nodded to him as I sipped from the water.

"Yeah. I'm okay." I said, "must have ate too much, or something." I said shaking my head then put my glass onto the bedside cabinet.

"I've left them talking about ballet. A conversation I'm sure you'd fit right into, but I could hear you so I figured I'd come and see if you were okay." He said, I nodded to him. "It's not school is it?" he asked, I frowned at him, although I ensured I made it soft. "You're not worried, or scared about anything? You want to go back on Monday?"

"Yeah, course I do. I don't know maybe I got a bad piece of chicken or something. I don't feel sick anymore."

"Okay." He said softly, then he stood from my bed. "You want to talk though, you can. Yeah?" he said, I smiled at him then nodded.

"Yeah." I said.

Chapter 5

"Good work first years. You've really come on leaps and bounds since your first week." Arlo said happily after he'd watched our warm up. "Now the exciting part." He added he sounded very happy with himself, I looked across at Kian as he laughed and leant on the barre. "As you know Christmas is rapidly approaching."

"It's October." A boy at the front said, Arlo looked amused.

"Yes, and in ballet world that means Christmas is next week." He said simply, we all laughed. "Every year we put on a Christmas ballet. This year is no different." He said, I raised my eyebrow at Kian as he did back.

"This year we are putting on Matthew Bourne's Edward Scissorhands." He said, everyone in the class gasped, "but before your auditions commence, I am here to remind you. Although you will be auditioning with an Edward solo, the main roles will go to Second years. You will be chorus dancers." He said, most of us nodded, because that was fair. "So, we will begin rehearsing. Your auditions will follow next week, you have a week to perfect this dance. Let's get started." He said clapping his hands, so we turned to look at the floor where Arlo stood. He danced through the solo for us, before he began to teach us it.

"This dance is a Pas De Deux." Arlo said as we formed lines to practice. "However, it is not in hold. This is danced alongside the female lead; you do not touch at all during this dance.

You will notice the Edward character never actually touches his ballerina, throughout their Pas De Deux sections, especially. There are lifts but he never actually touches her."

"That's because he has scissors for hands." Kian said, we all laughed as Arlo did, he pointed at Kian, that was all he needed to do.

"This is a very beautiful dance, of course, Bourne's choreography is always beautiful, but if I set the scene for you." He said, we all tittered as Arlo grinned. "It is snowing. Outside of the house. Edward is craving a statue of an angel. This bit of choreography is not necessary." He said,

"He stands strong. His arms raised into fifth." He said, so we all did, raising out arms into fifth position, "he brings them down before he even thinks about beginning to move, and then, he watches." He said, as the music worked through, "and now he joins in, with a petit jeté." He said, then danced through the section of music, he turned to look at us when he finished then started the section again.

"Extension is important for Edward." Arlo stated as he watched us dance through the section. "His movements cannot be small. He literally has scissors for hands." He said as he extended his fingers. "Make sure even the people sat in the gods can see your fingers." He said, Kian laughed beside me, which made me begin to laugh.

We got through the entire audition piece as we hit the half way point of the lesson so Arlo split us into two groups of eight, and got us to run through the dance multiple times.

"Brilliant boys, you're doing brilliantly." He said then leant on the barre behind him. "Let me tell you a bit more about this production as we dance." He said, I smiled as Kian rolled his eyes at me as he stepped into his extension.

"This will be a spilt production, as there are thirty-two first, and second years. We will have a cast of sixteen each night. The first cast will perform a matinee and an evening, as will the second cast. You boys will be split amongst the chorus unless one of you excels in your audition." He said, it was clear he thought that unlikely, I decided that was because the second years were so good, not because we were crap.

"When will auditions be Arlo?" Kian asked, as he continued to dance through, Arlo smiled at him.

"Next Thursday." He replied, Kian nodded back, "ensure you do not overwork this dance. We will rehearse it again next week in our lesson, and of course feel free to rehearse it in your own time, but do not get over familiar with this dance. That is how you become complacent, and I will not have any complacent dancers."

"It's easy." Kian said as he began on his treadmill, I ran alongside him, having now learnt how to turn my own treadmill on, and off. "The Edward solo. I like it but I figure it's easy."

"Nicer problems to have." I said, Kian laughed. "I like it but it's a bit boring for me." I shrugged.

"Well, you'll get to have your excitement in Pas De Deux this afternoon." He said, I laughed, "Abi will definitely put that sense of excitement back into you." He said, I smirked then shook my head as I laughed.

"It's been like six weeks and she despises me." I stated, "I've never known hate to grow in a person so quickly." I said, then looked back at him as he was laughing.

"Ever think she hates you so much because she wants to have sex with you."

"Give over. I can't even lift her up, she won't want to have sex with me." I said, he titled his head at me in a totally smug way that told me, he thought I was talking sheer bullshit.

"I think the opposite."

"Course you do." I said, he laughed then lifted his arm to read his watch, he hummed.

"Want to join me for some lunch, before Pas De Deux?" he said, I hummed. "Okay, I'll rephrase that. You're coming with me for lunch." He said, I rolled my eyes as he slowed down his treadmill, I followed suit.

I dabbed the back of my neck with my towel as Kian collected his bag, getting his phone out and reading it. "Margo's in the canteen, come on." He said, so I followed him. I went to sit beside Margo as Kian went through the food queue. He came back with a quiche,

"See I thought that looked nice, but I also thought it looked oddly healthy." Margo said, he laughed as he picked up his fork.

"Heaven forbid." He teased, then began to chase her with his fork. She laughed as she jumped off the seat and ran to the dessert section.

"Well done First Years, you're beginning to work together beautifully." Miss Olivia said as she weaved herself amongst us. She nodded to me as she passed me, so I smiled back as I let out a breath and held Abi's hand above her head as she pirouetted, she went onto the arabesque, barely holding my fingers as I walked around her.

"And fish dive." Miss Olivia said, then turned to watch as we all did the lift. I succeeded in that lift, because it was low. It didn't actually require me to lift her above my shoulders. "Lovely." Miss Olivia said, she almost sounded amazed, it made me laugh until Abi shot me a look that suggested I shut up. "Please practice through again." Miss Olivia said, as she turned to look through something.

"It's my nineteenth birthday this weekend." Kian said, I turned my head to look at him as Abi and Margo pirouetted.

"What are you planning? Night out?"

"No." Kian said thoughtfully, "in fact a night in. I thought we could get some drinks in. Watch a film or something of the sort. Nothing to wild."

"Shh." Abi said, I rolled my eyes as I walked around her.

"Maybe order a pizza." Kian said, then he tapped my back with his hand, I turned my head. "Oh, and invite Connor." He said, I laughed.

"Would you like a side of condoms with that?" I asked, he laughed as I lifted Abi into the fish dive, I began to laugh as Kian over dipped Margo so she could touch the floor, almost falling out of the lift. They were both very amused by it.

"Kian and Margo." Miss Olivia said, I looked at her as she was looking back at us in the mirror. "Do I see you, not being sensible?" she said, Kian laughed as Margo did.

Miss Olivia however did not look impressed, I watched her for a few moments as the music ran through again. She circled her hand, telling us to keep going through it.

"Connor likes you, a lot." I said, Kian grinned.

"Good." He said quietly, I smirked at Margo as she smirked right back.

"Less talking. More dancing." Miss Olivia said, I bit my lip, seeing as Margo and Kian looked at each other and exchanged a mock scared look. I heard Abi hum, I sighed as she went into the arabesque.

▾▾▾

"I have a question for you." Kian said, as he reappeared from the bathroom, I looked him over trying to figure out why he'd been in there so long.

It turned out he'd shaved.

"Go ahead?" I said sitting up from my pillow, and crossing my legs on my bed, he came to sit opposite me on my bed.

"I was thinking about our deal with sex." He said, I raised an eyebrow at him.

"Me and you? You're great. Very attractive, but I don't think so." I said, he laughed it sounded more like a sigh as he leant his head back looking up at the ceiling. "You mean the deal…" I said, as he lowered his head to look at me again, "…Like how we know not to come in."

"Yes." He said, I smirked slightly.

89

"Planning on sleeping with my best friend tonight, I see." I said, he laughed. "Or you better be, you're not metaphorically cheating on him?"

"Yes, I plan on sleeping with your best friend tonight." He said, "and I'm not just throwing it on him out of the blue. We've been talking for weeks, since we met." He said, I nodded to him then I shrugged.

"I don't know…" I said, because it had not been a question I'd asked Max and Cameron, it hadn't occurred to me at all that sex happened in the dorm rooms.

"I mean we can go cliché and put a tie on the door or something, but then I also don't want to kick you out tonight just so I can have sex, because that's not fair."

"I'm glad you see that." I said, he laughed. "I could stay with Margo." I said, he laughed.

"And Abi?" he said, I rolled my eyes.

"I take it Connor's place isn't an option?" I said, he frowned at me. "Connor lives alone." I said,

"Curfew." He said, I shrugged.

"If you don't come back until the next morning, you're not breaking curfew." I said, he laughed. "And maybe if there's a tie on the door, that means stay out." I said, raising my arms to him, he smiled slightly.

"Okay, I'll keep an eye out for that." He said amused as he stood from my bed.

"Hey, I could have sex. You don't know." I said, he turned to look at me. "I like girls, and boys. There is range." I stated, he laughed as he walked back around his bed and picked his phone up, he smiled as it as he typed into it, then he looked up surprised at the knock on the door. I stood and answered it, walking backwards as Margo came into our room.

"I couldn't deal anymore. I had to leave her." Margo said then sat on Kian's bed. "She was condemning everything. Drinking, eating, having friends." She said rolling her eyes, "and I've had to spend the whole day with her, because it's a Saturday." She stated shaking her head, she looked at Kian briefly. "Happy Birthday by the way." She said, Kian began to nod.

"Cheers." He replied, I laughed.

"Your gift, from me is going to be the copious amount of alcohol I'm going to buy." She said, "so tell me your spirit." She declared, I looked at Kian as he smirked.

"Don't buy him Malibu." He said, I laughed as he turned to look at me, he seemed to examine me. "Bottle of vodka." He said nodding, I nodded back. "And some beers."

"Beers aren't a spirit Kian love." Margo said, it made me smile.

"It's my birthday. My word is law." He replied, I gasped at him whilst pointing at him. "I like that rule, can we enforce that every birthday?" I asked, he laughed as Margo shook her head a smile on her face as she left our room.

"Connor's outside." Kian said, I looked towards him. "Do you want to meet him?" he asked, I reached for my phone swiping away the lock screen to see a message from Connor also telling me he was outside, so I nodded to him.

"I'll go meet him. You can make yourself look pretty." I said blowing him a kiss as I stood from the bed, he laughed holding his finger up to me as I left our room.

Connor was stood on the other side of the student entrance into the dormitories. He seemed surprised when I opened the door to him.

"Aw you shouldn't have." I said once I clocked the bunch of flowers in his hand, he laughed his cheeks going a little red as he held the flowers behind his back.

"Shut up." He replied as he laughed. "I also brought." He said reaching into his bag, he pulled out a bottle of gin.

"You brought gin."

"Yes, yes I did." he replied as he read the bottle. "There's been many of fun nights created by this bottle." He said, I sighed as I laughed then nodded my head down the corridor, so he began to follow me. "This is like a proper school isn't it." he said, I frowned at him. "Like I expected it to be all ballet like, but it looks like a proper school." He said, I raised an eyebrow at him.

"Oh shut up." He added I laughed then knocked him in the direction of our corridor with my hip. "Do you know if…" he began, then he sighed and looked at me, "at risk of sounding like a needy other half, has Kian mentioned me?" he said, I laughed then nodded.

"Yes, he has mentioned you." I said, he smiled to himself before looking back at me. "You're so going to get laid tonight." I said, he laughed as he looked at me.

"Really?" he asked, I nodded to him then stopped outside of our door. "Awesome." He muttered I laughed as I opened the door, Kian turned and smiled at us, so I turned my head to look at Connor who was smiling back at him.

I figured it was awkward standing between them so I went to sit on my bed. I watched as Connor awkwardly held the flowers out to Kian, then I smiled as Kian's whole expression lit up then he smelt the flowers. They both looked at me, I looked away as they stepped towards each other and kissed.

"This is beautifully awkward." I said, they both laughed as Kian went into the en-suite. He came back with our empty soap dispenser, although now it was filled with water and the flowers sat in it almost perfectly.

"I got Black Swan." Kian said, then looked at Connor, "because you know, ballet film is mandatory." He said, Connor laughed.

"I have a liking of ballet films. They were the only thing on when Jacob was in charge of the television." He said, turning to look at me I winked at him.

"I've also got the password to my brothers Netflixs. So…" Kian said shrugging dramatically at us then he opened his laptop.

We had figured out a few weeks back that his laptop had a suitable sized screen to be placed on the chest of drawers for us both to watch from our beds. It was also loud enough not to be a problem. It had been a great discovery and we'd gone through many series since we'd discovered it.

Margo returned with two bags that clinked together as they moved then began to pour drinks for us. She sat herself on the opposite end of my bed, as I sat at the head. Kian and Connor sat in the middle of Kian's bed, leaning back against the wall with the six pack of beers on Connor's side and the bottle of vodka lying next to Kian, then I started the film, Kian turned out the lights from his bed.

"Please remain quiet during the feature presentation." Kian said, I began to laughed as Margo held her drink up to me, I clinked my glass against hers as the opening titles began.

Margo kept our drinks filled to the top as we watched the film, she didn't let my drink drop below halfway, so I began to feel giddier and giddier as the night went on, which, I swear is the only reason I began to giggle like a child when I turned to look at Kian's bed to see they'd given up watching the movie and were more interested in each other's mouths.

"You know, I'm all for this relationship." I said to Margo, she frowned then looked towards his bed and began to laugh as well. "Just with less tongues. You know."

"I know." she agreed, I laughed then covered my mouth.

"You're trying to get me drunk."

"Honey, I don't need to try." She replied, grinning at me as I held my glass out to her again.

"I'm thinking of ordering a pizza." Margo said as the credits ran up the laptop screen, I nodded to her slowly then glanced at Kian as he hummed then got off his bed.

"I think we're going to bow out." Kian said, Connor grinned he seemed quite pleased with himself, then he looked at me, so I blew him a kiss, he winked back then blew me one back.

"Fine, fine you two go and have sex. We'll order pizza then. Right Jacob."

"Right!" I stated as Connor stood from the bed, he came to me kissing the side of my head.

"Don't get too drunk Ballerina." He whispered in my ear, I smiled at him as he began to laugh then he took Kian's hand.

"I'll see you tomorrow morning." Kian said as they left our room.

"I wouldn't count on it." Margo said, they both laughed then she turned to me. She ordered pizza on her phone then she grinned. "I have a game we should play."

"A game?" I repeated, she nodded.

"Truth, Dare or Shot." She said happily as she produced multiple coloured shot glasses.

"I've never played this." I said, she laughed.

94

"No, really. I'm shocked Jacob." She said, I smiled. "So it's simple. Every round, is truth, dare or shot."

"Can I back out?" I asked, she hummed.

"You can back out of a dare, but only by taking a shot. The same with truth."

"Deal." I said holding my hand out to her, she took it and shook it. Then placed the shots in lines of five, she filled the first row with vodka, the second with gin, the third with tequila then she started again.

"Youngest goes first." she said, I laughed.

"April, twenty-third." I said, she grinned at me.

"February, twelfth." She replied, I tutted then I hummed.

"Shot." I said,

"Fair game." She replied lifting her hands up as I reached for the first vodka shot, I threw it back then threw the little shot glass off the bed. "Shot." She agreed, grinning at me then took her own. There were almost ten glasses on the floor when I gave.

"Truth. Truth. I choose truth." I said, she grinned at me.

"Have you…" she said, then she hummed, "have you ever kissed a girl?" she asked, I looked down at the shots before us. "I know you've kissed a boy." She said grinning, so I shook my head.

"I haven't kissed a girl." I said,

"Ooh." She cooed at me, "truth." She added, I smirked.

"Have *you* ever kissed a girl?" I asked, she laughed shaking her head at me.

"No, no I haven't. You're right it seems like something I'd have done." She said, I smirked as she laughed.

95

"Dare." I said, she smiled at me as I grinned back at her.

"I dare you," she said, then leant a little closer to me. "To kiss me." she said, I laughed as I leant towards her.

"Surely, I'm meant to dare you to kiss me?"

"Double dare." She said, I laughed.

"Double dare." I agreed amused,

"You can take a shot first. If you're nervous." She said, I shook my head, moving closer to her whilst trying to ensure I didn't knock over any of the shots. She leant her nose against mine, so they were touching then she tilted her head, so I followed suit, following her lead and kissing her.

"Good morning." Kian said, I groaned at him then moved, feeling as a sharp pain travelled from my shoulders down my back, I opened my eyes then shut them again because it was too bright.

"You must've had a good night." he said amused, I opened one eye and looked up at him. I touched my face feeling the frame of my glasses. I opened both of my eyes, finding I was sat on the floor of our en-suite between the toilet and the shower. "Margo's asleep in your bed, and here you are." He said amused then held his hands out to me, he helped me stand.

I groaned once I did touching my head because it hurt then I walked to the sink, leaning my elbows on it, and putting my head into my hands.

"If I were a detective and had to figure out what had happened, I'd say you and Margo had a bit to drink after I'd left and you came in here to throw up, and feel asleep."

"I might've come in here to pee." I replied turning to look at him, he laughed.

96

"You didn't. Hate to break that too you." He said, I groaned, "I on the other hand did come in here to pee." He said, I laughed as I turned back to the sink, taking my glasses off and putting them alongside the sink as I washed my face. "Mind if I pee?" he asked, I waved my hand in his general direction.

"Please, feel free." I said, then ran my fingers through my hair. "We played a game truth, dare or shot." I said then put my glasses back on, Kian laughed.

"You let Margo peer pressure you into a drinking game."

"I did." I agreed, then I turned to actually look at him, "I kissed her."

"You what?" he said, then looked up at me.

"She dared me too." I said, he laughed as he flushed the toilet then came to stand beside me at the sink, he knocked me to side so he could wash his hands. I groaned and leant my forehead against his shoulder.

"You're hungover."

"I agree." I replied, he smirked. "How did sex go?" I asked, Kian laughed then leant his head on mine.

"The sex went really well." He said, I smiled into his shoulder. "And was a lot of fun." He added. "I'm back so early because Connor had to go to work, but we totally agreed we'd have spent most of this Sunday in bed if we could."

"It's Sunday." I groaned; Kian laughed into my ear. "I need to text Cameron." I said shaking my head at him, "I am not going home today." I said then I sighed as I went back into the bedroom, Margo was still asleep on my bed, and multiple shot glasses were scattered around the floor of it.

"It looks like you guys had a fun night." Kian said amused, "I'd say I wish I was here, but I really don't."

"How do I kick her out of my bed without being a dick? I want to sleep." I said, Kian laughed as he stood and walked to Margo, he shook her shoulder a few times until she woke up.

She groaned at him, as he moved away just about dodging the hit she aimed at him. "Come on my love. I'll take you back to your room so you can sleep it off." He said, she sighed but nodded to him getting out of my bed, and wrapping her arm around Kian's hips. "I'll come back and clean up. Go to sleep Jacob." He said, I nodded to him as he laughed and left our room.

I took my t-shirt off when the door closed, then let my jeans fall to the floor. I stepped into my bed, picking up my phone as I did, and laying back as I searched through my texts until I found Cameron, I sent him a text, telling him I wasn't leaving my bed today then leant my phone on my chest as I closed my eyes. it vibrated against me as I was drifting off into sleep. I opened the message then I laughed.

IMessage

Cameron: I remember it well. Get some rest, we'll see you next week. C x

I turned over when I woke up, frowning at Kian's silhouette before I put my glasses on, he smiled at me once he saw me, I frowned back at him, then sat myself up. He was sat in the darkness just his bedside lamp on beside him, a pair of headphones over his ears, a note pad on his legs, he appeared to be writing something.

"Evening." He said, I groaned.

"Evening." I repeated, he nodded as I rubbed my eyes under my glasses.

"Okay, so maybe it's not fully evening, it's just turned five." He said, I looked at the window, our curtains were drawn. "It's dark." He added amused, I groaned at him. "Too much to process?" he asked, I nodded. "Well wake up. I'd like to gossip about your best friend." He said, I laughed as I swung my legs out of my bed.

"I need the toilet." I mumbled, "then, yes talk about Connor to your hearts content." I said, he grinned as I stood and went into the en-suite.

I felt unbalanced as I stepped into the en-suite, so decided leaning my hand on the wall behind the toilet was the best option to keep myself from falling over. I leant my head against my arm, closing my eyes as I peed. I squeezed my eyes shut against the pain in my head then I gasped as I remembered the rest of the game with Margo. I washed my hands then went back into the bedroom, Kian raised an eyebrow at me as I reappeared, so I went to sit on his bed.

"What? What have you remembered from last night?" he said, I looked at him. "You had that look on your face, the sober slash hung over realisation of a drunken night." he said, "so what did you do?"

"I fooled around with Margo." I said, his eyes widened but he did a very good job of keeping his voice level.

"Fooled around like?"

"Like…" I said, then tried to resist making hand gestures. "She dared me to strip, so I double dared her, stating as long as she did too." I said, Kian laughed. "Then, she took a shot, so I also did, and then she dared me to touch her. Fuck, I went from being a girl virgin to touching a girl last night." I said, he laughed.

"It tends to happen like that." He replied, I rolled my eyes. "You…" he said, then he sort of stuttered.

"She touched my dick." I said, "I didn't dare her to do that. She gave me a handjob. I, returned the favour."

"Jacob." He said, it almost sounded like a laugh so I groaned again, into my hands. "Did she want you too?"

"Yeah." I said nodding, "I asked her over and over, and over. I wanted her too. God, I had fun." I said, he began to laugh, nodding to me.

"As did I." he said,

"As did you?" I replied, he nodded.

"We officiated it."

"I know you had sex."

"No, I mean we officiated the whole boyfriend thing, before we slept together, we were talking about us that cliché conversation, and he said he'd very much like me to be his boyfriend, and I very much agreed, so now. I have a boyfriend." He said, I smiled at him then I stood picking up my phone and taking it back to my bed.

"And he didn't inform me." I said as I flipped through all of my messaging apps. "Well, I guess I've moved down the pecking order." I said, Kian laughed as he moved off his bed, he picked off his own phone.

"Come on, let's get something to eat." He said, I looked at him rubbing my hand over my stomach, I shook my head.

"I think I'm still hungover. I don't think I could stomach anything." I said, he began to nod.

"Come with me for the company then?" he asked, I nodded to him. "And to see Margo." He added, I laughed biting my lip as I shook my head at him. I followed him into the canteen, choosing a table as Kian went through the queue. Margo came to sit next to me as Kian reached the drinks.

"Still hungover?" she asked, I nodded to her, she laughed.

"Yep, me too. However, my memory is crystal clear." She said, I looked at her.

"Mine too." I said, she laughed, I instantly relaxed although I wasn't aware I had been so tense.

"Regrets?" she asked, I shook my head. "Good." She replied then she smiled at me. "None from me too." She added, then kissed my cheek and stood to go to the food counter.

Chapter 6

I sat on the floor of the studio I'd rented for the hour.

I sat for a few minutes just looking back at myself as I tied my pointes. I ensured I tied them properly, pulling up my sock and wrapping the black ribbons around tightly, until I tied the knot behind my ankle. I folded the top of my sock back over the knot until it sat right, then I moved onto my other foot.

Max had frequently told me to wear my socks under my pointes, he'd sat opposite me on the floor, pulling my foot against his calf as he tied my ribbons around my ankles. He told me it'd stop my pointes rubbing, it'd help with the pain.

He had obviously lied, but had placebo-ed me long enough for me to get through the most painful period of breaking in my pointes. I still wore thick socks whenever I was breaking in pointes, even though I was well aware they did very little to actually aid the process.

I stood myself at the nearest barre, alternating my feet onto and off pointe. I rose onto pointe as I let go of the barre. I was still warmed up from my lessons this morning so I walked back into the centre of the room. I still alternated my feet onto and off pointe until I rose on both feet, lifting my arms into fifth.

I closed my eyes as I counted the beats in my head then I began to dance the Edward solo, smiling to myself as I rose into my arabesque, I looked at myself in the mirror holding my arabesque then I sighed happily as I let it drop, and I moved across the floor into the following extension, *then* I stopped listening through the music as it continued. Arlo had taught us the next section, but had said we would only need it if we progressed and had to do a Pas De Deux audition. It had involved multiple lifts and, it finished with a kiss.

I smiled to myself as I created a circle with my pointe then stood back up on them, holding my arms back in fifth as the music looped and started again. I danced through to the arabesque, raising myself up.

"You dance en pointe?" I heard, and I fell out of the arabesque, catching myself before I actually fell to the floor. I turned quickly, looking at Abi who was stood in the doorway, a duffle bag over her shoulder, her pointes tied together over the strap of her bag. She wore what looked like a leotard, but looked far softer and had shorts, she wore it with legwarmers, which reached her thighs, I was obviously spending far too long look at that area of her body. "Jacob." She snapped at me, I looked back up to her face.

"Yes." I said, then I nodded to her. "I dance pointe."

"I booked this studio."

103

"So did I." I said, she sighed. "Leave."

"No." I said frowning at her. "We're dancing to the same music, make do." I said, she scoffed, throwing her duffle bag onto the floor, the blocks in her pointes hitting the floor with a sort of trotting noise. I looked at her as she walked around the perimeter of the studio until she reached a barre and she began to warm up. I watched her for a few minutes then I circled myself starting the dance again.

"You're off time." Abi commented, I didn't turn to look at her.

"You're dancing the female." I replied, then actually turned to look at her as she stood, her arms folded watching me, I frowned back at her as the music played on behind us.

"Oh, I *presumed* with your pointes on, you were dancing the female." She said, I laughed, it almost came out like a bark.

"You think you can do better?" I said, she nodded to me walking to the centre. She met my eyes then began to dance to the part of music that we were instructed to stand strong during. I covered my mouth as I watched to ensure the smile that was growing on my face didn't come through.

There were multiple pirouettes in the section she danced, and it made me smile to think of how the flowy skirt, that I'm sure who ever was playing the principal ballerina would be wearing, would raise and fall as she spun. Then she stood, her own frame strong as she stood in the position that my dance section started with, she tilted her head at me as if she was asking me to join in, so I did. Ensuring I started perfectly on time. I could have sworn she smiled at me as we danced alongside each other, until I stopped for our pause section, watching as she pirouetted around me.

We soon ended up dancing into each other.

"Perfectly on time." I said frowning at her as she frowned up at me, then she hummed as if she didn't want to agree with me.

"You should do the audition en pointe." She said, I frowned at her, she began to nod. "You dance really well, en pointe." She added,

"Thank you." I said, but I heard the wariness in my voice.

"Do you know the Pas De Deux section?" she asked, I shrugged lightly as I continued to alternate my feet on and off pointe.

"Firsts don't need to do it." I said, she raised her eyebrow at me.

"Oh." She said, then turned away from me. "So, you don't know it." she added, I rolled my eyes.

"I know it." I said, she scoffed. "I'm surprised you'd even consider letting me lift you."

"You're my Pas De Deux partner." She replied turning to look back at me, as the music looped again.

She began the dance without thinking, and I joined in with her when I was supposed to, until we danced into each other again, and I walked away. She ran up behind me, lifting my arm over her shoulder and starting the step sequence, until she jumped and I lifted her with just my knee. We spun together when I placed her down, then broke apart, running in our own personal circles.

I held my arms straight watching as she barely lifted herself off the floor and somehow landed in my arms, letting me lift her, then she led me to my knees, she nodded at me briefly, so I nodded back as she slipped her foot between my legs and leant onto my shoulder.

I impressed myself as I kept my balance, stretching my arms out as she almost lay vertical on my shoulder, until

I turned and placed her down, but kept my arm around her waist, turning us both back and smiling as she pointed her toes out, lifting her arm into fifth.

She landed strong, watching me as I knelt up, holding my arms out then I stood, she walked back towards me. I lowered myself from my pointes, almost smiling to myself because I was still a head and shoulders taller than her, I looked down at her until she wrapped her hands around my neck, pulling my head down to her and kissing me.

We ran together down the corridor, to my room, as it was the closest. I opened the door taking a step in then looking around.

"He's not here." I said, turning my head to look at Abi, she bit her lip then nodded to me so I opened the door further letting her in.

She placed her duffle bag against the wall then walked towards my bed as I attached the tie Kian had hung on the mirror beside the door, onto the doorknob. I closed the door behind me, leaning on it for a few minutes then I walked towards her sitting beside her on my bed and kissing her. She laughed against my mouth, then held my chin, stroking her fingers over my cheeks, I smiled at her, she smiled back, then we began to kiss again, until we'd moved so we were lying on my bed.

I ran my hands down her bodysuit, and found myself pleased that it was as soft as it looked, she laughed softly so I looked up at her then began to chew on my lip as she pulled down the straps, pushing the top of the bodysuit to her hips so I could see her baby pink bra. I ran my fingers up her stomach, tracing her bra then reaching for the straps, pulling them down until she began to laugh, so I met her eyes. She

106

smiled softly at me as she reached behind her back, she brought the bra strap with her then held it up, before dropping her bra off the side of my bed.

I watched it until it hit the floor before looking back at her. My eyes danced over her body until I gave and moved closer to her, kissing her neck, then her chest, kissing down her body then back up, feeling as her breath quickened under my lips, so I continued to move her bodysuit down, pushing it past her hips then losing my breath, so I met her eyes again.

"What?" she whispered as I knelt myself up, pulling her bodysuit and legwarmers down in one go.

"You're not..." I said, she laughed quietly behind her hand.

"You're not supposed to wear knickers under a leotard." She whispered, I smirked. "Didn't you know that?" she added, quirking an eyebrow at me, I shook my head softly then let my eyes travel down her body, taking in every detail I could. "You can touch me." she whispered, I sucked on my bottom lip. "I want you to touch me." she added, then took my wrist, moving my hand closer to her, until she gasped. I gasped with her.

There was a knock on my bedroom door. I frowned at it.

"Yeah?" I asked, the door opened, Kian's head appeared around it, I frowned at him. "Tie on the door." He said, untying it from the door and holding it up to me, I laughed quietly and looked back down at my phone. "Or did you just do that for fun?" he asked as he came and sat on the end of my bed, he tied the tie around his wrist.

"It was definitely fun." I said, Kian's frown became curious.

"I'm sorry. What?" he said then moved closer to me until he was sat at my feet.

"Where you with Connor?" I asked, he scoffed.

"Jacob." He said, I tilted my head at him. "Yes, I was."

"He was texting me all afternoon." I said frowning, Kian laughed.

"I know." he replied, then shook his head. "What did you do this afternoon?"

"I had sex." I said, he almost choked.

"With who exactly?" he asked, I looked away from him.

"Do you know girls don't wear knickers under their leotards?" I said, Kian rolled his eyes. "It's given me this whole other view point. Especially in Pas De Deux." I said, managing to sound as surprised as I'd felt earlier this afternoon.

"Jacob." He said, "Pas De Deux?" he added as he looked at me, then he gasped. "You had sex with Abi." He said, then he laughed, "what the actual fuck?" he added, I figured I must have been blushing up a storm. "How?"

"Well, I…"

"Please don't describe the mechanics of sex to me." he said, I laughed because I was literally just about to.

"I was practicing Edward." I said, he nodded because he'd seen me leave for the studio this afternoon. "I decided to practice Edward en pointe. That is kind of irrelevant. She came in, she stated she'd booked the studio. She didn't seem too impressed that I was there, but I told her we could just dance to the same music." I said, he smirked as I continued to tell him, then he stopped me.

"I'm going to pass on the details of straight sex, knowing she has a baby pink bra and doesn't wear underwear under her leotard is enough." He said raising his eyebrow at me, I laughed. "How do you feel?" he asked, I shrugged at him.

"I don't know. Weird. I guess."

"Weird?" he repeated amused, I nodded.

"Like even though I've had a shower my bed still smells of her perfume and stuff." I shrugged as I stroked my duvet.

"Do you regret it?"

"I don't know." I said, he hummed.

"Are you hungry?" he asked, I began to nod.

"I could eat." I said, he smiled at me then he stood nodding to me, so I stood with him following him out of our room to the canteen. I went through behind him, getting two sausages and some mash, then smothering it in gravy and following Kian to the table he'd sat at beside Margo. I glanced at her almost embarrassed then frowned at the two of them as they examined my plate.

"What?" I said,

"You have food." Margo said, Kian hit her arm shushing her as he did.

"Yeah?" I said, Kian shrugged.

"Just surprised you went for the bangers and mash." He said, then moved some lettuce pieces around his plate before eating them.

I woke up with a start. The room was dark except for the orange light that shone through the window, we'd discovered that was the light on the side of the boarding house that guided people down the path.

It created an orange streak down the middle of our two beds, it didn't affect either of us at all. I looked at the end of the stream of light then I sat up. I touched my

109

stomach as it churned. I swallowed hard, groaning quietly as I felt my mouth fill with saliva then I got out of bed, hitting the wall around the light switch until the en-suite light came on.

I went in and barely lifted the seat before I was throwing up into the toilet. I sighed folding my arms on the toilet tank and resting my head on them, taking in a few deep breaths until I felt like I could stand up, I flushed the toilet then washed my hands and my face. I jumped as I looked in the mirror and saw Kian so I turned to him.

"Okay?" he asked frowning at me as he leant on the doorframe, I shrugged at him.

"Sorry I woke you up." I said, he shook his head,

"Are you okay?" he asked again as he stood himself up properly. I nodded to him.

"Yeah. Yeah, I'm okay." I said, he sighed nodding to me.

"Good." He said, "now get out, I might as well pee now I've stood up." He said, I laughed as I wiped my mouth with the back of my hand then stepped out of the en-suite, closing the door behind me, sitting back on my bed. I lay down under my cover as Kian came out of the en-suite turning off the light as he did. I looked at him as a light lit up his face, I presumed it was his phone.

"We've got about three hours before we have to wake up." He said, ending the sentence with a yawn.

"Goodnight Kian." I almost whispered as I closed my eyes burying my face into my pillow.

"Goodnight."

♥♥♥

"Take a seat first years." Madame Rose ordered so we did. I hugged my pointes closer to my chest as I sat myself in the boy's line.

Madame Rose had insisted we all sit in and watch the auditions. I figured she wanted us all to suffer watching the same dance thirty-two times. The second years were first up, so were sat on the opposite side of the three little chairs and the table, that Arlo and Miss Olivia were currently sat on, leaving the centre seat for Madame Rose.

"We will call your number. You will stand centre, say your name then wait for the music to begin. We will not give you any hints or any help. We want to see your musicality; we want to ensure you can dance to cues. Call backs for the Pas De Deux auditions will be this afternoon. If you are not called back, I expect you to use your afternoons wisely. Parts will be posted this evening." She stated, "so, let's begin." She said, then took her seat, she flipped through her clipboard then she placed her hands together on the table top. "Number one please." She said, a second year boy stood from his seat, then stood before the table. His feet in first position as he rested her hands against his abdomen.

"Wow." Kian muttered; I dragged my eyes away from the attractive second year in front of us to look at Kian.

"I agree." I said, he laughed as the music began, so I looked back at the second year as he stood, his arms in fifth waiting for the cue in the music.

"Number twenty-seven." Madame Rose said as she swapped her papers around on the desk, I looked at Kian as he took a deep breath then he stood, he nodded to me so I nodded back as he took his place on the floor, and answered Madame Rose's questions.

I smiled as I watched him, placing my pointes on the floor beside me and began to put them on as Kian went into his last extension. "Thank you, number twenty-seven." Madame Rose said, so Kian took his seat, he picked up my pointe before he sat on it then sat, twirling the ribbons around his fingers, until I took it from him.

"Twenty-eight." Madame Rose requested, Abi stood from the row behind us and took her position. I watched her until the music began then looked down again. I fixed my ribbons even though there was nothing to fix.

"Can't even look at her." Kian whispered, I glanced at him. "That good, or was it that bad?" he added, I laughed making him smile, then looked towards Madame Rose,

"Thank you. Number twenty-nine." She said, I swallowed then I stood taking my place in front of the table. I watched all of them as their eyes travelled down my body and stopped at my feet, there seemed to be a silent discussion when each of them reached it.

"Right." Madame Rose said, then nodded and the music began. I met each of their eyes then stepped into position, holding my frame strong, then raising up onto pointe as I lifted my arms into fifth.

"Jacob." Madame Rose said so I relaxed my final position. I nodded to her.

"Yes, Madame Rose." I replied then began to squeeze my fingers, pulling them all individually.

"What footwear are males required to wear for warm up, repertoire, auditions and exams?" She asked, I sighed.

"Flat ballet pump. Black." I said, then looked at my feet, I resisted at all costs pointing out that my pointes were black.

"So, why did you feel it appropriate to wear pointes Jacob?" she asked, I looked down, "Jacob, look at me when

112

you are speaking." She added, so I looked up and met her eyes.

"I thought it would enhance my performance." I said,

"This may be, but pointes are not appropriate footwear for a male audition, do you understand?" she asked, I nodded once. "Also, this production does not have any numbers performed en pointe, by neither females, or males, so if this was an attempt of showing off, or an obvious disregard for the rules. It was unacceptable and you will not do it again."

"Madame Rose."

"You'll be lucky if you get a role in this production." She said, I sighed then watched as Arlo and Miss Olivia began whispering to Madame Rose. "Enough." She declared, "sit down Jacob. Number thirty."

I wasn't allowed to leave the studio following my audition, not until we'd gotten through number thirty, thirty-one and thirty-two. I stood and left orderly with the rest of my class once we were dismissed, following them into the canteen for lunch.

"Jacob?" Kian said, I shook my head at him, as I got a tray and began to let myself through the food queue. Abi was on the other end of the queue.

"Jacob?" she said, I shook my head at her as I actually turned to look at her.

"Did you know?" I asked, she frowned at me. "Did you know Madame Rose would be pissed off at me? Did you know that there was no pointe in this show? Did you know all of this?"

"No, Jacob. I didn't."

"Did you sabotage me?"

"Don't be so dramatic Jacob, of course I didn't sabotage you." She said, I shook my head at her.

"Whatever Abi." I said then took my tray,

"Jacob... I'm sorry." She said, I shook my head at her and walked away from her, slamming my tray onto the table that Margo was sat on.

"Jacob it's okay."

"No, it's not." I said simply as Kian came to sit down.

"It is Jacob. It is." She stated, I sighed.

"Don't eat that." Kian said, I looked at him as he shook his head. "Don't." he said,

"Whatever." I muttered, picking up the bread roll I'd put on my plate and took a bite out of it.

"You're going to overload on carbohydrates, and you will be sick." He said simply,

"I don't care." I said, "I don't care at all." I said, then picked up the two other bread rolls that were on my plate. I left my tray and plate on the table and left towards my bedroom. Slamming the door behind me, then sitting myself on my bed, finishing off my rolls.

I scowled at the door when I heard a knock, I waited for it to go away. There was a second knock.

"Go away." I shouted towards the door, it opened.

"No chance." Connor said, I frowned at him as he came towards my bed, I pulled my knees closer to my chest, resting my head on my knees. "Kian called."

"I guessed." I murmured,

"Want to talk about it?" he asked, I lifted my head to look at him. "Okay, so I'll talk." He said then came to sit on my bed. "Kian said something like, your audition went wrong and you got pretty upset by that." He said, "then, he

114

said you made yourself sick." He said, I looked towards the en-suite where I had been throwing up not five minutes before he knocked.

"That doesn't matter." I said, he sighed. "I wore my pointes for my audition, Madame Rose was not happy with that, and Abi told me I should, and now I'm angry at her because she fucked me over, even after I slept with her."

"Wait, what?" he said, I shook my head,

"I got so angry because I am fucking good at pointe and ballet, but she told me I might not even get a role in the ballet because of my stupid decision to trust Abi, or as she said my showing off and obvious disregard for the rules." I muttered,

"So, you're pouting because you made the wrong decision in an audition."

"When you say it like this, it sounds petty and stupid." I muttered,

"It kind of is." He whispered, knocking his foot against mine. "So, should we talk about the actual issue here?" he asked, I looked at him. "You made yourself throw up." He said, I shook my head at him lowering my head back into my knees.

"Okay, okay. I'll take a different approach." He said, I looked back up at him wiping my cheeks violently as tears rolled down them. "Lie down." He whispered, I frowned at him but I did, lying on my side resting my hand under my head, he lay opposite me once he'd taken his shoes off, I watched his face as he went through his pockets, until he pulled some earphones out, he pulled the one nearest to me out of the knot it had formed in his pocket.

Then he held it up to me, I didn't take it, so he put it in my ear, putting the other in his then putting his finger on his lips, I nodded to him as he lifted his phone between us. I

115

couldn't see what he was scrolling through until it started in my ear. We didn't talk, he wouldn't let me, every time I went to open my mouth he put his finger back on his lips, shaking his head at me, so I soon quietened. Closing my eyes as the song played through the earphone, until it ended and the next one began.

"Go on." He whispered, I looked at him,

"I got nothing." I whispered, he smiled. "Is this what you used to do?" I asked, he nodded.

"Not even used to, still do." He said, I met his eyes. "This technique works better when I'm sad." He said softly as the violin instrumental continued into my ear. "Just listening to one song all the way through, then figuring out things. My therapist always said to me it was a skill to listen, and when you listen you appreciate." He said then he blushed,

"You've never told me what happened during your therapy sessions."

"I wasn't allowed to." He said raising his eyebrow at me, I laughed quietly. "Like Jack, he had therapy every Friday, but was never allowed to tell me what for, or what happened in them." he said, I nodded slowly. "Although admittedly, I enjoyed music therapy so much that I inflicted it on everyone." He said amused, I laughed as I sighed. "It helps. A lot." He said nodding, I nodded back.

"What did you listen to when you were angry?" I asked, he frowned at me as he looked back down at him phone.

"You angry?"

"Very." I replied, he nodded then pressed down on his phone, the song switched instantly, it almost made me jump. "I remember, when I was angry, when I was younger Max would make me dance." I said as I listened to the song,

Connor nodded he didn't shush me. "I remember you used to throw things." I added, he smirked at me.

"Only if I was just a little angry." He said, I almost laughed.

"Oh, no I remember. You went really quiet. It was scary."

"I went really quiet for a lot of reasons."

"Yeah, but if you were angry, you went quiet, and your music got louder." I said, he nodded as I looked at him, straight into his eyes as the chorus kicked in.

"You look strange without your glasses on." He said, I smiled, it made him smile back.

"Madame insists I wear contacts." I said,

"Now," Connor said, I looked at him, "let's start with you had sex, with a girl?" he said, I nodded.

"It was intense. We dance together in Pas De Deux, but my god she's hated me since we started, turns out…"

"She didn't hate you, she wanted to sleep with you. Sounds familiar." He said, I laughed.

"It was good. I guess. We just sort of had sex, although I don't think I did it too right." I said, Connor smirked so I hit his chest.

"As Ste used to say…" he said, I frowned at him. "Practice makes perfect." He said, I laughed shaking my head at him as he smiled at me. "Is she the one who suggested you dance on pointe?" he asked, I nodded. "And?" he asked, he sounded mildly confused.

"And it wasn't a good idea."

"You're blaming her?" he asked, I shrugged.

"I guess. Even though it was my fault." I muttered, Connor nodded to me then looked back down at his phone, changing the song to one of his violin instrumentals, it was far softer in my ear.

"So, what are you going to do now?" he asked, I shrugged at him. "Going to mope about it, and be a big idiot?" he asked, I shook my head. "Going to get up out of bed and continue with your life?"

"Tomorrow." I muttered, he nodded softly.

"That's better than nothing." He said thoughtfully then ran his fingers through my hair. "I think you should talk to Max." he said, I frowned.

"What good would that do?" I asked, Connor sighed.

"He'll be able to help. You know he will. He'll be able to sympathise with your pointe problem, he'll be able to give you advice and will understand exactly what you're going through."

"He'll just be ashamed of me."

"He will not." He replied, I looked away from him. "I haven't heard anything more ridiculous in my life." He said, I shook my head at him, we both turned to look at the door when it opened. Kian leant on it before even attempting to come in,

"They released the list." He said as he closed the door, I sat up, watching as the earphone fell out of my ear and onto my lap, I could still hear the music coming out of it.

"Who are you playing?" I asked, he sat on his bed.

"I'm just a chorus member on Thursday's shows." He said, then he smiled softly at me. "As are you."

"Really?" I questioned, narrowing my eyes at him, he began to nod. "A second got Edward, and the ballerina, most of the seconds are performing Wednesday, whereas the two seconds that got Edward and the ballerina for Thursday's show are performing with a first year chorus." He said nodding, I nodded back, then looked back at Connor as he squeezed my shoulder and ran his fingers down my back.

118

"It'll be fine." He said into my ear, I sighed but nodded to him as he kissed my shoulder.

Chapter 7

I looked at my phone as it lit itself up, on and off it alternated between Cameron's name and Max's name. Neither of them had called, it was just a continuous stream of texts.

I figured they were working together, or at least sat next to each other, and had reacted verbally to my initial text that had started off their flow of replies. It stopped buzzing as I looked at it again, watching as my screen faded to black

"Are you going to get that?" Kian asked, I shook my head then looked from my phone across the canteen table at him as he pointed a piece of lettuce at me,

"I'm ignoring it for the time being." I replied, he frowned, "I told them I wasn't coming home this weekend, which means I'm not helping Max in Immediate Pointe, which will be what his texts are about. Cameron's will be about how he's probably brought something to roast." I said then looked back at my phone again, "both are using our group chat for evil." I said, Kian laughed then shrugged.

"And why aren't you going home?" he asked, I muttered looking down at my plate. It was full, or at least the edges were, I'd pushed all my food into the brim of the plate, so it looked like I'd given it a good go.

"Are you going to eat that?" Margo asked, she obviously wasn't fooled by the empty circle on my plate. I frowned at her. "Can't let good potatoes go to waste." She said, then looked at Kian, "am I right?" she added, he laughed as he poked his fork through a tomato, a beetroot and a little block of cheese.

"Seventy-seven calories, I can take them or leave them." he replied, I laughed as he smiled at me. "I thought you were going home this weekend." Kian said frowning at me, I looked at him, "I've arranged to go out with Connor." He added, I began to nod.

"I'll be fine alone, you know?" I said, he laughed nodding to me almost dramatically. "Besides I won't be alone, I have Margo... I have...." I said, Margo began to shake her head, I sighed.

"Abi is pissed off at you." She said, "she won't even acknowledge your existence right now."

"Why?" Kian asked, Margo laughed,

"Well, Kian. When you sleep with a boy that then shouts at you in front of the entire canteen just under a week later, you tend to want to make said boy an eunuch."

"A what?" I said, Kian laughed so I looked at him,

"She wants to castrate your balls." He said, I winced.

"I should apologise to her." I said, they both nodded back to me.

"I agree." Margo said, I sighed. "But maybe wait a bit. She still seems quite angry."

"And you should never provoke a girl when they're angry. I learnt that the hard way." He said, "especially not two of them, my god."

"Your sister?" I asked, he nodded slowly as if he was traumatised by the memory. "Do you know how hard it is, when your Pas De Deux partner, is also your sisters' best friend. They tend to conspire."

"Poor Kian." Margo cooed, "now can I have your potatoes, so we can get to our show rehearsal?" she asked, I sighed spinning my plate around so she could take the potatoes, I watched her take the first two with her fork, then picked up my phone, scrolling down the messages that alternated between Max and Cameron.

"They making you feel like a bad son?" Kian asked, I began to nod.

"The worse."

"Our two Edward's, front and centre please." Arlo said as he stood against the barre putting his ballet shoes on, he was leaning on the barre us firsts had taken, whilst all the seconds stood on the opposite side of the room. Two boys moved themselves away from the barre and stood in the middle, they smirked at each other when they did.

"We will practice as a big group." Arlo explained as he stood in front of the two seconds. "Then we will perform in our two separate groups. I expect you to be watching if you are not performing, there are always things you can learn." He said, more in a pointed way towards the seconds. "You will all be a part of a chorus number, a Pas De Deux sequence and an all-male number.

We will also select the strongest dancers to make cameos, or to dance in the background. Of course, our

Cavalier and ballerina will be centre stage for the majority, but that does not mean that you cannot be seen."

"No small roles, just small people." Kian murmured, I laughed,

"I thought it was there are no small roles, just small actors." I said, Kian smirked.

"But we're not actors." He said, then he grinned, I smiled back.

"Centre floor." Arlo ordered, we stood in lines of four, he nodded to us, happy with the formation then he began the soundtrack.

He let us listen through it the first time, ensuring we noticed the accents and the change in pace, then he began it again and started to show us the dance. I marvelled around the room as the Seconds followed without hesitation, their lines perfect, their footwork nearing perfection every time. We danced through it once then Arlo lifted his hand, circling it towards us.

"Back row to the front." He ordered, so we swapped. I kept my eyes on Arlo as I danced, trying not to think about the rows behind me who were watching me dance, or judging my waist line and lack of padding in my shorts. I closed my eyes as the song began again, just listening to the music, hearing what Connor had said, over *and* over again.

You have to zone out of everything, the only thing that matters is the music. Listen to the notes, enjoy the harmonies, appreciate the arrangements.

"Beautifully danced Jacob." Arlo said, I opened my eyes looking at him as he nodded to me. "Nice and strong Kian, keep it up." He added, Kian smiled next to me, I saw it in the mirror. I laughed softly as I looked down. "Okay. Firsts take a seat under the barre." Arlo said, "make sure you keep yourselves hydrated. Keep drinking. Seconds centre floor, with Wednesday Edward. I'd like to see you dance through once." Arlo said, then came to the barre we were at, he drank from his own water bottle as the seconds prepared on the floor then began to dance through.

I swirled my water around and around in the bottle not quite drinking it, until Kian placed his hand on the lid, stopping me swirling it.

"You're making me need the toilet. Please stop." He said, I laughed seeing his smile as the music came to its end. Arlo stood himself from the barre, walking to the group and talking to them individually. Some were positives, some boys he just picked out to compliment them, others needed improvement, then we swapped, the seconds sitting in front of us, watching as we danced through.

▼▼▼

I was still lying in bed when Kian returned from his Saturday morning run. He'd decided a few weeks back that he was going to take up running of a Saturday morning, and for some bizarre reason, he woke up unbelievably early to do this run.

I was awake when he came back, he always stated it was a miracle that I had managed to wake up, so I lay resting my head on my arms as I looked at him sat on his bed.

"You should try a good run." He said, I groaned back at him. "Get them endorphins going." He added amused, I shook my head.

"Aren't you going to get enough endorphins from this afternoons activity?" I said, Kian laughed shaking his head at me, I sat up. "Are you telling me you and Connor are not going to have sex?" I said, Kian laughed as he stood from his bed.

124

"I never said that." He said then went into the en-suite, he turned back before he closed the door. "It is likely." He added then shut the door, I laughed as I lay back down.

I had almost fell back asleep when Kian came back out of the en-suite, I watched him as he walked from the en-suite to his drawers, he turned to look at me once he'd put his boxers on, and threw his towel into our wash basket.

"Coming to breakfast?" he asked, I groaned at him making him laugh. "Come on." He pushed so I sighed sitting back up and pushing my quilt back, going into the en-suite. He was impressed when I reappeared, and even more impressed when I was dressed.

"When are you meeting with Connor?" I asked as he sat opposite me with a bowl that looked like it was full of yogurt. He began to sprinkle blueberries and raspberries on top of it.

"Not until this afternoon." He said, then he laughed. "We're going to eat; I believe he said something about the cinema then we're going back to his."

"Staying over?" I asked, he shrugged.

"We'll see, I'll let you know though, especially if it's getting close to curfew." He said, I nodded to him. "What are you doing?"

"I was going to go to the gym." I replied, then looked down and away from him.

"Muscle?" he asked, I frowned at him. "Weight lifting." He said, I shrugged.

"I'll run on the treadmill for a bit." I said,

"Don't run for too long." He said, "Miss Olivia wanted you to gain muscle mass, not lose weight." He said, "but I'm not one to talk you out of those endorphins." He said grinning at me, I laughed. "Are you going to talk to

Abi?" he asked, turning to look towards her, I followed his gaze at Abi as she sat on a different table with a bowl in front of her.

"Do you think she'll attack me?" I whispered, he laughed as he scrapped the bottom of his bowl with his spoon.

"I think the longer you put it off, the more pissed off she will be." he said, then he sighed. "What I learnt, quickly was you usually just have to admit you're wrong, even if you're not." He said, I almost laughed. "You also should never say I told you so, if they ultimately admit that you were right, they have a huge dislike for that."

"Noted." I said, he laughed as I sighed and looked back towards Abi.

I stood at the end of the treadmill, trying to unknot the earphones Connor had left in my bed. I knew he had hundreds, upon hundreds of pairs of headphones, and earphones so he wouldn't miss them, especially as they were a generic blue pair that appeared to knot easily.

I finally succeeded in unknotted them, then plugged them into my phone, scrolling through my music apps until I decided on a playlist. I stood on the edges of the treadmill slotting my phone into the little hold, and my water bottle into the cup holder then started it.

I closed my eyes as my walk became a jog, running the beat of the music I could hear. I ran through the pulsing in my head, as it grew more intense, hitting my forehead like a pin, so I squeezed my eyes tighter.

Keeping up the pace as the treadmill got quicker.

Until I felt my breath get knocked out of me. I held the supports of the treadmill, lifting myself up so I could stand on the edge of the treadmills, folding my arms on the support and resting my head in it, feeling the sweat as I dripped off my hair, my heart beat pulsing through my head as I tried to regain my breath.

"I think you need a break." I heard; I didn't look up because I didn't want to. "An ice cream?" I heard, I laughed and looked up taking my glasses off to wipe my face with my t-shirt then put them back on turning to look at Margo who was stood at the end of the treadmill. She'd turned it off, I took the earphones out.

"Why an ice cream?" I asked, then I frowned at her. "It's winter."

"Ice cream is both a snack and a drink if you leave it long enough." She said, I laughed. "Come on Jacob. Don't push yourself too much. It's a Saturday." She said, I nodded to her, taking a step off the treadmill and feeling as my knees became jelly.

Margo laughed looping her arm around mine and walking me through to the little coffee area, that apparently also sold ice cream. I got a little bowl with three scoops of chocolate in, whilst Margo got strawberry, pistachio and praline, she told me not to be so boring then laughed as we sat on a couch to eat it. The coolness of the ice cream calming my head almost instantly as I let it melt on my tongue.

"So, we going to talk about why you're killing yourself on a treadmill?"

"I wasn't." I said, she laughed.

"I haven't seen a boy that destroyed since, well…" she smirked at me, I almost choked on the piece of melting ice cream.

"How is sex so casual to you?" I asked once I'd done coughing, Margo laughed.

"Is that a distraction technique?" she asked, I shrugged at her nodding as I did, she laughed. "Sex is different to everyone Jacob." She said, I sighed.

"You sound like my Dad." I said, she laughed.

"Well, it is, your virginity is completely different to your fourth, fifth, or seventeenth time." She said raising her eyebrow at me, I frowned back at her.

"So, when we fooled around. That meant nothing to you?" I asked, she sighed.

"What did it mean to you?" she asked, I shrugged looking away from her, she touched her spoon against my arm, I jumped.

"I really liked you." I said, she frowned.

"Liked?" she repeated, I shrugged.

"Yeah, I guess it's now liked. I don't know. I think I like Abi." I said then sighed, "but I don't know, it's all too complex."

"Because you guys had sex?" she asked, I nodded. "I have no strings attached sex. Which all that means is everyone gets off and there's no commitment. Feel free to call me a slut but it just makes things easier… more pleasurable." She said, I laughed, it sounded embarrassed.

"But what if you don't get off?" I asked, she laughed.

"Oh Jacob." She said, then hit my knee, "I always make sure I do." She said, then she frowned at me, "didn't you?" she asked, I began to stutter. "Jacob…" she said, I looked at her. "Just tell me this… are you happy with who you lost your virginity too?" she asked, I looked back at her.

▼▼▼

"If you are not dancing you should be drinking." Arlo shouted as the girls danced their chorus number. Miss Olivia

128

was also shouting at the girls, whilst Madame Rose stood and critiqued everything from the corner.

We were in the main theatre, although they hadn't actually put the stage out yet, or the seating bank. Madame Rose had insisted on one big rehearsal a week, which meant all thirty-two students of first and second year, and every member of teaching staff they had in the school.

We had danced through most of the first act, with Arlo reminding us every single time we breathed that if we weren't dancing, we should be drinking.

I'd stopped doing that after the first number as the water was sitting heavily in my stomach, every time I had jumped, I had felt the water slosh around so I didn't drink any more at risk of throwing up.

"Gentlemen on stage." Miss Olivia requested, so we moved, all standing in our first position and almost instantly began to dance. "Be strong gentlemen, your frames are slacking." Miss Olivia shouted over the music. "Stop complaining seconds." She added, I heard laughter behind me, but I daren't turn my head to look. The Seconds had been talking through most of the dancers, mostly complaining about how long it'd be before they could smoke again. I'd tried to zone them out time and time again, but I ended up listening to their conversations more than not. Arlo had noticed and told me to pay attention a few times but each time it had been quietly and without making a show of me.

"Liquid Jacob." Arlo commented raising his eyebrow at me as I walked away from the floor again, I picked up my bottle and turned away from him, resting my head against the wall as my head began to pulse. I closed my eyes tight until I was called back to the floor.

"You alright son?" Arlo asked as he walked past me, he placed his hand on my shoulder so I looked at him, I watched as he examined my eyes, I nodded back to him. "Keep drinking yeah, if you need a minute, just leave don't worry." He said, I nodded to him again as I held my arms in fourth and began to dance through.

I listened as Miss Olivia critiqued the ballerina whilst Arlo shouted at the second years playing Edward, they shouted over each other. Their voices piercing through my headache as they shouted. I took a big swig out of my bottle when I went to the sides again, coughing after I did, trying my hardest to keep the water down, then I wiped my head and my neck with my hand towel.

"End of Act One." Miss Olivia called, so I ran to the side, standing behind the chair that indicated the wing. I watched the beginning of the dance, gripping onto the chair tightly as I felt myself begin to sway. I closed my eyes taking in a deep breath as the swell in music came up that indicated I needed to start dancing so I moved to the centre of the floor where I'd been placed.

I kept my eyes closed as I danced hoping I wouldn't bump into anyone, until I stopped, touching my stomach as I felt a wave of water move through my stomach. I took another deep breath as I felt my gag reflect reacting, I closed my eyes, hoping I wouldn't throw up.

Which I didn't.

I swallowed it back down then turned to continue the dance but felt as my knees weakened, my head felt light and then it went dark.

"Alright move away. Go for a break everybody." I heard Arlo say but I couldn't see him, not well anyway, it was like when I wasn't wearing my glasses but instead of just fuzziness, I could see white dots. "Don't fuss. Get out." Arlo ordered; I closed my eyes again then felt a hand on my forehead.

"He was drinking, wasn't he?" Miss Olivia said, there was no reply.

"Kian..." Arlo said,

"He hasn't been eating." Kian said, then I felt a hand on my stomach, "it's been weeks, but I wasn't here this weekend. I don't know... did he eat this weekend?"

"Only ice cream." Margo said, "I found him in the gym. He had run himself to almost exhaustion so I suggested ice cream, he ate it but I didn't see him Saturday night, or Sunday. I didn't think anything of it."

"Has he been keeping food down?" Arlo asked, there was no reply. "Okay." He said, "Jacob." He said softly, it must have been his hand against my head. "Jacob, open your eyes." he said, so I did, looking up towards his voice. "Okay, we're going to take you to your bedroom okay. Get some food down you." He said, then he began to whisper, I didn't hear it all but I did hear.

"I'll call his parents."

I woke with a start, I touched my quilt then lifted it to find I was just in my boxers, I could feel the coolness of the sheets against my back, as I continued to sweat.

I swallowed hard, feeling as it got harder and harder until I sat up, I searched around my bed hoping there was something closer than the toilet to throw up into.

There was a bucket at the side of my bed, so I threw up into it, then I sat on my bed and I cried, until there was a knock on my door. I looked at it, then went to welcome whoever knocked in, my voice felt hoarse as I began to talk, so I swallowed hard, even though a few tears still left my eyes. The door opened anyway.

"You're awake." Arlo said, he sounded surprised I looked at him, I frowned confused at him because I could see him, then I rubbed my eyes, groaning as I did and taking the contacts out. "Okay." Arlo said softly, he placed something on the end of my bed, then I felt him take my hands.

He ran his fingers down two of mine, I presume taking the contacts off my fingers, then he passed me my glasses, I put them on then looked at him, he lifted my chin, looking straight into my eyes nodding his head towards the end of my bed, so I looked towards it. "I brought you some soup." He said, I scowled at it. "You need to eat it Jacob." He said as he pulled the tray closer to me, I sighed as I leant back against my headboard and actively attempted to eat the soup. "I've called your Dad; he's coming in for a chat this afternoon. I'd like you to be present at this meeting."

"My Dad?" I repeated, he nodded as I cringed in-between slurping soup. "Which one?" I asked,

"Mr. Whelan." He said, I sighed.

"Shit." I sighed.

"Finish your soup. I'll send Kian to collect you this afternoon, but only if you're up to it." he said, I nodded to him.

"Arlo." I said as he stood, he turned to look at me, "how badly have I fucked up?" I asked, he tilted his head at me.

"Come to the meeting if you're up for it."

Kian appeared what felt like hours later. I had remained lying in my bed for at least an hour before I felt too grubby and forced myself out of bed for a shower. I had felt one thousand times better once I had, then I sat on my bed in my joggers and the school hoodie because they were both soft and warm. I hadn't touched my phone; I was too scared to.

"How are you feeling?" Kian asked, I looked at him from where I'd perched on the edge of my bed hugging my knees to my chest.

"Like shit." I said, he smiled, "but better. I've kept the soup down." I said looking at the empty bowl that was still at the end of my bed.

"That's good." He said softly, "I've called Connor."

"Snitch." I said half-heartedly, he smiled.

"He said he's available for hugs whenever necessary and suggested you go with him to your old home." He said, I sighed.

"I take it my Dad's here." I said, Kian nodded.

"Good luck." Kian whispered, I nodded to him standing from my bed and walking towards him. He slid his arm around my waist cuddling me close to him, and walking with me down to Arlo's office. He kissed my cheek when we were outside, then he knocked, I nodded to him when Arlo welcomed me in. Max was sat on the chair opposite Arlo's desk, they both looked at me when I walked in.

I froze.

"Come take a seat Jacob." Arlo said, so I did closing the door behind me. "I have informed Max of what happened this morning. I have also spoken to Kian and Margo who have both informed me that they have noticed you haven't been eating." He said, I looked down at my legs. "Jacob this is serious." He said, I looked at Max as he frowned at Arlo. "You understand students can only remain in this school if they are healthy, and are in control of their wellbeing. If this becomes an issue at any point there are counsellors and wellbeing officers on hand to talk to."

"I understand." I muttered,

"So, I'm sure you also understand that you cannot remain here whilst you are unwell." He said, I looked at him,

"You're kicking me out."

"No." Arlo snapped back at me, "I am putting you on sabbatical."

"Sabbatical?" I repeated, Arlo nodded as Max did.

"I have spoken to Max in length before you arrived. We both agreed this is what is best for you." He said, I frowned at him. "You will not attend any lessons, or take part in the Christmas ballet." He said, I went to retaliate, Max put his hand on my leg, it stopped me instantly.

"Come January, if you are in a better place. If you are eating, and are healthy you can begin to attend lessons again. Our counsellor will begin to meet with you regularly and then, if they feel you are appropriately recovered, and you also feel you are able you can begin boarding again."

"Arlo." I moaned, he sighed,

"Obviously this is a sensitive subject, and it can be difficult to understand what young ballet dancers go through, as a parent." Arlo said, I saw Max smirk but he was trying to be the adult here.

"I understand completely." Max said, "as a ballet dancer myself." He added then looked at me, I looked back at him.

"I knew, I knew you from somewhere." Arlo said, I frowned at him as Max did. "You competed didn't you, years ago? You won gold."

"Arlo?" Max said, Arlo nodded to him, "Arlo won silver." Max said to me, I frowned at him,

"Maxwell Whelan. Of course, Max." he said, Max almost laughed.

"You know each other?" I said frowning at them, Max nodded to me,

"Very well." He replied, I groaned.

"You slept with my teacher." I said, Max looked at me. "Can we get back to me actually? I don't want to know that." I said, Arlo nodded looking back at me.

"Let's talk Jacob."

"This is your fault." I said as I threw my bag at the couch, Max turned to look at me,

"Excuse me?"

"This is all your fault." I stated, "why didn't you tell me?" I shouted as I pushed him back, I saw his frown as he grabbed for my arms.

"Tell you what Jacob?" He said, holding onto my forearms as I tried to fight against him. "Jacob, what?"

"I'm too fat to be a ballet dancer." I shouted back at him, he grabbed me harder so I looked away from him.

"No, you are not." He stated, I shook my head back at him.

"I'm too fat, too short and don't have a big enough dick. Why didn't you tell me?" I shouted then pulled my arms out of his grasp, I turned away from him, crossing my arms over my stomach as I did.

"Jacob I didn't tell you, because it's not true." He said, I looked down as I felt tears running down my cheeks. "You're healthy. Actually, you're exceptionally healthy for a boy of eighteen. Your weight is in perfect proportion to your height, and I'm not even going to acknowledge your worries about your penis." He said, I looked at him.

"Jacob." He sighed, I looked away again, until I felt his arms come around my shoulders, his chin on my head. "You're perfect Jacob." He whispered into my hair, I shook

my head, sniffing in between the tears falling to my cheeks.
"I don't have this perfect ballet body." He said, I leant my
head back, I felt it as it rested on his chest. "I've never had
this perfect ballet body."

"Frankie said..." I said in between tears,

"Frankie said I was perfect for Pas De Deux." He
whispered, I sighed. "I was never stick thin. I never had an
impressive bulge." He said more into my ear, I laughed then
covered my mouth.

"You can dance Jacob. You're an amazing ballet
dancer, and that is what matters. Not how much you weigh,
not your height, not how big your ballet belt is. How well
you can dance." He said, then squeezed me tight, I closed
my eyes. "Your teachers will be harsh on you. Yeah? But
you should only be listening to the ballet technique, not
anything about your weight." He said, so I turned to look at
him, then wrapped my arms around his waist, he hugged me
back, leaning his head on mine, placing a kiss on the top of
my head, then cuddling me tighter.

Chapter 8

I stepped through the little cut out door of the garage
walking up behind Connor who was under the hood of a car.

      I decided not to bother him, *or* startle him, instead I
just sat on the table top that held a lot of tools I didn't know
the names of. It wasn't too long before he looked up, turning
towards me, smiling as he took out a pair of earphones and
coming to me, he almost lifted me off the table as he hugged
me.

      "Sorry I'm getting you all oily." He said into my ear,
but didn't let up the hug. I just hugged him back tighter.
"Kian told me everything." He said, then he turned to look at
me, I looked back at him. "How are you taking it?" he asked,
I shook my head at him.

"We just keep talking about it. I'm done with hearing about it, but they're both in a show come next week so I should get some relief." I said, he shook his head at me.

"I won't talk about it then." He said, I tilted my head at him. "I am however sorry; I'm going to visit the home this afternoon." He said, I nodded.

"I know." I replied, he frowned at me. "Kian told me." I added almost mocking him, he laughed as he wiped his hands on a rag. "I want to come with you." I said,

"Are you sure about that? It'd seem you'd rather forget where you came from?" he said, raising his eyebrow as he turned away from me and looked back into the hood of the car, I began to nod slowly.

"It's been strange." I said, he looked at me over my shoulder. "The idea of boarding scared me; I was terrified it was going to feel like being back at the home." I said, he turned completely to me. "And I know I should appreciate how the home was. I remember talking to Jack about his previous homes and they sounded like genuine nightmares, but as amazing as our home was, it was still a home." I said, Connor nodded.

"I'd agree but I don't know any different." He said, I looked down. "I get what you mean though feeling like boarding would be like going back. Did it?"

"No." I said shaking my head, "not at all."

"Are you embarrassed that you grew up in care?" he asked, I looked at him. "I'm not going to judge what you say, especially given you're now a student at this prestige ballet school, which is kind of what is making me ask the question?"

"I'm not well, this isn't fair." I said, he didn't drop his stare, so I rolled my eyes. "I'm not embarrassed." I said,

"I just, don't want to be defined as that kid who grew up in care and was a success story."

"Any kid that makes it out of the care system whether it's through adoption, or turning eighteen is a success story Jacob." He snapped, I sighed, "but I understand. I think… I think it's a good thing you want to come with me, there's someone you should definitely talk to." He said, I sighed.

"Don't get pouty Kennedy." He said simply so I laughed. "I finish at twelve, okay?" he asked, I turned to look towards the round white clock on the wall, the little red hand was ticking around, whilst the other two hands told me he only had ten minutes left. "Come help." He added beckoning me to him with his finger, I shook my head. "Ballerina, get your hands dirty." He stated, so I went to him, standing beside him knocking his shoulder against mine as he explained what was going on under the hood of the car.

My legs felt a little weak as we walked from Connor's car to the home. It hadn't changed, at all and *that* for some reason sent a shiver down my spine. Connor took my hand as we began up the stairs to the front door.

"It's okay." He said, I looked at him. "You'll see a few ghosts but no poltergeists." He said, I laughed shaking my head at him as he grinned at me then he rang the doorbell. "And the kids are at school, so…" he said as the door opened, my face broke into a smile the moment I saw Ste, his appeared to do exactly the same thing.

"Connor." He said nodding, Connor nodded back then let go of my hand. "Jacob." He said then he stepped towards me and hugged me, I hugged him back my grip tightening almost instantly. "I believe there's something you need to tell me." Ste said once I'd finally given up the hug, I looked away from him as he squeezed my shoulders.

"I agree." Connor said, I looked at him as Ste let us into the house, "Is he in?"

"Of course he's in." Ste replied amused, "but he's working so don't bother him. It's hard enough to get him working in the first place." He said amused, Connor laughed.

"I got into the National Ballet School." I said, because I figured out what he was talking about. Ste nodded to me.

"Congratulations." He said happily, "I was over the moon to hear the news." He said, I looked down. "Connor told me." he whispered, I laughed as I looked at Connor, "He also told me you're currently on a sabbatical."

"Things got a bit out of hand." I said, he rubbed my shoulder.

"If you want to talk?" he said, I nodded to him,

"Thank you." I replied, he smiled as he looked back at Connor.

"I have a list for you. Which I let the kids compile themselves so, good luck." He said, Connor laughed.

"Great." He said, Ste nodded.

"I'll go and get it, and him for you." He said, then he smiled and walked towards his office, I went to follow him but Connor took my hand, leading me into the rec room. Which to me looked exactly the same except the computers we'd had had been replaced with laptops.

"Look." Connor said, as we walked towards the mural that we'd painted when we were nine.

The house had been renovated, and in that the rec room had been built. Ste had let us decorate it with paint and spray cans, and one of the older kids, who was insanely good at graffiti art had wrote the house name on it. We all signed it when it was finished, and then any new kids got to sign it when they'd been in the house long enough.

I walked towards the mural, smiling to myself as I ran my fingers over my name, my handwriting was not the neatest on the wall, the letters in my name all different sizes.

"They still do it." Connor said, so I looked towards where he was stood, he pointed up the wall to where a group of names were that I didn't recognise. "Jack and I, we made sure the newbies did it, then it became tradition." He said, then he smiled at me. "The little ones used to choose a name on the wall and ask us to tell them about the name they'd chosen." He said, I laughed.

"What did you say about me?" I asked, Connor smiled.

"Ballerina." He replied, I laughed as he held his hand out, so I took it and let him lead me to the office,

"Some people would like to see you." Ste said as he leant on the door of the office, he passed Connor a piece of paper then turned to look into the office. "You can take some time out; the kids aren't due home for a few hours." He added amused, then he smiled at us. "You will teach ballet to our little dears, and I'd like you to talk to Riley, he likes cars. A lot." He said amused, Connor laughed.

"I'll talk to him, might be able to get him to the garage."

"That'd be great," Ste said, his sigh sounded happy. "He's taking his theory in a few weeks. He loves cars probably as much as you love ballet." He said, I laughed then looked at Connor.

"That's a hell of a lot." I said, Ste laughed as Jack appeared in the doorway, pushing his shirt sleeves up as he smiled at us. I marvelled at how much he actually looked like an adult, before my brain connected that it was Jack before me.

"Jack?" I said, he laughed,

"Jack." Connor said, he sounded quite affectionate then he hugged him, they kissed each other's cheeks. I frowned at Connor as he took a step back, he tilted his head at me, it kind of told me he'd explain later.

"Go on, be free. I want you back by half two though." He said, Jack nodded to him.

"I'll be back for Emmett's daily football tournament." He said amused, we both laughed as Ste smiled at him and went back into the office. "He likes to play football against me, always has. He especially likes to beat me."

"But..." Connor said,

"Oh, I let them win." Jack said amused, as he walked us to a coffee shop, we sat around a little round table on tall chairs. "Drinks on me, what do you want?"

"Latte." Connor said, I raised an eyebrow at him, so he laughed.

"Are you sure?" I said, Jack nodded as he went into his wallet. He held a card up to us. I recognised it, because it looked like the one Ste used to carry around.

"Yeah. On me." He said,

"Mango cooler." I said, he nodded, I touched Connor's hand.

"We started having sex when I was fifteen." He said, then he looked straight at me, I raised my eyebrow at him.

"So, when you told me you'd lost your virginity, to some guy. It was Jack?"

"It was Jack." He agreed then he exhaled, "and pretty much every time following until a few months ago."

142

"Shit." I said in a laugh, Connor smiled at me, "why didn't you tell me?"

"Because it was Jack." He said, then turned his head to look at him. "I loved him, and although I know you changed your mind on him, I still felt as if..."

"I'd judge you?"

"No." He said, then he laughed softly. "Yes. Will you honestly sit there and look me in the eye, saying you wouldn't have judged me, even a little?" He asked, I shrugged so he smirked.

"Why did you guys stop having sex?" I asked, "or were you boyfriends?"

"With lack of a better word." He said, then he looked down. "It got strange." He said, "I'm sure Jack will tell you why he's at the home, but he was eighteen. He quickly found out everything about everything.

He knew all my therapist notes, all my triggers, all about me, and although it was a comfort when I was sixteen, when I left the home it got a bit, I don't know, irritating." He sighed, "he appreciated certain things, like he appreciated that I like to listen to music during sex."

"I can fully believe that." I said, Connor smiled at me.

"Kian enjoys it far more than I'd have ever imagined." He said, then he shook his head as if to get him back on track. "It was kind of like, every sentence went something like I know I shouldn't say this because it'll have this effect on you, but if we do this it'll calm you." He rolled his eyes, "I got to this point where I was pissed off with him. I told him I wasn't my disorder. If anything, that's a minuscule part of me. I might have crossed the line." He said, I frowned at him,

143

"I asked him if he wanted me to associate him with his depression, if he'd prefer me to dance around it every single time we met up." He sighed as I chewed on my lip. "We agreed there and then, that it stops. We always agreed the moment it wasn't working anymore that was it, and well that was it."

"Then I introduced you to Kian."

"Then, that." He agreed I smiled as Jack came towards the table. He placed the plastic cup down in front of me, the the mug in front of Connor, he placed his own mug down then took the tray back to the table. He retook his seat. "Tell him how you ended up in the home." Connor said, Jack smiled after drinking from his mug.

"He knows that. He was there on my first day when I was fifteen." He said, then he smirked at Connor as he laughed,

"You work there?" I asked, he nodded.

"Now I do." He said, then placed his mug down. "Obviously I was never adopted." He said, I frowned at him. "I was a little shit, for starters, but ultimately I didn't want to be adopted, so whatever. I was talking to Ste before I tuned eighteen. He likes to know if we have prospects.

I told him I had no idea what I wanted to do, who I wanted to be, but I did mention to him that the idea of being a therapist intrigued me." He took another sip out of his mug as Connor and I did.

"Obviously that didn't come off, but Ste suggested I did health and social, so I did, but I stayed in the home. He had me do odd jobs, and once I learnt how to drive he started to get me to ferry the kids to and from extracurricular.

I did a qualification in social work when I was nineteen, then I looked into residential worker. It was the beginning of this year I got a job officially, and I actually love it. The kids are amazing." He said softly, then smiled at Connor, who smiled back.

"You're almost like a different person." I said, Jack nodded.

"I feel like a different person. I helped one of the kids recently, he was feeling low. Many adoption meetings had fell through, he was not in a good place. I got him out of the dark.

Well, I won't take all the credit. He worked damn hard in himself but he didn't do anything..." He said, then stroked his wrist until his fingers knocked against his watch. "...Extreme." He said, then he looked at me.

I closed my eyes, because the night, when I was fourteen that I'd found Jack in our bathroom with bloody wrists still haunted me sometimes. "Connor mentioned to me that you were going through battling some mental demons." Jack said, I looked at him. "He's been gushing about you being in this ballet school for months no word of a lie, but recently he said he was worried about you." He said, I looked at Connor.

"Well, I was." He said, "still kind of am." He added, I sighed.

"I'm by no means suggesting that you talk to me, or that I'd be any kind of help, but if you want…" Jack said, I looked at him.

"What made you so..."

"Depressed?" Jack asked, I sighed but I nodded. "I figure it was multiple things." He replied. "There was definitely not one definite thing. There was my parents dying, my shithole of a home. You know, my life was in fact a bed of roses." He said,

"So, why did you do it once you got a good deal?"

"Because it scared me." He said, I frowned at him. "I was waiting for something to go wrong, and when it didn't go wrong."

"You made it go wrong." I said, he nodded.

"I never did it again." Jack stated, "after then, because Ste was so attentive, even you and Adam, there was such love there the thought never actually occurred to me again."

"So, you're not depressed anymore?" I asked, he laughed softly.

"Sometimes. Yeah, I am. I feel better but I'm not cured. It's not like you flip a switch and turn the depression off, it's more of a dimmer switch."

"Some day's it's less, some days it more." I said, he nodded.

"How did you get to this point though?"

"I admitted I had a problem." He said softly, I sighed. "I admitted I had depression, but that didn't mean that it was my fault." He said, I looked at him. "Connor said you haven't been eating, but you won't admit it." he said, I shook my head.

"That wasn't what was happening, I was just missing some meals. I didn't."

"And throwing them back up?" Jack said, I winced.

"Madame Rose told me I needed to lose weight, so did Miss Olivia." I said, Connor frowned at me, I frowned right back at him.

"Kian told me that they wanted you to gain muscle." He said,

"Yeah, code for lose weight." I said, they both shook their heads almost in perfect synchronization. "What?" I asked quietly,

"Jacob, they wanted you to be stronger, not thinner."

146

"And even if they wanted you to lose weight, stopping eating is not the way to do that." Jack said, I scowled at the mango cooler in front of me, every sip I'd taken had tasted remarkably like cardboard.

"You don't understand ballet school is hard." I stated, I saw as Jack touched Connor's elbow, it was as if he was telling him not to reply.

"Okay." Jack said, I looked at him, "okay, yes ballet school must be difficult, I can't imagine I've ever done something as physically demanding as ballet school." He said, I looked at him. "But anorexia is never the answer. To anything."

"I'm not anorexic." I said, Jack raised his eyebrow at me, "I'm not. In our monthly medical checks the nurse said I was an average and normal weight. So did Max." I said, Jack sighed. "I'll be fine." I stated, "I will, I'll be back in school in January. It'll be like nothing happened; I made a mistake." I stated, "I just made a mistake."

"This was by far the best room of the house." Connor said from behind me, it didn't even make me jump as I stood in what had been my bedroom, and then Connor's. Now it appeared to belong to a very young boy given the toys that were scattered around the room.

"I want to be alone."

"No knock policy." Connor replied, I turned to look at him as he smiled at me. "Brings back memories?" he asked, I nodded.

"When we kissed." I said, he laughed as he came to stand beside me,

"Your first pointes."

"You sewed the ribbons on for me." I replied, he smiled.

"The first night I was here, when we were four." He said, I laughed in a sigh.

"You came in here and we slept in the same bed."

"Ste didn't even tell us off, he just smiled at us and told us it was time for breakfast."

"Our first day of school." I said, Connor nodded, "Ste got us both ready in here, and told us to look after each other."

"The first time we watched porn." He whispered, I laughed covering my mouth,

"Adam caught us." I said laughing,

"The day you got adopted." Connor said, I turned to look him. "You brought me in here, and you told me that you wanted me to have your bedroom." He said, I nodded, "and that night." he added,

"What happened that night?" I whispered,

"I slept in your bed before moving any of my stuff over. I cried for most of the night." he said, I hugged him almost instantly, he laughed into my ear as I cuddled him. "I'm sorry if you felt ambushed before." He said, I looked at him. "I'm just sick to the stomach worried about you." He said, I nodded.

"I know you are." I whispered, then I swallowed hard, "I'm going to see the school counsellor tomorrow." I said, he nodded lifting my chin.

"Tell me what he says, okay?" he asked, I nodded. "And come downstairs. Ste wants you to teach ballet to a group of very excited little girls." He said then began to laugh, so I laughed with him.

▾▾▾

"Thank you for coming to see me." the school counsellor, *who* had told me I could call him Ash said, as Max and

148

Cameron sat either side of me on the couch opposite from him.

I'd already been in his room for half an hour, we'd gotten as far as introducing ourselves to each other and then sat in silence for the remaining twenty-seven minutes and fifty-four seconds, until he gave and invited my parent's in.

"I have spoken with Jacob's teachers, and I am aware of the incident that happened last week; however, Jacob still seems a little reluctant to talk to me." Ash said warily,

"Is that because he's attractive?" Cameron whispered directly into my ear, I laughed looking at him, I saw as Ash smiled, so I looked back at him.

"How about we start with the incident, and not focus on the lead up to it." Ash said, I eyed him warily, "Arlo, said he noticed you not drinking in between your dances." He said softly, he didn't say it as if it was a question, it was simply a statement.

"No." I said, he seemed mildly surprised I'd replied to him.

"Why is that Jacob?"

"Because I didn't want to throw up." I replied, every adult in the room looked at me, but I kept my eyes firmly on Ash's.

"Did you feel sick?"

"After I drank the first bit of water. Yes."

"Did you inform Arlo, or another of your teachers?" he asked, I shook my head. "Any of your friends?" he asked, I shook my head again. "Why not?"

"They were all busy. I was busy."

"Okay." He said nodding. "Had you eaten prior to this rehearsal?" he asked, I shook my head slowly to him. "Why is that?"

149

"I forgot." I whispered,

"And the night before?"

"I forgot." I repeated, I saw Max wince out the corner of my eyes, so I turned my head so I couldn't see him at all

"Okay." Ash said warily, "were you afraid you'd throw up, if you ate?" he asked, I nodded to him, he began to nod back. "Jacob, have you been feeling self-conscious about eating in front of your peers?" he asked, I shrugged at him. "Do you eat of a night?"

"No." I replied, he ticked something on his sheet.

"Have you been exercising more often?" he asked, I nodded,

"But I'm at a ballet school. I have to." I said, Ash nodded although I don't believe it was an agreement.

"Jacob, have you been having erections, wet dreams, or masturbating?" he asked, I sat up with the shock of the question, I felt Cameron touch my shoulder so I looked at him.

"I, I…" I said, then I thought about the answer, I shook my head frowning at him as I did.

"Have sexual experiences been, at lack of a better word, disappointing for you?" he asked, I nodded almost instantly because after listening to Margo, Kian and Connor talk. Sex was not supposed to be as disappointing as it was.

"Have you been drinking excessive alcohol?" he asked, I frowned.

"No." I said, he nodded to me.

"Have either of you noticed a difference in Jacob?" Ash asked, I looked at Cameron first, who looked over my head at Max so I also looked at him.

150

"He stopped coming home." Max said, Ash frowned as he nodded. "To help with immediate pointe, and for Sunday lunch." He said, Ash scribbled something down.

"I feel like he's lost a lot of confidence." Cameron said, I turned to look at him as Ash nodded, "He used to be so ballsy, shit wouldn't stick to him, should we say." He said, Ash nodded,

"When did you notice this change?"

"Just before he came here, then it's gotten gradually more noticeable over the last few months." He said, "I mean, I know we've only had him for four years but I've noticed it recently."

"Four years?" Ash repeated, we all turned to him, "you adopted him?"

"What, you thought we made him?" Max said, I felt as Cameron hit Max's arm behind me, Ash shook his head, he almost looked embarrassed.

"What are your professions, please?" He asked,

"I'm an actor." Cameron said, "mostly in musicals."

"And is that stable?" Ash asked, I saw as Cameron scowled.

"I've been employed every year we've had Jacob." He replied, Ash nodded quickly,

"And yourself?" Ash asked,

"I'm a ballet teacher." Max said, "and a dancer."

"Where you Jacob's teacher?" Ash asked, we both nodded. "Okay. Jacob, you are showing very clear signs of anorexia." He said, I went to argue, "but, looking at your medical records and health checks your weight has remained constant, and healthy.

With this in mind, I believe your diagnosis is atypical anorexia. However, this is early onset, and it's good that it has been caught so quickly, that means your recovery can begin quickly, and you are likely to have a full recovery." He said, then he looked at Max, "Jacob has been very dependent on you Max, for I presume how long he has known you.

To have gone from such a loving environment, which I presume your teaching would've been towards him, as he is your son, to a prestige ballet school, is a massive change in his life, and there are probably a lot of feelings and unresolved emotions within Jacob right now. However, as you are a ballet dancer also, there is the element that Jacob could be comparing himself, and his achievements to yourself, as he will be doing with his classmates." He said, I looked at my hands. "Your roommate?" he said, I looked up at him.

"Kian?" I replied, he nodded to me,
"What do you think of him?"

"He's an extraordinary dancer. It's all so effortless for him and he's in amazing shape. Although he did admit to me that he pads his ballet belt." I said, Ash smiled sympathetically at me,

"What? Did I answer it wrong?" I asked, Ash shook his head.

"No, not at all Jacob." He said, then looked at Cameron and Max, they all spoke without using words for a little bit. "There are a lot of things you can do as a family to support Jacob. Such as timetabled meal times, if you sit to eat the same meal which is planned as a family it can make mealtimes easier, and also Jacob, make sure you remain in contact with your friends. Go out with them, see them, talk to them. Okay?"

"Okay." I whispered, Max and Cameron nodded either side of me.

"I'd recommend no ballet until recovery is taking place. We will meet regularly and together we will decide when it's best for you to begin dancing again." He said, I'm sure I whimpered. "Do you have any questions?"

The journey home was quiet, the quietness remained until we got into the living room, and I just couldn't handle it any longer. I watched as Cameron opened the double doors leading to the couches then went to go sit down as Max went towards the kitchen, and then, I began to cry.

Feeling as it completely overpowered me, so I fell to my knees burying my face into my hands. There were arms around me the moment I touched the floor, so I turned myself so I could hug the arms back.

"I think you've needed to cry for a while haven't you." Cameron said, I nodded to him as the tears continued to flood out of my eyes, he sat us down, letting me stay in his arms until I felt drained and I couldn't cry anymore. Cameron kissed the side of my head as I sniffled.

"I must be a huge embarrassment to you." I said, then turned my head to look at Max, "you're both so perfect." I said in-between sniffles, "and I let you down."

"You did not let us down." Max said coming to crouch beside next to us, "Not at all. Not one bit. We will get through this."

"Together." Cameron said, I looked back at him. "We will figure this out and you will be okay. That is the most important thing to us Jacob, that you're okay, and you're happy." He said, he began to nod to me, so I nodded back.

"I know it's hard. I know ballet school can be difficult but you can get through it. If you want to." Max said, I looked at him,

153

"How do you know?" I said. "You never went to the National Ballet School." I added as I stood from Cameron's arms, he reached for me tugging on my arm, telling me to calm down, but I didn't want "You never went, you don't know what it's like there. You don't have a clue." I stated, "you sent me into that not knowing and letting me believe I could do it, and I can't, I can't do it." I shouted then left the living room, running up the stairs to my bedroom.

I didn't look up when I heard the knock on my door. I also didn't welcome the knocker in, but he came in anyway.

"Ready to talk?" He asked, I didn't respond to him. "Okay. I'll talk you listen." He said then came to sit on my bed.

I still didn't look up at him.

"I want to tell you why I didn't go to National Ballet School, or into the Royal Ballet." He said, I glanced at him as he sighed. "I had a boyfriend in school, I think I told you that when you asked, when you were little." He said, I nodded. "Billy." He added, I raised my head to look at him.

"He broke up with me when I was sixteen because he didn't think we could do a long distance relationship." He said, I frowned. "I was heartbroken because he was my first ever boyfriend. He was my virginity, and I knew he still loved me as much as I loved him, but he broke up with me and he went to National Ballet School to complete his studies." He said then inhaled, "When it came to my turn for auditioning, when I was eighteen Frankie and I went to the induction day." He said, then looked directly at me,

"I was apprehensive about auditioning anyway, honestly, but I saw him as we were on our tour. I saw him and his new boyfriend and I knew I couldn't audition. He was only in his second year, I'd have had to have completed my first year with him in third, with him so close to me but not available to me." He said, I frowned.

"We had agreed we'd get back together when I went to National Ballet School. That was the plan, then he'd live in London whilst I finished studying. He broke my heart all over again the moment I found out he had a new boyfriend." He said then sighed. "Yes, I know what you're thinking, I didn't go to the National Ballet School because of a boy." He said, then met my eyes.

"Which is exactly what happened. I threw away my chance at the company, I threw away my chance of becoming a principal because of Billy, because he broke my heart and I couldn't bear to be around him. I don't regret it though." He said then looked at me, I shook my head because I knew he couldn't regret it. "I'd have never of been the World Champion if I went to National Ballet School, I'd have never competed. I'd have never done Musicals, I wouldn't have met Sam. I wouldn't have met Cameron." He said, then laughed sadly, "I'd have never of met Cameron." He repeated then looked at me, he put his hand into my hair. "We'd have never adopted you."

"I'd have never learnt ballet." I replied to him, he smiled before closing his eyes I pretended to ignore the tear rolling down his cheek.

"I know you're confused." He said, then opened his eyes. "I know you're angry, and excited, and..." He said then looked at me and smirked, "horny. You've been in a ballet bubble for so long you forgot to experience the real world and it's all hitting you at once. I forgive you for what you said"

"I don't forgive me." I replied,

"Well, you should." He said then tugged on my hair lightly. "But don't forget Jacob, we're here. I'm here if you need to talk, if you want to just figure things out. We won't judge you. Ever." He said, I looked down.

"I'm sorry." I said, then sniffed hard to try and disguise the quiver in my throat. "I'm so sorry." I repeated, he hugged me. "Can I stay here?" I asked, he nodded from in the hug.

"Of course you can. This is your home." He said then looked around my room, I followed his head around, my grades five to eight sat on my bookcase, alongside pictures that were took from various concerts and performances.

My first pair of pointe shoes sat above my desk on a shelf with the pair Max got me for my eighteenth and a rainbow pair, I'd spray painted with Connor. On my desk was a framed picture of Connor and I, *I* think we were sixteen in it. I turned from looking at the picture back to Max. "You chose the wallpaper." He said, I laughed as he stood from my bed. He got almost halfway before I decided I didn't want him to leave.

"Max?" I said, he turned to look at me, "I think I made a bad decision." I said almost frowning at him, he frowned back. "I think I regret having sex with someone."

Max passed me a shake bottle with something brown in, I frowned at him as he also sat on his bed,

"Protein shake." He said, I frowned harder at him as I hid underneath his quilt, I flicked the lid of the shake open and closed a few times. "It's chocolate." He added, I looked at him until he sighed. "You'll be able to keep it down better than food, and it'll fill you up better than drinks. It'll stop you from feeling hungry."

"It'll make me fat."

156

"No." he said warily, "it'll help you gain muscle mass." He said, I looked down. "Now talk to me." he said,

"I slept with my Pas De Deux partner." I said, he began to nod almost instantly. "But I don't regret doing that." I said then I sighed, "I don't know how to explain it." I said, then I gave and drank some of the shake, Max raised his eyebrow at me as I frowned at the taste. "I regret that I've ruined any opportunity I might have had to actually have a relationship with her."

"Oh." He said softly, "why?"

"Because I shouted at her." I muttered, he frowned. "I fucked up my audition. Huge style. She suggested I do it en pointe, and I did. Madame Rose didn't like that, at all." I said shaking my head, he shook his with me, "I shouted at her. Publicly and now, I think she actually hates me." I said, I saw as he kind of agreed. "I regret shouting at her more, but I was so angry…" I said, then I looked at him, "I was so hungry." I added, he hugged my shoulders.

"We'll figure this out okay." He said softly, I nodded to him as came under the cover with me.

"This is vile." I said, he laughed taking the shake from me, drinking it then covering his mouth.

"Yep. That's definitely vile." He said, I laughed quietly as I continued to drink it, watching as Max searched through the Netflix's until he found a reliable ballet film for us both to watch.

Chapter 9

"Dress tech." Cameron shouted towards the living room. I looked at him from my seat at the kitchen table, he glanced at me, just waiting,

"Time?" Max replied, Cameron smiled.

"Noon." He replied then came to sit opposite me to finish eating his breakfast,

"Rehearsals over then?" I asked, Cameron nodded slowly to me.

"Show opens the first week of December." He said, I nodded back to him.

"And the run?" I queried as I flicked the lid of the shake bottle open and closed, Cameron sighed.

"Are you okay?" He asked, I shrugged.

"We got put into a list. Kian sent me it" I said, Cameron laughed so I looked directly at him, he covered his mouth.

"Sorry, I was just having school memories." He said, I frowned at him then shook my head.

"I'm a pretty sorry number." I said, Cameron smiled.

"I usually came ninth out of twelve." He said, then raised an amused eyebrow back at me. "Your placement on a list doesn't define your worth." He said, I shrugged again. "And you've had a pretty crappy term, no?" He said, I nodded, because I really had.

"Don't tell Max." I said, Cameron frowned at me,

"Why?" He whispered, so I looked down,

"I don't want to disappoint him." I muttered, Cameron nudged my hand with his,

"You Jacob would never disappoint Max. Max is the proudest of you I've ever seen. You got into the National Ballet School, and that is amazing, *oh* and he's also usually pretty proud that you can dress yourself, feed yourself and go the toilet on your own." He said, I laughed.

"You guys didn't get me through toddlerhood." I said, he smiled back at me.

"No, but Max loves you so much he might as well have birthed you himself." He said, I looked into my bowl to smile, then up as Max came into the kitchen.

"You said noon, right?" He asked, Cameron nodded back to him. "Dress tech." He repeated, Cameron nodded again,

"Come sit, eat something." Cameron said pointing at the chair between us; Max sighed. "Sit. Eat. There's nothing to do, or nothing that you can do." he said, then laughed, "I love your neurotic self but... To an extent."

"I'm not neurotic." Max said pointing at his chest as he sat down,

"I'm on Max's side here." I said, Cameron laughed loudly.

"Well, I'm not surprised." He stated, I laughed then bit my lip.

"Oh, you made him laugh. Bonus points." Max said, Cameron winked back at him.

"Can I come to your rehearsal?" I asked looking between them, as they looked at each other. "Just to watch." I added, Max spoke to Cameron with just his expression, I still hadn't completely cracked their expression code yet.

"Yes." Max said, "it might be good for you." He added, I nodded to him then drank from the shake bottle.

I sat between them in the stalls as their director sat on the end of the stage, he spoke exactly like I imagined a theatre director would, he spoke as if he had a dream. All that he was missing was a silk scarf and a melodramatic backstory.

When he stood up, everyone else did, all leaving the stalls and going to the stage. Cameron stood alongside Sam Bing, as they read through Sam's copy of the script. Max sat on the other side of the stage, tying his pointe ribbons.

"Let's warm up, then straight in. Okay?" The director said, they all agreed then spread themselves out on the stage.

Max stood next to Cameron; I saw as Cameron grinned as if he was prepared for whatever Max was going to do to him.

They did some breathing exercises, then sang alongside the scales, *which* they did twice over before the director made them jog on the spot whilst still singing. Then they went into a dance warmup, stretching every part of their bodies. That's when I saw Max's mischievous smirk, as he reached for Cameron and began to tickle him, getting squeaked at as a response, I laughed covering my mouth as Cameron punched Max's arm, then went straight back into the stretch, they continued until the director clapped his hands,

"Narrator front and centre." He requested, so Cameron did so, "dancers in the wings. Everyone else off stage." He stated, everyone scurried leaving just Cameron stood centre stage. He walked backwards until he was stood where he should, he clicked his fingers and a spotlight appeared. He looked up happily as the house lights went out, and the stage went to black,

"Right, from the top." The director said, and the music began, it sounded like an orchestra warming up, until Cameron clicked. The sound echoing around the theatre and the spot light shone down on him, he smiled, a quick almost sinister smile then he began to sing.

I moved forward in my seat, leaning on the one in front of me as the stage gradually got lighter, and lighter until it was completely lit and all the dancers were stood as if they were statues around him.

They only began to move when Cameron touched them, and even then it was slow aerobatics. I watched as he walked up to Max, he took his hand, then smiled as Max raised his leg vertical to his body. Cameron let go as he sang his next line, leaving him stood with his leg vertical until he turned to the audience and they all began to dance together.

All moving perfectly together, until Cameron stopped and they surrounded him doing their aerobatics again until the song finished, and Cameron clicked his fingers again, making the stage go dark.

161

Max came to sit next me when they hit the interval, Cameron was sat on the stage alongside Sam as they received notes.

"So?"

"He works hard." I said, Max smiled then tried to hide it behind his hand. "Like I never quite realised how hard Cameron has to work."

"You thought ballet was harder?"

"Well, stricter." I said, Max nodded.

"Admittedly. I like doing musicals because I can relax slightly, the choreography can sometimes be more intense though." He said, I laughed as I nodded. "Not just ballet."

"Is this supposed to be a life lesson?" I asked, Max laughed,

"No. You love ballet, I'm not telling you to get another hobby. I just think it's good for you to see that ballet isn't the be all and end all, or, that ballet dancers aren't the only ones who work hard." He said, I sighed but nodded to him,

"I placed tenth on the assessment list." I said,

"Tenth?" He repeated, I nodded.

"I know it's shit." I said, Max laughed.

"It's not Jacob, it gives you room to improve." He said, I looked at him. "To be number one by second year." He said, I shook my head, agreeing with him. "Then you're doing just fine. Tenth overall, or tenth male?"

"Overall. There's not enough males to make a list." I said, Max smiled at me again, so I broke and smiled back at him.

"Act two beginners, to the stage please." I heard so I turned to look for the voice.

"You'll be fine Jacob." Max said as he stood, I nodded back to him as he left the stalls and went back onto the stage.

I warily went into the kitchen after I heard Cameron shout my name. He'd disappeared into the kitchen the moment we'd returned from their dress tech and Max had disappeared upstairs to have a shower, as he had lessons to teach this evening. Cameron turned to smile at me, so I frowned back at him.

"Come here." he said, I shook my head. "Come." He repeated, so I *went*. "You're helping me make tea." He said, I shook my head almost instantly.

"No, no I…"

"Pizza." He said, "quick and easy." He said, so I looked at his face I began to nod as his expression literally screamed 'please'.

"What do you want me to do?" I asked, Cameron grinned then put a lump of dough that was wrapped in cling film down in front of me.

"Roll that." He said amused, "try and get it circle shaped." He added as he sprinkled some flour onto the countertop. I unwrapped the dough then began to roll it, as Cameron got the toppings out. "We can either have three individual pizzas, or one big one?"

"Max like's olives. Three individuals please." I replied, Cameron laughed nodding to me as he assessed my dough rolling skills. He seemed to approve, then helped me cut it into three, I rolled out two of them, as Cameron rolled out the third.

"Just in time." Cameron said, so I turned my head to look at Max as he came into the kitchen.

163

"For?" Max asked, then kissed Cameron's cheek, Cameron laughed whilst threatening to touch him with his floured hands.

"To choose your pizza toppings." I said, Max oohed and stood on the other side of Cameron to top his. Cameron took a picture of the three pizzas before we cooked them, smiling at us both as he turned away with his phone, typing into it then placing it on the kitchen table.

"Now the fun part." He said, I raised my eyebrow at him as Max laughed and ate some cheese off the top of his pizza, then put the three of them into the oven. "Cleaning up."

"Oh give over." Max said laughing as he held his hand above Cameron's head, he barely had time to register it before Max began to sprinkle flour over him, I almost instantly began to laugh as Cameron scooped up some flour.

"I have just had a shower you can't." Max said backing away, until he walked into the dish washer. Cameron threw the flour anyway, so Max grabbed him, turning him around to face me. "Go on." He said amused, I bit my lip. "Throw it." he added, I took a handful out of the bag,

Cameron began to shake his head at me as he tried to escape Max's grasp, then he screamed in amongst laughter as I threw the flour at him. Max let Cameron go the moment I had so I ran, hiding behind the kitchen table as Cameron got the bag of flour. I screamed ducking under the table as Cameron began to throw it.

We all sat around the table, all freshly showered when the timer dinged to indicate the pizzas were done.

"Going to be hot." Cameron said as he placed the three pizzas onto the table, he passed me the pizza knife, nodding to me as he took the trays to the sink. I cut each of the pizzas into quarters.

"What are you going to do when your show starts?" I asked, Max frowned at me as he took his first piece of pizza. "With evening classes?" I asked, he began to nod because he understood.

"As the show runs through December, Frankie's going to teach the classes," he said, I must've looked surprised, "and do a winter show around February time." He said, I nodded back to him then reached for my own piece of pizza.

"That makes sense." I said nodding, he seemed to agree.

"Thought it was the easier option, than teaching multiple classes in the interval." He said, I began to laugh then ate some of the pizza, I watched as Cameron smiled at Max, who smiled right back.

Cameron came to sit next to me on the bathroom floor once I'd done throwing up. He didn't speak when he came into the bathroom, he'd just sat beside me wrapping his arms around my shoulders until I looked at him.

"It's okay." He said simply, I shook my head, "it is, you won't get better overnight. You'll never get better overnight, but the fact that you want to get better is good Jacob." He said, I whimpered as I leant my head on his shoulder.

"I enjoyed making the pizza." I said, he laughed softly.

"Yeah, that was fun." He said nodding, "and you know what, that's good enough for today." He said, I looked up again. "And you did eat it, so there's definite progress." He said, I nodded to him as he hugged my shoulders. "pretty

165

soon you won't have to drink those retched shakes again."
He said, I began to laugh as he did too. "Now come on." He
said then stood, I stood with him. "I'll get you some water."
He added as he led me out of the bathroom.

"I don't appreciate you working in alliance with my
fathers." I said as I walked down the path of the carpark
towards the supermarket, Connor laughed as he shook his
head.

"I apologise I needed food." He said, turning his
head to look at me, I smiled at him so he laughed. "I'm not
working in alliance, I swear." He added, I laughed.

I'd called him earlier, begging him to let me go out
with him, just to get me out of my house. Max and Cameron
had both approved of my day trip as I ate a bowl of cereal,
and hadn't yet recreated it, when I'd arrived at Connor's flat
he had announced he had to do a food shop, and that he'd
appreciate my help. I'd complained to him for most of the
journey to the supermarket.

"Cameron had us make pizzas." I said, "I know what
he's up to." I added as Connor put a pound into a trolley,
then rolled it towards me, I began to push it.

"What do you mean? What he's up to?"

"Ash told them, we should eat together as a family
and eat the same food. It'll make me more likely to eat it."

"Did it?" he said, I sighed. "Right." He said
nodding,

"Ash also suggested I help in preparation, ergo we
made pizzas."

"I did eat it." I said, "but I threw it back up." I
added, Connor winced. "I'm not doing it on purpose." I
stated,

"I know. When I was talking to Kian, all about you, totally about you he said he could tell you weren't actually purposely doing it.

However, killing yourself on a treadmill was questionable." He said raising his eyebrow at me as we walked down the fruit and vegetable aisle, he picked up some bananas.

"Yeah, I admit that was stupid." I said, as he opened the bag of bananas, he pulled one off, passing it to me, so I took it as he pulled another and threw the bag into the trolley, he began to eat the one he was holding, so I copied.

"You've never actively done anything that involved exercise." He said amused, I laughed with him because it had been all too true. "There's a kid in the home like that now. He hates all kinds of physical recreation. Ste stated that it's one activity of your choice and a sport." He said laughing, I nodded.

"I remember all too well; it's why I did swimming for ten years." I said, Connor laughed.

"I loved football." He said nodding, I nodded back to him because I *knew* he had. "This kid goes to a gaming club every week, and every week he tells Ste he won't do exercise, it's humorous." He said smiling at me as he picked up some ready meals, "I'm going to buy their presents next week, if you wish to join me?" he said, I looked at him as I finished the banana, then I nodded, he smiled at me as he turned the end of the trolley towards the next aisle. "I'm thinking of buying this kid a headset for when he plays games on the computer." He added, I smiled,

"Connor." I said, he looked at me, "have kids someday." I said, he laughed. "Please." I added, "Kian likes kids. I'm sure it wouldn't be too difficult to persuade him to elope." I said, he grinned as he picked some tins off the shelves.

"Speaking of Kian…" he said, I frowned at him, "I'm going to watch the ballet. The evening performance Kian requested, because then he can come home with me and stay at mine." He said then waved his hand at me, sort of saying that fact was not necessary. "Do you want to come?" he asked, he winced as he did, I winced back because I didn't actually have an answer to that question.

"I don't know." I said softly, Connor began to nod. "I think I might have to ask Ash if it'd be wise to." I added, he smiled and nodded to me.

"Course." He said, "just let me know. I mean it's almost guaranteed I'll be having sex with Kian that night, so I fully understand if you do not want to come with me." he said, I laughed as he grinned at me then turned the trolley into the next aisle.

I went home with him, as I promised I'd help put his shopping away, so I did.

"Staying for some tea?" he asked, I looked at him as I closed the cupboard, I'd put all his tins into.

"What's on the menu?" I asked, Connor smiled.

"I was thinking soup honestly, I brought a chicken and sweetcorn mix." He said, I nodded to him.

"That sounds good." I said, he seemed pleased as he got a pan out of the drawer and put it on the hob.

I went to stand beside him, as he opened the packet and poured the soup into the pan. We sat opposite each other on his couch to eat. He had decorated his couch with numerous sequined cushions that changed colour when you stroked them, the one behind him had a K written into it, the blue sequins against the silver background, the one behind me had a star, but I had ran my hand over it a few times and began to write a J into it.

He laughed as he saw what I was doing, shaking his head at me, so I pointed at the cushion behind him, he laughed as he looked over his shoulder.

"He does it every time he comes over." He said as he stroked down a few of the silver sequins. "I decided to just leave it this time, see what he does." He said amused, I laughed as he placed his now empty bowl onto the table, I copied.

"I feel as if we haven't gossiped nearly enough about Kian." I said, Connor began to laugh.

"You probably know him better than I do." He replied, I nodded waving my finger between us,

"Gossiping goes both ways Connor." I said, he grinned then he nodded to me.

▾▾▾

"Connor has invited me to watch the Christmas ballet." I said, Ash nodded to me as I rubbed my thighs with the palms of my hand. "I couldn't work out if that'd be good for me to go to, or not?" I asked almost frowning at Ash who was tapping his pen against his chin.

"I think this is something only you can fully decide for yourself."

"Starting to sound a bit like a mystical mentor there." I said, Ash laughed briefly.

"Jacob, how are you finding not doing ballet?"

"It's killing me." I admitted, I'd waved it off to both Cameron and Max the multiple times they'd asked because I didn't want to make them feel worse, although I'm sure Max knew, or at least some part of him knew that it was killing me not to be doing ballet.

169

"Do you feel watching ballet would make those feelings more prominent?" he asked, I looked at him,

"But I'd be going for my friends, not…" I began then I lost myself.

"I believe this is truly only a decision you can make yourself." He said, I frowned at him.

"I thought you were supposed to be helpful." I said, he laughed briefly, and inwardly I was glad he understood it was a joke.

"How are meal times for you?" He asked, I hummed at him.

"I am continuing to throw up big meals." I said, he nodded,

"What are we labelling as a big meal?" he asked, I shrugged.

"I don't know, a lot of food. I suppose, meals that aren't soup, or cereal." I said then winced, he began to nod.

"But you're keeping soup and cereal down?" he asked, I nodded, "small victories." He said happily, so I smiled back at him.

"Small victories." I agreed.

Corinthian tapped my shoulder, as I sat on his till point, I turned to look at him then took the tea he was passing me. I turned back to Max and Frankie as they sat on the floor of the shop multiple pointes surrounding them, and ballet wear magazines open in front of them.

"I wanted to talk to you." Cory said, I looked at him as he leant on the till, watching Max and Frankie himself and sipping at his own tea. "I've spoken to Max, and of course Cameron and they have a brilliant perspective on the whole thing but I feel like I'd only get a genuine one from you."

"On what?" I asked,

"Frankie and I are looking to adopt." He said, I looked at him, "we just don't know how to approach it." He said, then he frowned at me, so I frowned back. "I mean, we don't know if we want to adopt a baby, or... Not."

"Everyone adopts babies." I said, "it's very common and usually there's a long waiting list to adopt a baby. You either get a freshly made baby, or one that's still cooking." I said, he laughed. "I mean you can do the cool thing where you mix your sperm together and have a surrogate but, that's not really what you're asking is it." I said, Cory laughed. "We always said once you turned thirteen that was it. If you hadn't been adopted, you're not going to be."

"Were you, or were you not fourteen?" He said, I nodded.

"I was rare, but Connor was never adopted, nor was Jack. Ste told us it was becoming more frequent that kids stayed in the home until they were eighteen. Adopting was becoming less common, as was fostering." I said, then I sighed and looked at him, "I still haven't answered your question, right?"

"Right." He replied amused,

"I guess I can't tell you what kind of kid you should adopt. You work here, so you can do the school run. Frankie," I said then frowned in his direction,

"Frankie has just retired from dancing in ballets. He's between jobs right now." He said,

"So technically you could adopt a baby or a toddler, but they need a lot of love, as do the little kids in homes. Up until their about nine or ten, they need so much love because they're aware that they don't have a mum or dad, but can't always comprehend why. I remember it well," I said, then looked at him.

171

"It sounds twisted, messed up but I was almost envious that Connor's parents had died. That was such a simple black and white situation. We were babies but we both understood perfectly what that meant. Ste struggled telling me why I was in care, every time I asked he struggled, because how do you say to a four, five year old that their mum gave them up at birth.

I'll never know why, and I can't work out if that's a shitty part of the deal or not." I said, then I sighed. "My point though, although kids are cuter, they need so much more love because sometimes they just feel as if no one wants them." I said, then looked at him,

"And your view on adopting a twelve, thirteen year old?"

"You'd make their year. Their life." I said, he smiled.

"You'd recommend it?" He asked, I shrugged,

"I'm bias." I said, then I laughed. "You've got a fully-fledged little human if you get a twelve year old. I mean, I was ballet mad from when I was about five, but by twelve, I was a ballet force." I said, he began to laugh.

"And obviously with us being gay?"

"Kids don't care, so long as you love them." I said then looked towards Max and Frankie again.

"So, maybe stop being so hard on Max." He said, I sighed.

"I'm not doing it because he's gay."

"That'd be quite hypocritical of you, no?"

"I'm bi," I said, he raised his eyebrow at me, so I laughed. "Fair." I said, he smiled. "He knows I'm sorry."

"I know, and you know he loves you." He said, I nodded.

"You'll be a good dad." I said almost frowning at him. "Careful though, you might accidentally get a football

172

mad kid, who can literally list off every player since time began."

"I wouldn't be surprised." He said amused. "I'll talk to Frankie, but thank you. You've given me somethings to think about." He said nodding then looked back towards them, so I did as they both stood.

"What do you think?" Frankie asked, I began to laugh as they both presented their Christmas tree made of pointe shoes to us with their arms.

"Awesome." Cory said nodding, I continued to laugh as Frankie came over to Cory leaning towards him and kissing him.

"Do you mind if I take the prodigy?" Max said, they both laughed.

"He is your son." Frankie said, Max laughed as I jumped off the till, and put my coat on. I watched Max hug both of them, then he walked towards me. He led me out of Cory's shop and down the street, we didn't really talk as we walked. I let him lead the way, not bothering to ask where we were going because there was no chance he was going to tell me. Until he cleared his throat.

"It's Christmas." He said, I bit my tongue so I wouldn't reply with a snarky remark. "Which means my favourite thing is in town."

"Your favourite thing?" I asked, then I actually looked at him. "The Nutcracker?" I said, he nodded.

"However, not the traditional Nutcracker this year," he said as we rounded the corner to the theatre,

"Bournes." I said then I smiled at the huge poster on the front of the theatre.

"I have two tickets." He said, so I smiled at him. "If of course you still like me enough to join me."

173

"Of course I do." I said, he smiled at me so I nodded. "Thank you, dad."

Chapter 10

I took a deep breath as I took the seat beside Connor. Our hall looked completely different with the stage built and the seating bank pulled out. I almost couldn't recognise it, which humoured me, if only lightly as I'd been so wary of going back into the hall, since the last time I had, I'd blacked out.

Connor had held my hand most of the way, until we got to our row of seats and he had to turn sideways to walk down, so had forgone my hand, and continuously checked to make sure I was actually following him.

"Good?" he asked when I finally sat down, I nodded to him then looked over his shoulder as he read the programme. There was a long description of the show over the first two pages, I guess it was for the non-ballet fans who'd been forced to come and watch as their child, or sibling was performing.

The next page was the running order, the scenes and where they were set, then there were some photos. The Second playing Edward, and the ballerina got their own headshots and a quote underneath from both of them, both stating their joy that they'd gotten the role. Below, was a group photograph, it was my class, all stood in boy girl pairs, except for Abi, who was stood in the centre holding fifth position. Underneath in an extraordinary small font was all of their names, left to right.

"So, which girl did you sleep with?" Connor asked as he searched the photograph, I laughed.

"This isn't a fun game." I replied as I moved the programme a little closer to me, putting my finger above Abi's head. "I fucked that up." I said, he nodded although I could tell it was totally wary.

"What are you going to do?" he asked, I sighed.

"Turn over a new leaf." I said, his eyebrow raised. "I'm going to apologise to her, when I see her again. Straight out apologise, and although I'm sure that won't change very much and I've probably left it too long now, it might create a little bit of harmony. Then I'm going to not focus on it anymore, and just treat it as a learning experience."

"Ash is working wonders on you, isn't he?" Connor said, I almost laughed.

"I ate some of Max and Cameron's takeaway on Friday, and I didn't throw it back up." I said, Connor smiled at me.

"That might be the best news I've heard all week." He said nodding, I nodded back, then turned to look at the stage as it lit up, and the music began to play.

Arlo appeared beside me when the interval began, he must have spotted me during the first act as he slid into the seat beside me without a thought.

"I'm glad you came Jacob." He said as I looked at him, I nodded back to him. "How are you feeling?"

"Better." I said, then I sighed, "but it's slow and steady. Ash, and Cameron keep reminding me that it's not going to happen overnight." I said, he agreed,

"We look forward to having you back in class. Although I think these guys are ready for the break." He said amused, so I laughed because I figured that was what he expected. "They've been working very hard." he said, probably more for the benefit of the rest of the audience,

"I'm hoping to be back in January." I said, then I chewed on my lip. "But Ash said we have to get through Christmas first, then he wants me to do ballet with Max, or by myself for a bit." I said, Arlo began to nod.

"How is Max?" he asked, I laughed for real that time.

"He's fine. He's actually in a musical currently." I said, Arlo nodded he looked intrigued.

"He wasn't too hard on you?" he asked, I looked down.

"I think Jacob's been harder on Max." Connor said, I scowled him but only briefly.

"Oh. Well, stay in touch Jacob, yeah?"

"Yeah." I said nodding, as he smiled and stood, Connor and I both watched him leave the row we were sat on.

"Who was that wonderful being?" Connor asked, I laughed. "My male technique teacher." I said, Connor tutted, "he's slept with Max." I added, Connor almost choked.

"What?"

177

"Years ago. I think. Prior to a competition, apparently, they slept together, I didn't exactly dig deeper into any details." I said, Connor hit my arm,

"And why not? Max's sex life is amazing." He said, I laughed, it became rather nasal so I covered my face embarrassed. "First Samuel Bing, then, this Arlo, and of course you're exceptionally beautiful father Cameron."

"Your crush on Cameron concerns me." I said, he winked as the music for the second act began.

Margo appeared first when we stood in the parents meet and greet area, she appeared then she was hugging me, and I was hugging her back, so tightly.

"I have missed you Jacob." She said into my ear, I nodded because I was sure if I spoke, I'd start crying. She let go first, but only to turn to present me to Kian, he smiled at me then came to me and hugged me himself.

"How are you Jacob?" he asked, I began to nod to him, taking a deep breath as I did.

"I've missed your company, for sure." I said, he grinned at me,

"Do I dare ask when we might see you back?" Margo asked, I hummed at them then crossed my fingers.

"January." I said, "Even if it's just dancing and not boarding, I'm hopeful." I said, they both nodded with me, "I just have to get through Christmas. It's my next achievable goal." I said, then looked at Connor as he smiled back at me.

"Now I better get you home." Connor said, "otherwise I'll have a pretty angry Max on my back. I'll drive you home, and Kian…"

"I'm yours." Kian said nodding, Connor grinned then looked away from me embarrassed as he did. I hugged Margo again, giving her an extra squeeze then walked with

Kian and Connor to the carpark. "I'm going home for Christmas on Monday." Kian said more to Connor, "after this week, which was unbelievable." He said nodding, then he looked at me. "We've missed you so much." He said, I laughed. "What did you think though? Did we deliver?"

"You were amazing." I said,

"I concur." Connor said, Kian laughed,

"You're already getting laid tonight, you don't need to work for it." he said, I laughed as I got into the back of Connor's car.

"You've got yourself a good boyfriend there, I am mildly jealous." I said, Connor winked at me as he got in the driver side then grinned at Kian who grinned right back as they both put their seatbelts on.

I groaned into my pillow before giving myself the motivation to get myself up out of bed and strip the sheets. It was almost muscle memory now, stripping back the sheet, the quilt and my pillows, wrapping them up into my pillowcase and taking them downstairs. I startled as I walked into the kitchen, finding Cameron stood at the counter with a cup of something. He raised his eyebrow at me, I did it back.

"Everything okay?" He asked, not at all fighting the smirk on his face, I rolled my eyes holding the pillowcase to him.

"I had a sticky dream." I said, he laughed softly then took a sip out of his mug.

"You know where the washing machine is." He said as he turned to lean on the countertop, he watched me as I filled the washing machine. "It's been a while." He said, I laughed.

"Are you making small talk?" I asked, he shook his head as he drank from his mug.

179

"No. I'm just happy to know you're eating again."
He said, I looked at him. "One cannot produce a sticky
dream, without energy, without food in their stomach." He
said then he smiled. "So, in a way I'm glad." He said, I
laughed, shaking my head at him. "Hey, you should be glad
too. You've never had to do the walk of shame down the
corridor with at least two of your dorm mates because, they
so have to see this, to the *only* male teacher in the whole
school to express you've had a wet dream and need new
bedding." He said, I laughed ensuring I covered my mouth
as I did. "It happened at least bimonthly, in my dorm."

"To you." I replied, ensuring he understood how
much I was mocking him, he obviously did the way he
quirked his eyebrow back at me.

"Until I began sleeping with Max." He said, I
groaned covering my face.

"You win." I said, he laughed.

"Come on. Let's go up. I'll get you some fresh
bedding." He said, I nodded to him as he put his mug by the
sink, an action I'm sure Max will be displeased with in the
morning, then began to lead me up the stairs. I waited
outside when he went into his bedroom and to the airing
cupboard. He reappeared with the pile of bedding in his
hands.

"Thank you." I said, he nodded to me.

"Goodnight." He whispered, I smiled at him as I
turned back to my bedroom.

"Goodnight."

▼▼▼

I remembered the Christmas' in the home vividly, and I
remembered them often. It had started with a pantomime. Ste
and Diane took us to a pantomime every year, it was the one

180

night we could get away with buying sweets and slushes in the foyer.

We were always very excited and almost unruly but it was Christmas and Ste and Diane let us off at Christmas. We always got a McDonalds on the day we went to see the pantomime, we took up multiple tables and all somehow ended up getting the same toys in our happy meals, but they had stuck with me, for the years after, when my pantomime trip became ballet trips and our once a year McDonalds had become far more frequent.

I had agreed, after much badgering from Connor to accompany the home and him to the pantomime that Christmas, he stated it be good for me, *then* Ash agreed and suddenly I was an additional adult with two teenagers to keep an eye on.

Connor had been showered in hugs when we'd gotten out the car, mostly by the younger children, then a teenage who had dark purple hair had bumped shoulders with him, and whispered something to him that made Connor squeeze him tight in a hug.

"Don't worry they're not as scary as you think." Ste said as we stood on the edge of the curb watching the kids as they grouped, they weren't running wild, they weren't actually doing anything but talking to each other, so I looked at Ste.

"We were not as good as this?" I said, Ste laughed.

"What are you basing that on, the yearly pantomimes? Or the party you once went to, when you drank at fourteen?" he asked, I laughed. "They're just kids. The girls can be a bit feisty, the boys are pretty laid back, well most of them anyway. They love Connor, and they adore Jack. I'm pretty certain they'll have a fondness for you too."

He said, I nodded as I let my deep breath out. "How are you feeling anyway?" he asked, I looked at him.

"I kind of wish people will stop asking me that." I said, he nodded as if he completely understood, there was no hurt in his expression, just complete understanding.

"That makes sense. Okay, how about I ask, any plans for Christmas?" he said, I smiled at him.

"Apparently Cameron has planned something which I am so beyond wary about, but Christmas kind of runs the same. We go to see a ballet, eat out on Christmas eve, then Christmas day is presents and dinner and alcohol. Usually." I said,

"That sounds good." He said, I agreed.

"And your Christmas?" I asked, he smiled fondly towards the kids as Jack gathered them around the poster of the pantomime and took a picture.

"Oh, standard." He said, I smiled. "Pancakes…"

"For breakfast, presents after breakfast, then you'd just let us play, all day." I said, Ste nodded.

"When all the kids go to bed, Diane and I would stay up with any of you that were over sixteen at the time, we'd have a drink whilst watching a film, or some sort of sitcoms Christmas special." He said, I smiled.

"I didn't know that." I said, he shook his head.

"It was a secret." He said putting his finger on his lips, I laughed as Diane clapped her hands to get all the kids' attention, then she began to ferry them into the theatre.

"Riley passed his theory." Connor said as we walked behind the group into the theatre, I frowned at Connor so he laughed. "The teenager with purple hair…" he said, I nodded. "He passed his theory. He's the second kid ever to pass their theory whilst they're still living in the home." He said, I laughed.

"Says the first." I said, he nodded,

"Says the first." he agreed, "I'm so proud of him." He said in a sigh, so I nudged my elbow against his. "Shush." He said, as we took our seats.

I lay looking at Connor in his bed. He'd driven me back to his flat after we'd crowd controlled in McDonalds, we'd both decided it was a far wiser decision for me to sleep over at Connor's than go home to an empty house as Max and Cameron's run was well underway.

I had sent a text to Cameron, informing him of my whereabouts, and letting him know what I'd eaten so far, he had replied during what I presumed was the interval with a few very happy emoji's.

"You didn't tell me that you've drank with Ste on Christmas." I whispered, Connor laughed quietly as he lay looking back at me, he was playing with the aqua sequin cushion he had on his bed, the hot pink K was evident in it, Connor appeared to be stroking it back to the blue.

"He'd let us have either one glass of prosecco, a can of beer or a mixer, and only one." He said softly, "he said, it was better that we learnt about drinking, and drank appropriately with them, than getting drunk in an alleyway somewhere." He said, I nodded because that logic was sound.

"Even if we had our first drink at fourteen." I said, Connor laughed.

"I was thirteen." He replied, I grinned, "and it was a blue WKD. We were rebels."

"Totally." I agreed amused, he grinned at me.

"Do you remember our first real drink?" he asked, I squinted at him, so he shook his head. "Your eighteenth?"

"Oh my god. I got so drunk." I said, he nodded whilst not hiding his laugh.

"And you weren't the only one." He said, I frowned at him then began to laugh myself.

"Max." I said, he began to nod.

"Max." he agreed, then he sighed but it sounded amused. "I've missed doing this with you." He said, I smiled at him,

"Thank you." I said, he frowned,

"For missing you?"

"No, for persuading me to go tonight, I didn't realise how much I needed that, but I did."

"They're pretty great kids." He said nodding, "and helping out is the least I can do, especially after Ste and Diane were parents to me." he said then he smiled at us. "Sorry. To us." He said, I nodded then smiled when he kissed my forehead.

▼▼▼

We had a family meeting, and all agreed that we'd forgo our annual Christmas ballet, given Max had already taken me to see the Nutcracker, and instead, Frankie, Cory, and Cameron's twin brother Caspar accompanied me to watch Pippin.

"Has there been any progress with the adoption?" I asked Cory as we took our seats, Frankie and Caspar had both well disappeared, probably to the merchandise store.

"Some actually." Cory said nodding, "when I spoke to Frankie he said both babies and teenagers scare him." He said, I laughed, "so we thought we'd look about seven, eight." He said happily, I smiled back at him. "We are waiting for our documents to be checked and approved and then, it looks like we're moving forward."

"That's exciting." I said, he agreed as Frankie reappeared passing Cory a plastic cup with some sort of drink in it, Caspar passed me one from the other side.

The first time I'd officially met Caspar had been at a huge family event. All five of Max's sisters had been present and I had spent a fair bit of time trying to learn their names, when I felt like I'd achieved something I went to find Cameron for some comfort. It had turned out that instead I found Caspar, and had just began talking to him, I had recited all of Max's sister's names at least three times before Caspar stopped me and informed me that he wasn't my Dad, I was confused, definitely as I was still fourteen, having been adopted just three months earlier, and hadn't been informed that Cameron actually had a twin.

Later, I'd sat in the garden with Caspar, and Cameron and after getting over the initial shock that they were in fact completely identical, I sat listening to Caspar playing his trumpet. Now, I could tell Cameron and Caspar apart, although that was aided by them having different haircuts, I however still did not know which of Max's sister went with which name.

"Thank you." I said, Caspar nodded to me as he took his seat. "Did you bring your trumpet?"

"Of course." He said amused, "Cameron hates it after many years of having to hear me learn it." he said happily, I heard Frankie laugh so I looked at him.

"I often wished I had a brother, but listening to these two, I'm glad I didn't." He said, I began to nod.

"I have a not biological brother. Does that count?"

"Does he do mean things to you?" Frankie asked, I shook my head, "doesn't count." He said, so I began to laugh then turned towards the stage as the overture began.

Caspar stayed at our house on Christmas Eve, he had for as long as I'd lived with Max and Cameron, and I presume he had before that. There had been big hugs when Max and Cameron had come off the stage, and confirmation of the time of Christmas dinner for Frankie and Cory before we took our separate cars and went home.

I went to change into my pyjamas when I returned, laughing when I saw Christmas pyjamas on my made bed that hadn't been made this morning, all tied up in a ribbon. I pulled out the top, smiling at the long sleeved grey top, and red pants that were covered in Christmas trees, candy canes and reindeers.

Cameron seemed pleased when I reappeared downstairs.

"You really don't torture him as much as you should." Caspar said as he passed a beer bottle to Cameron, Cameron began to laugh.

"I'm too traumatised." He said then took a sip out of his bottle, I frowned at him. "Our Mum, and grandparents used to work together and give us the worse Christmas pyjamas they ever could."

"Most years they matched." Caspar said then sat on the couch, so I sat next to him, Cameron on my other side. Max came into the living room, two bottles of beer between his fingers, his phone in his other hand and his own pair of Christmas pyjamas on.

"We were going to order a takeaway." Max said, I looked at him, "what...?" he began, then looked at Cameron, so I also did.

"How do you feel?" Cameron asked, I nodded slightly. "How about you get the appetiser box, and you eat some of that rather than a meal?" he said, nodding to me, then to Max, we both agreed with him. "You know what I'll have." He said to Max, Max smiled as he nodded to his phone, "and Caspar?" he asked, Max sighed and went to sit beside Caspar to take his order.

"I'm pretty certain he always orders the entire menu." Max said more to me when he gave up and passed his phone to Caspar to let him do it, then he passed the second beer bottle to me, I pushed the lime that was wedged into the neck of the bottle into the beer then took a sip,

"He's not old enough to drink, no way." Caspar said as he handed Max's phone back.

"You went to his eighteenth." Cameron said amused, Caspar shook his head to me so I began to laugh then drank more of the beer.

I sat on the edge of the bath rubbing my forehead and running my hands through my hair, as my glasses sat on the toilet tank as they had become overly foggy. I coughed a few times, leaning over the toilet again just in case then I looked at the door as it opened, Cameron came in, passing me a bottle of water, then he sat next to me.

"Can I blame the beer?" I asked, he sighed as he began to rub my back, "I was getting better."

"You are getting better." He said, I closed my eyes as I leant my head against his. "You really are Jacob. To be fair, it was probably partially the beer and partially the greasiness of the takeaway." He said, "that's what I get for letting Max order it." he added more into my ear, so I began to laugh.

"I'm sorry." I said,

"For what?" Cameron asked, I shrugged.

"Ruining tonight." I said, he laughed so I opened my eyes.

187

"You have not ruined tonight. You threw up. Granted it probably ruined tea for you." He said, I nodded. "But it didn't ruin the performance we put on, it didn't ruin the catch-up I got to have with my twin brother, who I see twice a year, if I'm lucky. It didn't ruin the fun we had downstairs watching the film, it didn't ruin anything." He said, "besides, Max is well asleep, and probably has been for a while, and Caspar is, doing whatever, he is doing, only I know you've thrown up. Right now, and I will tell Max but not the moment I go to bed." He said, so I looked at him, he was too close for me to actually see him properly, to make out any of his features, he was horrendously blurry, so instead I just moved my head towards him, leaning it on his shoulder, he hugged me the moment I did.

I finally made my way downstairs after lying in bed for a few minutes contemplating if I actually wanted to get out of bed and be officially awake yet. I ultimately decided I did, and put my glasses on to make my way downstairs. The doors leading to the living room were still closed, I presumed no one had even attempted going into that part of the house yet, as they always waited for me to make the first move. Instead, the kitchen door was open and there were very happy sounds coming from it, so I walked towards it. Caspar was sat at the table with Max, they were both very amused by whatever Cameron was doing at the oven.

"Merry Christmas." Max said, so I looked at him then I smiled at him.

"Merry Christmas." Caspar said, as Cameron did. Max and I laughed at the same time.

"He's got this perfect, he knows to only come down after my first few failed attempts at pancakes." Cameron said, then placed the plate of little round golden pancakes in

188

the middle of the table, so I sat at the table, picked the top pancake and began to eat it.

"First few failed attempts?" Max repeated, as Cameron sat on the chair beside me, "I think that's being polite." He added, I began to laugh as Cameron gasped and threw the dishcloth at him.

We all sat on the floor when we got through the doors of the living room, to where the Christmas tree and presents were hiding. They had always sat on the floor with me, as we opened presents, and if ever I asked if they wanted to sit on the couch they'd both complain loudly at me, Cameron shouting that he was still young, whilst Max shouted about being a ballet dancer. I soon figured it was easier just letting them sit with me, unless I wanted a laugh from all their shouting.

"That one's yours." Max said, pointing at the silver present, so I reached for it stroking the wrapping paper when I rested it on my knee.

I remembered being very overwhelmed the first Christmas I spent with Max and Cameron, after having so many in the home, and only getting one present being presented with more than one had completely shook me, and I hadn't really known how to respond to it, until Max and Cameron explained the resting behind each of the gifts and why they had waited until Christmas to give me them.

It had made a little more sense to me, and I had opened them all, thanking Max and Cameron after every tear of the wrapping paper.

I had spoken to Cameron later on that afternoon as he added the last touches to our dinner, I explained to him what had happened, and he had smiled, and took me into their bedroom. He showed me a snow globe that he had on the top of his chest of drawers, it was of Broadway, all the theatres with their brightly coloured billboards, and when it was shook it looked like it had begun to snow.

He told me Max had brought him it, for Christmas, the first Christmas they were together, Cameron was just eighteen and had been with Max for a grand total of sixty days at that point, he had whispered to me that he was counting them at that point because he still didn't believe he was actually Max's boyfriend. He hadn't gotten Max anything for Christmas, having only been together eight weeks or so, he hadn't even though they were doing presents. He had been so shocked that Max had gotten him something, when he initially saw the present, and then he was overwhelmed by the complete beauty of what Max had brought him. He hadn't completely known what to do or how to receive the gift but, he told me, he knew the moment he'd opened the gift that Max loved him, and that he most definitely loved Max. Then, he told me that Max loved me so much he couldn't quite bring himself to stop buying things for Christmas, then he hugged me.

It was the first time he'd ever hugged me.

"These are yours." I replied, passing them both a gift bag, they matched with each other as Cameron's was cream with gold spots, and Max's gold with cream spots.

"We told you, you didn't have to get us anything." Max said, so I laughed.

"And I told you, I would." I replied, he smiled at me

"Yours is there." Cameron said, so Caspar looked behind the tree, "didn't think we'd leave you out." He added, Caspar laughed as he pulled out the green shiny parcel, we all opened them together.

My package turned out to be a grey jumper, which when I unfolded had Ballet. Sleep. Repeat. Wrote on it, I laughed standing to hug both Cameron and Max then watched as they opened theirs. I'd gotten them both a water bottle each as they frequently mixed up their water bottles. I had personalised them with their names, in big block letters down one side, and Max's had little ballerina's in different positions on the opposite side to his name, whilst Cameron had music notes.

They pulled me down together, kissing both of my cheeks then let me go, I got to the doors when they exchanged their presents for each other, I didn't see what they were but I left as they kissed each other.

Connor was the first of our Christmas dinner guests to arrive. He'd been coming for Christmas since I'd moved out of the home, because it would never have felt like Christmas without Connor. He hugged me once I opened the door.

"I have literally been Santa Claus this morning." He said, I began to laugh as he looked at me, "nice jumper." He added,

"Right back at you." I replied, as I took in the purposely ugly Christmas jumper he was wearing. "When you say literally?"

"Red suit, beard." He said, I laughed. "I took the kids their presents. Well, I called Ste and said I'd bring them on Christmas Eve, and he simply said no, so I asked when and he said Christmas morning. It was nice." He said nodding, I nodded back to him. "And I got pancakes." He added as I led him into the living room.

"Spoke to Kian?" I asked, he nodded a blush covered his cheeks almost instantly, so I nudged my elbow against his.

"We spoke last night. Wished each other a merry Christmas and you know, all that." He said, I raised my eyebrow at him. "And we had phone sex." He said, I began to laugh.

"I talked to him a few days ago." I said, then I smiled. "We did not have phone sex." I added, he shook his head at me then held the gift bag out to me that was in his hand, I took it in both of mine, peering into it then I began to laugh.

"You enjoyed the ones on my couch so much, I thought I'd get you one of your own." He said, then he smiled. I laughed as I reached under the tree and passed him, his present. "Where are the adults of the house?" Connor asked as we both sat on my couch, I laughed.

"Kitchen. I believe their scheming something." I replied as I got the cushion out, it was a beautiful emerald colour, until I ran my hand over it and it became aqua.

"I made sure I got you boy colours." He teased, I rolled my eyes at him as he pulled his tongue at me as he pulled out the vinyl, he'd hinted at months ago, he smiled at it, then kissed my cheek.

"I see me with my boy colours did well." I said, he laughed, we both turned when the doorbell went again.

"Jacob?" I heard from the kitchen, so I stood.

"Got it." I replied, as I walked towards the door. I opened it to Cory and Frankie who both seemed very happy to be there.

"Cutting it a bit fine." Max said as he appeared in the living room, they both laughed as Frankie walked towards him to hug him. "Dinner is ready." Max said, "and I warn you, it's pretty exciting." He said, then led the way into the kitchen where Cameron was lighting the candles on the table.

There were two dipping cheeses on either end of the table with multiple crackers surround them. Once they were completely eaten, Cameron and Max stood to give out the main course. I was the last to receive it, and I looked at it as confused as everyone else did.

"A whole Christmas dinner in a Yorkshire pudding." Cameron said then he took his seat, "the meat, the vegetables and some gravy." He said, then he smiled at me, so I smiled back at him. "Not too much." He added, I nodded.

"But do help yourselves to the potatoes." Max said as he placed the serving plate in the middle of the table.

Chapter 11

I stood alternating from foot to foot, raising onto and off pointe as I scrolled through Max's tablet, I just wanted one song to dance to, until I found a playlist that Max had named '*Jacob*'. I opened it, I smiled as I began to scroll down it.

It had my warm-up song and the song we'd battled pirouettes with for the first time, what followed was every performance song I'd ever danced too. I got to the bottom, reading the song I'd danced to in Max's summer show before I went to the National Ballet School, I hovered over it for a few seconds then used my finger to slide the entire list back to the top.

I chose the first song I'd ever danced on the stage too, I closed my eyes as the song began, the bells ringing out, so I walked to the centre of the floor. I took a deep breath like I had when I was fourteen then I rose onto my pointes, smiling to myself as I began to dance.

I danced it step perfect, laughing to myself as I went into my extensions and pirouettes with such ease, I didn't even think as I started the pirouette section. I just spun, and spun, and spun until I stopped, holding myself steady as I went into my bow, I looked up quickly as I heard an applause.

"Sorry." I said quickly when I saw Max, he shook his head at me as he came into the studio.

"What for?" Max asked, I waved my hand above my head.

"Hijacking your studio. To dance."

"Heaven forbid a dancer, uses my dance studio, to dance." He said, I smiled as I looked at my feet. "You danced it as brilliantly as you did when you were fourteen." He said, "except, of course your pirouettes we're much cleaner, and I think you did about three more than choreographed."

"Course." I said, he smiled.

"Although, should I be worried about your extension?"

"Why?" I asked, Max laughed,

"Because it was starting to look better than mine." He said, I looked up at him.

"That's because I'm younger than you." I said, then pulled my tongue at him as he gasped, then pushed me backwards.

"I taught you everything you know." he said, I nodded to him.

"You did." I said, as I turned my head to look at him, "I just improved it." I said, grinning at him, he shook his head back to me then looked at his watch,

"You have to see Ash in an hour." He said, I nodded as I looked towards my phone. "Are you just hoping that Ash will approve of you doing ballet again?" he asked, I laughed,

"Okay, I broke the rules, but ballet." I said, Max nodded as he scrunched his nose at me,

"But ballet." He replied, "want to dance together?" he asked, I nodded slowly to him, then I frowned.

"To what?" I asked, he laughed as he scrolled through his watch, then looked at the stereo system as the music began, I shook my head at him, rising onto my pointes, so he also did, nodding to me, as I rose my right leg as he did too.

I looked at him in the mirror as we both held it vertical to our bodies, he nodded his head to me counting the beats, so I did it back, until we both got to five and dropped our legs to go into the jeté section. "Point your toes." I shunned towards him, making him laugh almost instantly,

"Oh Mr. Ballet School knows best, I see." He replied, I chewed on my lip so I wouldn't laugh out loud, as we continued to dance through.

"And what was your other one?" I said, he looked briefly at me as we both rose into an arabesque. "Oh yes. Strong." I shouted at him; he began to laugh.

"Strong." He shouted back, as we both prepared for the pirouettes, I looked at him, he nodded to me.

"Strong, strong, strong." We said together, I began to laugh as I went into my pirouette, still managing to keep my rotations going, even though I was laughing.

196

Max stepped out of the pirouette first, so I pointed at him then stepped out of my own section, taking a bow, he pointed back at me then turned around to look at the door where Cameron was leaning against the doorframe.

"You're breaking the rules." Cameron said, then he pointed at Max, "and you're even worse for breaking the rules." He said, Max looked at me, I high-fived him. "I've come to take you to see Ash, and to kiss you." He said, Max nodded he seemed quite happy with that.

"I can work with that." He said nodding as I leant against the barre then used it to sit myself down and take off my pointes, I glanced up between shoes as Max whispered in Cameron's ear, then they kissed.

"Come on ballet boy." Cameron said, so I laughed as I placed my pointes into my bag then stood,

"Let me know what he says, I've missed dancing with you." He said, I smiled back then began to follow Cameron out of Max's studios.

Cameron sat outside Ash's room. Ash had been I'm sure relieved when I finally began talking to him without the aid of Cameron and Max.

Our sessions had become more about conversing in the last few weeks, I felt as if we'd actually formed some sort of bond. As the week after Christmas I had found out that Ash, was Arlo's husband and they'd met during a production of Alice in Wonderland, where Ash was the tap dancing Mad Hatter, and Arlo the March Hare, this lead to the hour being filled by talking about the fact Ash could tap dance.

He spent the first five minutes of today session looking through the food diary he'd asked me to keep. I'd found when I opened it this morning, that I presume

Cameron had stuck multi-coloured smiley face stickers next to the days that I'd wrote I'd eaten everything and not thrown any of it back up.

"You're coming on brilliantly." Ash said, I nodded. "It's been a hard two months, I'm fully aware of how hard it's been, but your progress has been brilliant."

"I threw up on Christmas Eve." I murmured, "and New Year's, but I genuinely think I was drunk." I said, he laughed softly then placed his finger on New Year's.

"I agree with how empty your stomach would've been." He said, I looked down and smiled.

"Ash?" I said, he nodded so I inhaled. "School starts next week."

"Yes." He said, then he closed the diary. "Right, I feel you are ready to start dancing again. I know it's been hard to get through not doing ballet. I think that's been the hardest part for you? Right?"

"Right." I agreed, because I'd been binge watching ballet videos late at night on my phone, it had begun to feel like a dirty habit, as if I was watching porn, as I felt the need to hide it whenever I heard movement come from Max or Cameron's room.

"Which, I think is the reason you've been so progressive with your recovery." He said, "I worry that putting you back into the school environment might cause a regression."

"That's bad." I said, he nodded once,

"However, it is a part of your recovery and regressions happen, although we wish they wouldn't."

"So, I can't go back to school?"

"Now, I never said that." He said cautiously, "I feel as if going straight back to boarding wouldn't be the best of ideas, you should stay with Max and Cameron for at least another month." He said, I nodded. "And if you wish to help out with the classes Max teaches, that too I would say is okay."

"But I can't go back to school?" I repeated, he sighed.

"Jacob…" he replied, so I closed my mouth as I heard the '*let me finish*' in his voice. "I think you can go back to your repertoire classes with Arlo, and your classes with Madame Rose, however I feel that should be dictated by you, if you do not feel mentally up for Madame Rose's class, you should not attend."

"Okay." I said, "not Pas De Deux?"

"I don't think you're quite ready for Miss Olivia's lesson." He said, I nodded because I agreed. "Maybe in a month or so." He added, I sighed. "I would like to know what you do not want to do?" he said, I frowned.

"What?"

"In regards to classes, or sessions. For example, do you wish to take your exams?"

"Yes." I said nodding, "I want to take my exams, both my Christmas and my end of year." I said, then I looked at him, "I don't want to wear contacts." I said, he nodded as he wrote something in his book. "Or go to the gym." I added,

"I advise you don't do additional gym hours for the time being." He agreed, so I nodded.

"That's all."

"That's all." I replied, he nodded then flipped through his folder until he found a piece of paper, he passed it to me.

"Your winter term timetable." He said, I looked at him. "I would say, I'm happy for you to be present in your repertoire class first thing Monday morning."

"You're serious?" I asked, he nodded

"I want you to see me frequently, and to know that my door is always open if you need a mental health day." He said, I smiled at him, he smiled back at me.

▾▾▾

Max drove me to school on Monday. It had felt odd to wake up and to put my leotard and shorts on ready for a ballet class. Max had attempted to make breakfast, so it had become a do it yourself, yogurt and oats mixture. Cameron had appeared just before we left, he hugged me then watched us go.

"Okay?" Max asked as we sat in the car outside of my school.

"Nervous." I said then looked at him and frowned, "and I don't know why." I added, he smiled as he squeezed my shoulder.

"You'll be fine." He said softly, I nodded.

"I know." I replied, "so I don't know why I'm nervous." I added, he pushed my shoulder lightly,

"Go on. Go to class. Cameron and I will be home when you get back definitely, then Frankie said you were welcome to stay at his tonight." He said, I nodded to him then opened the car door.

"I'll see you later."

"Break a leg." He replied, I laughed as I got out of the car and walked into the office.

The lady smiled at me and let me in without questions, so I walked down to Arlo's class. Dodging the second years as they ran down the corridor towards Miss Olivia's studio. I let myself into Arlo's studio, creeping in behind my class as they all stood on the barres. Arlo was focused on scrolling through the music, so I threw my bag against the wall, changed into my ballet shoes then went to take up my position behind Kian on the barre. He turned to look at me when I touched the barre, probably to tell me to move back, and away from him. He didn't quite get the words out, instead he gasped happily then hugged me around my waist, picking me up as he did, so I began to laugh.

"I have missed you. So much." Kian said, "oh my god. You're back."

"I'm back." I said nodding, "for classes." I added as he put me back onto my feet. "I'm not quite your board mate again, yet."

"Gutted." He said, I smiled at him as he grinned back at me. "I'm so happy you're back." he said, then he spun to look towards Arlo as the warm up music began. I took a few steps back then began the sequence. Arlo smiled at me as he passed.

"Nice to see you back Mr. Kennedy." He said nodding to me as he continued to walk down the barre.

Kian had grabbed my hand the moment Arlo had dismissed us. He didn't even let me change my shoes before he began to run me down the corridor and towards Madame Rose's class, where the girls were finishing their pointe work. We both peered through the door, watching as they moved through their jeté session.

Madame Rose tapped her fingers against her elbow counting the beats until she clapped her hands, and the girls stopped, all standing in first position. Madame Rose said something, which I guess was dismissing them, as all the girls curtseyed to her then began to walk towards the barres to take their pointes off. Madame Rose turned towards the door, Kian and I ducked almost instantly, then began to laugh until the door opened to her on the other side. We both stood up straight as she looked between us.

"Mister Cunningham." She said, Kian smirked at her in a totally schmoozer kind of way, she sighed, then she looked at me. "Mister Kennedy, good to see you back." she added, I nodded to her. "However, as neither of you are required at my pointe work class, neither of you should be here."

"No Madame, you are correct." Kian said, I almost laughed as I looked at him. "But, as Jacob has only just returned, I thought Margo…" he said slightly louder, she turned towards the door, then stuffed her pointes into her bag to get out of the door. "Would like to see one of her best friends." He finished, grinning at me as he did, I laughed. Madame Rose went to reply, then outwardly sighed when Margo appeared beside her.

"Boys should not linger outside of girls classrooms." Madame Rose said then walked away, Kian began to laugh as I was almost strangled in a hug by Margo.

"Coming for lunch?" She asked, then she looked at Kian, I hesitated.

"Not right now." I said, then put my hand up before they began to shout at me. "I need to talk to someone." I added, looking into the studio, both Kian and Margo looked into the studio also then began to nod.

"Seat on our table. If it's needed mate." Kian said, then he sighed. "Make sure you eat something." He added, so I looked at him. "You always need a full stomach to withstand the attack of a girl." He added, then took Margo's hand and began to walk to the canteen. I watched them go then turned back just in time to catch Abi. I reached out for her then withdrew my hand, I figured the last thing she wanted me to do was touch her.

"Jacob." She sounded surprised, "do you feel better?" she asked, I nodded slowly to her then I sighed.

"I need to talk to you." I said, she nodded once.

"I think you do." She replied, then sighed. "Lunch?" she asked, then she winced. "Sorry."

"Lunch." I agreed, walking with her towards the canteen. We went through the food station together then she went to find a table as I picked up two bottles of water. I sat opposite her at the table. "I'm sorry I embarrassed you." I said,

"Oh, straight in there." She replied surprised, I nodded to her.

"I'm so sorry for shouting at you, for making a show of you and treating you as if you were… nothing."

"Was I nothing?" she asked, I shook my head,

"No. Not at all, and I regret not telling you that." I said, she looked down and away from me. "I'm sorry I ruined your virginity story." I said, she laughed, so I looked directly at her.

"What?" she said, she seemed confused.

"Well, now all you'll say is I lost my virginity to this dick, who acted like a complete tosser and ruined everything." I said, she smiled and touched my hand.

"No." she said, I turned my hand so I could hold hers. "I'll say it was with this really sweet, sensitive boy. Who got a little lost along the way." She squeezed my hand. "I want to be your friend. Honestly. I want us to be friends, but it's a bit difficult for me right now."

"I understand." I said, because I did, Ash had whacked - in a metaphorical sense - empathy and compassion into me throughout our sessions. He told me that if I apologised it was likely Abi would forgive me, but I had to be ready for her not wanting to be in my life, or be close to me, at least not straight away. I had prepared myself for that, but it still hurt me a little.

"I accept your apology." She said, then she came around the table and kissed my cheek. "Thank you." She added, I nodded to her. "Now, go and neutralise your nosy friends." She said turning her head towards the table Kian and Margo were sat at, both looking in our direction. They both looked away the moment we looked over, pretending to talk to each other. We both laughed when I stood, picking up my tray as I did.

"Don't forget to be generous." She said, I turned my head to look at her whilst holding my tray against my stomach, I almost instantly began to laugh.

"As long as you're generous too." I replied, she smiled at me.

"I always am." She replied, I grinned then began to walk towards Kian and Margo. I slid my tray onto the table top then took a seat.

"So?" Kian asked, I looked towards Abi as she took her empty tray to the clean-up station then left the canteen.

"I think we're going to be okay."

I actively searched out Frankie and Cory in Max's studio after Cameron had fed me my tea. I found them, in the furthest studio as I'd ensured I didn't come until I knew all the lessons were over, *they* were dancing together.

Frankie was wearing his pointes whilst Cory danced on flat ballet pump. Their steps were perfect, their sequences flawless but they couldn't have looked any more bored with what they were actually doing, I laughed as I leant on the doorframe watching them dance through *Hold My Hand*, the Pas De Deux section that they'd been doing in school assemblies since I was fourteen, *at least*. It was a beautiful dance, to beautiful music but they must've been sick of it by now. They kissed when it came to an end, then Frankie walked towards his water bottle, as Cory looked towards me, he smiled, so I smiled back.

"We have the prodigy." Cory said, Frankie began to laugh as he turned to look at me.

"I've never had to babysit an eighteen year old before." Frankie said, I pulled tongues at him, he did it back. "Did you enjoy school?" he asked, I nodded sighing as I did.

"I really did." I said,

"Do you want to dance?" Cory asked, I looked between them,

"And look as bored as you both did." I said, they both began to laugh as they looked at each other.

"Or we can go home and order pizza." Frankie said shrugging at me, I began to nod.

"That sounds like a plan I can get on board with." I said, they grinned as they began to pack up their things. They both put a pair of jogging bottoms on and a t-shirt then I walked down the stairs with Cory as Frankie locked every door behind us.

"So, have your parents given you up for sex tonight?" Cory asked as we left the studio, I laughed.

"Me being present has never stopped them beforehand." I said, Cory smirked at me. "They're weirdly open about their sexual conquests."

"Is that good or bad?" Cory asked, I cringed,

"Totally depends on the context." I said, he began to laugh as Frankie locked the front door.

"Max has always believed sharing is caring." Frankie said, I glanced at him as we began to walk to his car. "I think it's because he grew up with five sisters." He added. "There was always someone talking about boyfriends, and sex, and making a move that it's been drummed into Max that girl gossip is mandatory."

"You're as bad." Cory said as he unlocked the car,

"Excuse me, I'm allowed to talk to you about our sex life." He said, I began to laugh as I climbed into the back, I plugged my seat belt in as they both got into the car. "I'm going to order the pizza now, so that it arrives quicker." Frankie declared, then turned in his seat, passing his phone to me.

"You're revolutionary." I said as I scrolled through the website and chose my pizza.

We sat around the coffee table in Frankie and Cory's living room with three individual pizza boxes covering the entire table top. I sat on the side that I could lean against the couch whilst Cory sat against the arm chair and Frankie against the wall, underneath the television.

"You're on your second term, right?" Frankie asked, I nodded to him as I tried to catch all my toppings from my pizza.

"Scholarship." Cory said, I frowned at him as Frankie nodded.

"What scholarship?" I asked, they smiled at each other before looking at me.

"Every year, the National runs scholarship auditions." Frankie said, I nodded because I'd gotten that,

"It's gives the recipient of this scholarship, usually a boy and a girl, the chance to study their second year totally free of charge, anywhere in the world."

"Anywhere?" I asked, they both nodded.

"Paris, New York, Russia, Australia. Wherever there is a ballet school, they can go."

"Shit." I said, they smiled at each other. "Is that how you ended up in Australia?" I asked, Cory half nodded.

"The firsts do scholarship auditions; the seconds do company auditions." He said, I frowned. "Simply, there is an invigilator from every school, or near enough. So, Frankie danced for them first." he said, Frankie nodded.

"I didn't get the scholarship."

"Shocker." I said, they both nodded back,

"It actually was. He was pretty much guaranteed to get it." Cory said, "then the seconds dance for the same panel, but for a part in their companies. Nine times out of ten, everyone gets a company and a role, only about one in ten times does someone get a principal role." He said, I nodded to him,

"On the panel usually there's someone from the Royal Ballet,"

"Where you got your contract?" I asked, Frankie nodded.

"Where I got my contract. Someone from the New York Ballet, someone from the Opéra national de Paris, someone from The Vaganova Academy in Russia, and someone from the Australian ballet school. In first, they decide whether you get a scholarship, and are usually the top choices for where you study."

"In second, they decide whether they want you." Cory said, I looked at him.

"The Australian ballet wanted you?" I asked, he nodded,

"And the New York ballet, and the Russian ballet, *and* the Paris ballet…" Frankie said, Cory began to laugh.

"So bitter." He said, then began to tickle Frankie's stomach, Frankie almost screamed as he scrambled away.

"Why did you choose Australia?" I asked, Cory smiled.

"It was the warmest." He said, I laughed. "And having been friends with Sam, he sort of persuaded me to do it."

"Do you regret it?"

"Not one bit." Cory said shaking his head, "we were just guttered he didn't get the scholarship." He said looking at Frankie so I did.

"Would you have chosen Australia?"

"I'd have chosen wherever he did." Frankie said, I smiled.

"You guys are Pas De Deux partners, aren't you?" I asked, they both responded with unsure noises, so I laughed. "You dance Pas De Deux together?" I said, they both nodded, "I just have a question, that's all."

"What's your question?" Cory asked, I looked between them,

"How do you two separate sex from Pas De Deux?" I asked, Cory smirked so I sighed. "It's so orgasmic, dancing Pas De Deux, or at least dancing Pas De Deux right…. I know from." I said, then shook my head,

"From?" Frankie asked, I sighed as I closed my eyes.

"Before I, before I fainted, I slept with my Pas De Deux partner. After we'd danced together, now I'm worried I won't be able to dance with her, so I was wondering how you separate it?" I asked, Frankie sighed.

"We only began dancing together, after we'd slept together." Frankie said, I moaned slightly. "And we began to dance together because we were sleeping together. Max might have a better answer."

"Cameron's not a ballet dancer." I said, Frankie shook his head,

"No, but his first boyfriend was." Frankie said, "and he managed to separate sex from dancing with Sam." He said, I sighed.

"Honestly." Cory said, so I looked at him. "And this was drummed into me through Miss Olivia, Pas De Deux is an act. You isolate your feelings, your emotions, your love life and you dance."

"Obviously it's not that easy. Pas De Deux is so intimate, and when you do it right, it's exactly as you said, it's orgasmic." Frankie said, "Miss Olivia is understanding. She will swap your partner if you ask her too." He said warily,

"So, in other words. There's no way out." I said, they both shook their heads. "Well shit that is not what I wanted to hear." I said, they both laughed. "Tell me more about Australia." I said, "I'd like to hear more about Australia."

The spare room in Frankie and Cory's was the equivalent of Max's little box room that had more recently been infiltrated by me.

It held all their performance pictures, their medals, their trophies and a shelf full of black pointe shoes, all of them Frankie's. Seeing his was the reason I'd gotten my own pair of black pointes. Max had expressed his disinterest in them, and had told me a pointe shoe, was a pointe shoe regardless of the colour but Frankie had told me he preferred to wear black because it looked more like the ballet pumps males were supposed to wear rather than the pale pink pointes that were usually occasioned with ballerinas.

Cory made me jump when I was stood looking at them, stood ready for bed, just reading their medals, their trophies, their grades, their certificates and examining each and every one of Frankie's pointes, trying to figure out what had worn down the block, or split the soul.

"Okay?" Cory asked, I nodded to him before I looked at him, "Cameron asked me to make sure you didn't feel sick." He said but he said it warily, it made me smile a little.

"I've wrote in my food diary, but no I don't feel sick." I said, then I frowned at him. "I feel full." I added, "which admittedly, is stranger, because this is definitely the first time in a good while I've felt full." I said, he smiled although it didn't quite reach his eyes.

"I'll tell Cameron." He said, I laughed as I looked behind myself at my phone, I'm sure a text would come through in next ten minutes or so, as Cameron and Max's evening performance had definitely finished, and they'd be home pretty soon.

"You're definitely babysitting me." I said, Cory shrugged.

"Cameron and Max are worried about you." He said, I nodded. "In a parental sense." He added, I looked up at him, "Frankie and I are worried about you, in a ballet sense." He said, I frowned. "Did we put too much pressure on you?" he asked, I shook my head almost instantly, "Prodigy." He added, I sighed.

"No." I said, "no, you let me do ballet, you let me do it and love it." I said, then I looked down, "but I was confused."

"Confused?" he asked, I began to nod.

"When I started in school. None of you guys care about your weight." I said, then looked up Cory shook his head almost instantly so I frowned at him.

"Oh Jacob, we care about our weight." He said, then he sighed and went to sit on the bed, I sat beside him. "I

210

understand where you're coming from right, Frankie and Max, they are both literally perfect ballet dancers." He said, I nodded. "They have the right build, the flat stomachs, they're even well endowed." He said then sighed, I nudged my elbow against his, he looked at me. "It's difficult to be around such perfection, and neither of them understand that, I'm not going to lie to you. They find it difficult to understand why, say I might find an imperfection with my body and be worried about it because…"

"Because they've never had to deal with it." I said, he nodded,

"What made you aware of it?" he asked, I sighed.

"Kian." I replied, he nodded. "He calorie counts and works out; his body is fucking magnificent." I said, Cory laughed.

"How guttered are you that you gave him over to your best friend?" he teased, I smiled at him.

"I touched myself over him a few times. I got my reward." I said, Cory laughed. "He's not actually my type." I said warily, Cory smiled.

"You can have a type. You don't have to be worried about that." He said softly, I nodded. "What is your type?" he asked, I laughed.

"Feminine guys." I said, then I cringed. "Can I say that?" I added, Cory nodded so I laughed. "I like girls but only girls that are slightly,"

"Tomboyish?" he asked, I nodded.

"I feel like a bad bisexual." I said, Cory laughed then covered his mouth so I smiled at him.

"You know…" He said thoughtfully, "Frankie was pissed when I got so many company offers."

"And he didn't get a scholarship?" I asked, he nodded softly.

"The problem. I guess with our relationship, especially during school was that we were always competing. Even if we didn't want to be, we were in competition with each other, and allegedly Frankie was the better out of the two of us."

"I don't believe that." I said, he seemed surprised, "at all actually. Reading them, you're obviously the best." I said pointing at the wall, Cory laughed as he looked at the wall himself.

"The point I was trying to make..." he said, so I looked back at him. "Was that you're not in competition with Max. Although I know you feel like you are. You're not in competition with his dancing, his specialty, or his body. You are amazing Jacob.

Outstanding even. You realise you have been doing ballet for four years, four years Jacob and you have a place in the National Ballet School. That's almost incomprehensible." He stated, I laughed. "You don't get it? Do you?" he asked, I looked up seeing he wasn't saying it harshly at all, so I shook my head. "Perspective." He said, I nodded to him. "I started ballet when I was four. I trained until I was ten, and I got shit for it, but I stuck by it because..."

"Because you love it." I said smiling at him, he nodded to me.

"I started in the Astaire Academy when I was eleven."

"Where you met Frankie." I said, he hummed.

"Not until I was seventeen." He replied, then he laughed, "there's a lot that happened between my first year, and my sixth."

"Understandable." I said nodding, Cory laughed softly.

"It's quite difficult being in ballet school, and going through puberty late."

"Late." I repeated, he nodded as he sighed.

"It meant I wasn't able to do Pas De Deux, as I was smaller than ninety percent of the girls. I was also pretty weak, given my muscles just were none existent. It's why I didn't actually progress onto pointe." He said, I frowned at him. "I wasn't strong enough to, or at least that's what Madame used to tell me, I was not strong enough to do pointe, only demi-pointe. I was pretty much always never strong enough, always just okay and that's hard. Especially when dating Mister Overachiever."

"You love Frankie." I said, he nodded.

"With all my heart." He said simply, "I love that boy to death, but even though I would do anything for him, and I love him and know he loves me. It doesn't stop me feeling imperfect next to him."

"You know before, when I asked how you separate sex from Pas De Deux?" I said, he began to nod.

"Weirdly. I feel less conscious being naked with him, than I do dancing with him."

"Ballet is fucked up." I said, Cory laughed.

"Yeah, but isn't that why we love doing it." he said, I smiled at him. "I'm not going to tell you you're perfect. Okay?" he said, I looked up at him, "because I think that's wrong. You should never put perfection on someone. It can be damaging. It can ruin someone. So, you are not perfect. Not in any way Jacob." He said, I looked at him, "but you are an amazing ballet dancer. You are loved, so, so loved, by Connor, by Max and Cameron, by Frankie and I.

We all love you so much, we want you to succeed and you will. You've hit a bump in the road. We all do. For Max it was his first boyfriend." He said, I nodded because I

213

agreed. "For Frankie, it was when he broke his ankle." He said, I winced, "for me, it was depression." He said, I met his eyes. "But then, Max won gold. Frankie became a Principal. I, met Frankie." He said, then he smiled at me. "You're at a bump. You will overcome it."

"You think?" I asked, he nodded.

"I know." he replied, I looked down then I nodded.

"Cory." I said, he hummed at me, "you're going to be an amazing Dad."

"You think?" he asked, I looked up and smiled at him.

"I know."

CHAPTER 12

"Jacob, we don't want to do things too fast." Ash warned, I sighed.

"It's been six weeks Ash." I moaned, he nodded. "I want to board again." I said,

"I would rather you start back in Pas De Deux." He said, I moaned at him. "Jacob. If you begin to board again, you will have to be in charge of your own meal times, and what you eat." He said, I nodded.

"I know. I'm ready."

"Jacob."

"You don't think I'm ready." I said, he shook his head.

"That is not the problem. I'm concerned about the loss of support."

"Ash." I said, he sighed then began to flick through his book, when he'd found whatever he was looking for, he began through my food diary.

"Let's talk about the last week." He said, I closed my eyes.

"Thursday was a blip." I said, he nodded,

"I'm a bit concerned that it followed you throwing up on Wednesday."

"I was sick." I said, "Cameron will confirm that." I added, "he gave me orange juice."

"It was Cameron's fault?"

"Yes." I muttered, then I looked up. "The juice made me sick, and then I was just a bit… shook on Thursday. I didn't eat and by the time I was aware I hadn't eaten." I sighed, "I'm ready Ash." I said, he hummed then he rubbed his forehead.

"I want you to go to Pas De Deux." He said, so I nodded frowning at him waiting for his ultimatum. "But I want it to be a decision you and your parents make whether you are ready to begin boarding again." He said, I sighed because I couldn't figure out if that'd go in my favour or not. "Jacob, you understand, if you are going to board again, you will need to full board." He said, I frowned.

"Why?" I asked,

"Because the instability of half boarding may cause you to relapse." He said softly, I began to nod. "You can of course see Max and Cameron, don't think I'm saying that you cannot see your family, you just need to get some stability, a routine, set meal times." He said, I nodded.

"But it's up to Max and Cameron?" I asked, he nodded.

"It's up to Max and Cameron." He replied, "and you start Pas De Deux."

216

"And I start Pas De Deux." I repeated, he smiled at me, so I smiled back.

Miss Olivia seemed happy to see me that afternoon, when I walked in behind Kian and began to put my shoes on whilst leaning on the barre behind me, she nodded once to me then clapped her hands, calling us all into the centre. I stood awkwardly in my allocated spot, whilst Abi also stood awkwardly. Miss Olivia clocked us straight away, so I looked at her, meeting her eyes as they scanned over us both, I saw the thought process behind her eyes then watched as they jumped, I followed them watching as Kian lifted Margo by wrapping his arms around her waist, he lifted her and made her scream with laughter, when I looked back at Miss Olivia she seemed less than impressed.

"Jacob, Abi please." She requested, I sighed and walked towards her, standing beside Abi. "Rest of you please go through the fish dive." She said then looked at each of us in turn. "Your personal life stays at the door." She said, I looked down as Abi sighed.

"You know that's the rule of class, your personal life always stays at the door. You come to dance and that's it." she said. "However, you are both still students." She said, so I looked back up. "And sometimes, things in your personal life feel massive." She said, "I don't care what has happened. I don't want to know what is going on between the two of you, or what has happened between the two of you. All I want to know is, do you feel as if you two can work together?" she said, I looked at Abi who looked apologetic as she looked back at me.

"No." She said softly, I shook my head, letting out a deep breath as my heart was beating at about one thousand miles per hour at the thought of having to touch her.

"Okay." Miss Olivia said, then looked behind us, we both turned to look at Kian and Margo. "Gives me a good excuse to split them two up." She said, then she clapped her hands.

"Margo, Kian I am unimpressed with your unprofessionalism." She said, the entire class looked towards them, "so, I will be splitting you up. Margo, from now on your will be dancing with Jacob, and Kian, Abi. I'm sorry Jacob and Abi as you were beginning to work really well with each other." she said then she winked at us, as I walked back to my space, Margo came and stood in front of me.

"Now Jacob," she said, I nodded to her frowning at her lightly, "This is my waist." She added touching her waist, I began to laugh.

"Oh shut up." I said as she turned and took my hands placing them on her waist.

Max seemed unimpressed with the healthy opinion Cameron had placed in front of us. I was equally as unimpressed but hungry, so didn't think it wise to complain.

"What is this?" Max asked, Cameron sighed as he took his seat, he put some mayonnaise in the middle of the table.

"Chicken, and salad." Cameron said, he sounded defeated, because he knew that on the way back from Max's studio we'd definitely stop for chips.

"Great." Max said, Cameron began to laugh, burying his face into his hands and shaking his head.

"I give up with him." He said, I began to laugh as I cut into the chicken.

"I went back to Pas De Deux today." I said, making Max and Cameron look away from each other and at me,

"Miss Olivia swapped my partner, so I don't have to worry about awkwardness."

"That's good." Max said nodding, I nodded back to him.

"Ash thought you were ready?" he asked, I nodded,

"He also wanted me to discuss with you…" I began then I took a deep breath, looking at them both in turn. "Me boarding again." I said, Max began to nod as Cameron watched me, so I watched him right back.

"How do you feel about it?" Max asked, I sighed.

"I want to board again." I said, "I do, really. You both did it, you both get it."

"Yes." Cameron agreed, I could tell it was wary, I could also tell he was struggling with what else to say.

"Jacob, you realise you're going to be in charge of your own eating habits." Max said, I nodded to him.

"Yes, and I will have Ash on site, so I can go visit him whenever I need him, and Kian. Kian will not take his eyes off me."

"That's a lot of responsibility for an eighteen year old Jacob." Max said, I looked back at him.

"Nineteen." I muttered; he rolled his eyes.

"Jacob." Max warned, I sighed.

"Please." I said, then looked between them watching them both in turn. "Please let me board again. I need to. I need to be with my friends, I need to be fucking eighteen." I said, they both sighed together perfectly, I figured that was what happened when you had been together for as long as Max and Cameron had, and then you stuck an eighteen year old son on top of it.

"Come on guys." I added, "you, *you* should defend me." I said to Cameron, he frowned, "If you hadn't been boarding at eighteen, doing all your eighteen stuff you wouldn't have met Max." I said, he laughed so I sighed until I began to laugh myself.

"Jacob do you feel ready?" Max asked, I nodded, "and you promise to stay in touch, to talk to us, to talk to Ash."

"I promise." I said, he began to nod, as Cameron shook his head.

"If he gets up to what I was getting up to at eighteen whilst boarding, he isn't boarding." Cameron said, I saw Max's smirk instantly.

"I didn't realise I was that bad of an influence on you." Max said, Cameron moaned into his hands. "And I presume Jacob doesn't plan on taking part in a musical that will end up with him having a lot of sex with a ballet dancer." He said, it was my turn to groan as Cameron laughed happily.

"I'll be honest…" I said thoughtfully as I moved some lettuce pieces around my plate. "I do not plan on having sex. Much, or any for that matter." I said, then glanced at Cameron, "which is slightly disappointing, no?" I said, he nodded once so I smiled.

"Cameron and I will talk tonight. Okay?" Max said, I began to nod. "Then we'll talk to you. We'll come to a conclusion together okay? We're not making a quick decision on this."

"Doesn't my wellbeing come into this?" I asked, they both tutted at me,

"Funnily enough Jacob, that's our main concern." Cameron said, so I sighed.

"Except obviously when he's serving us chicken and lettuce." Max muttered, I smirked at my plate hearing Cameron's sigh as I did.

"You're spending your night off from your dancing job. Dancing. I find that weird." I said as I stood perfectly on line with Max, as we did arabesques.

"I doubt you find that weird." He replied, I laughed softly.

"True. Actually." I said, turned my head to look at him, he smiled back at me as I followed him out of our arabesques.

"Ballon." Max said, I frowned at his reflection. "Arlo said you struggled most with jumps. I was confused because that seemed odd to me, but…" he said then began to wave his hand at me so I began to jump. Laughing as he shushed me, telling me to make my landing softer. "Let's try a petite Cabriole." He said curiously, I looked back at him,

"Are you trying to bruise my legs?" I asked, Max laughed shaking his head at me,

"Do you remember them?" he asked, I waved my hand at him in an 'unsure' kind of way. "Okay…" he said then he smiled at me, moving to the middle the floor then lifting himself off the ground, he did a few, travelling across the floor until he stopped in front of me. "Ready?" he asked, I nodded to him, preparing then I began to move, closing my eyes and listening to him as he clapped his hands and said, "ka-bree-AWL, ka-bree-AWL, ka-bree-AWL."

"You worked me hard tonight." I said as I chewed on the top of my water bottle, taking breaths between sipping my water, I heard his laugh so I looked in his direction as he put his joggers on.

"Well, got to impress Arlo." He said, then winked at me so I laughed softly. "Your strength is coming back Jacob." He added, I nodded to him then took a bigger swig out of my water bottle. "I spoke to Cory." He said, I frowned at him as I turned towards him.

"We got a full update on their babysitting hours." He added so I'd laugh, which I did because it was expected of me. "Look, I'll be honest. It's likely Cameron and I will agree that it's right for you to start boarding again." He said, I tried to bite away my excitement. "But I want you to remember something." He said, then took my hand, turning me so I could look in the mirror, then he pointed at my reflection.

"That, who you are looking at right now, is your only competition Jacob." He said, I looked away from my reflection to look at him as he leant his head on my shoulder. "You are not in competition with anyone else, yeah, and you shouldn't use other people as a benchmark for your progress. The only competition is what you see in the mirror." He said, I looked back at my reflection.

"You?" I asked, he shook his head, almost frowning at me through the mirror. "Me." I said in a sigh, he nodded.

"Do you remember when you were fourteen?" he asked, I looked down, "the first lesson you came in, in a leotard, with your shorts and your first pair of pointes." He said, I nodded, he laughed a breathy laugh in my ear, "you stood in front of the mirror, right in this spot." He said, I laughed.

"I look like a real dancer don't I Max? One day I'll be bigger and I'll be able to balance on my pointes, and I'll be the best dancer, ever." I said, Max nodded so I met his eyes in the mirror.

"You weren't in competition with anyone Jacob, you were just dead set on being the best, and you will be, if you get out of your head." He said, I nodded to him, watching as his head moved with mine.

"You are now bigger, you can balance on your pointes, and you do look like a real dancer." He said, I slowed my nod until I turned towards him and hugged him.

▾▾▾

Kian liked to run on a Saturday. He usually went in the early hours of the morning, but depending on his Friday night the run could go on until eleven, or sometimes twelve.

He wasn't in the room when Max moved me back in that Saturday morning, but I had expected it to be that way. Max had attempted to stay longer but soon gave, after the fifth ding to his phone from Cameron who was reminding him he had a matinee in less than two hours.

He squeezed me in a hug, reminded me to keep in touch then he left. Kian returned a few minutes later, his earbuds in, his hood up. He threw his hood down then looked up as he pulled his earbuds out. He gasped the moment he saw me sat on my bed, so I waved to him.

"For good?" he asked, I nodded.

"For good." I replied, he laughed then came at me, scooping me up in a hug, the shortest hug I'd ever had with him,

"I'm sorry. I'm quite sweaty." He said shaking his head at me as he threw his earbuds onto his bed, I laughed.

"I do not care. Hug me." I said, so he did.

He came to sit on my bed after he'd had a shower, his hair still dripping as he took his seat.

"There's so much to tell you." He said, although he genuinely appeared confused for a moment, "I guess the most important one is Elijah's coming to visit."

"Elijah?" I asked, he nodded then he smiled.

223

"My best friend, who is currently studying in Australia, it's his spring break, and he's coming to visit because he loves me."

"So why is this a problem?" I asked, he laughed.

"Because I offered him your bed." He said raising his eyebrow at me, I gasped at him.

"Not even cold." I said, he began to laugh.

"He'll sleep on the floor. He's happy to do that." He said amused, so I smiled.

I could hear laughter and screaming as I got closer to the home. I looked up to the sky, appreciating how blue it was, the sun glaring down, with not a cloud in sight, the kids in the home were probably outside, even if it was against their wishes Ste and Diane had probably made up some excuse to get them all outside.

I went to walk up the big stairway towards the door, then stopped because I saw Connor's car. I walked towards it, then around it finding Connor under the hood with the tall purple haired boy who I believed was called Riley. Connor was pointing at things, talking quietly to him, until he looked up wiping his hands on a rag, and smiling at me.

"You came." He said, he seemed mildly surprised.

"Ste sent me a text, apparently he's being hounded for another ballet class." I said, Connor laughed then pattered Riley's shoulder, walking around him and to me. "What's he doing?" I asked, "your car broke?" I added, Connor laughed shaking his head.

"Good excuse to change the oil, refill the washer fluid. Riley enjoys it, and it saves me doing it myself."

"I'm pretty certain you're not allowed to use these kids as manual labour."

"I'm pretty certain he approached me and asked if he could do things to my car." He replied, then smiled at Riley as he looked towards us. "Go on, Ste's in his office I believe. Jack's the one making them scream in the garden." He said amused, I nodded to him turning towards the stairwell and making my way up them. I went straight to Ste's office, knocking twice then standing awkwardly outside of it, until he opened it.

"Jacob." He said happily, "thank God you're here. They almost made placards demanding another ballet lesson." He said amused as he shut the office door behind him,

"I'm not that good of a teacher. No way." I said, Ste laughed.

"You're just like Max." He replied, I looked at him, "they're used to that, they obviously enjoy that." He said, I shook my head amused as I followed him into the garden.

After I left the home, back when I was fourteen, Ste and Diane had finally caved and added Ballet to the extra curriculum list. After years of arguing with me about the expense and the dedication it took, they finally ended that battle and made a partner with Max, *who*, allowed any child who wished to attend ballet lessons, do so free of charge and only need pay for leotards and shoes.

It appeared to work well, as most of the little girls in the home took part in at least a terms worth of ballet lessons. Some stayed, but most didn't. It however didn't stop them from begging me to do a ballet class with them when I visited. I stood beside Ste in the garden as he laughed watching Jack running around the self-made football pitch, he had the ball, and also had five small children running after him in an effort to get the ball.

225

"Melody." Ste called out, the little girl at the back of the huddle chasing the ball stopped and turned, her long black plaits whipping themselves around. She had a blue gingham bow in one, the other however was bowless and when she smiled, she had multiple teeth missing. "Look who's come to see you." He added, she gasped happily, then ran away, Ste laughed as she grabbed another little girl who looked about her age, they both turned to look at me.

"Do you want to do it inside or out?" Ste asked, I looked towards the little patio set then nodded towards it.

"Out. It's such a nice day. It'd be a crime to stay indoors." I said, Ste laughed leaning his head back and shaking it.

"Don't start repeating my wisdom back to me." He said, then squeezed my shoulder. "Good luck." He added, I smiled as I walked towards the patio, I soon gathered a following of little girls, led by Melody. They all ran to the little fence around the patio and stood alongside it, resting their right hands on it, as if it was the barre then grinning happily at me awaiting my command.

"First positions ladies." I said, they all giggled because I'd called them ladies. "We'll start with a simple point." I said, Melody did it straight away, beaming at me because she knew how, she was on her fifth week of Max's programme.

"You have to make sure you don't squash the fairies." Melody stated, "don't you Jacob?" she asked, I looked at her then began to nod with some gusto.

"You have to lift your heel fair enough off the ground that a fairy can get underneath it." I said, whenever Max stated it to his new beginners there was always a slight laugh in his voice.

When Frankie teaches alongside him the laugh becomes far more verbal and Max usually has to stop teaching for a few minutes to regain himself. If Cory's in the room it's ten times worse, so Max banned the two of them from being in his beginner's class, because they make him laugh.

"Don't squash the fairies is, definitely, the best thing I've heard all day." Jack said, as I sat beside him on the steps leading up to the house, we both had a glass bottle of coke that all the kids had shunned us for as Ste gave us the prohibited item. The majority of the kids sat on the patio area with their own juice and a packet of crisps each.

"It's Max's favourite thing to say. He made it up in reference to the Sugar Plum fairy, and his best friend just twisted it, and made it…"

"Homosexual." Jack teased, I grinned at him then drank from the bottle. "How are you doing anyway? I've heard bits and pieces from Connor, but nothing substantial." He said, I began to nod.

"Better. Much better actually." I said, then looked straight at him. "I'm sorry for being so angry at you when you tried to help… I was just…"

"Hungry?" he asked, I began to nod as I sighed.

"I get it. A lot. Looking back on some of my behaviour, it was actually embarrassing, but I got better and, well, here I am."

"Here you are." I said looking back towards the patio. "I have to ask." I said, Jack nodded whilst also watching the kids. "Would you prefer everyone just forgot about your depression because it's over?" I asked, Jack sighed.

227

"It's not over." He said, we looked at each other. "It's quiet now. My therapist told me to think about it like the tide, when it's quiet, it's like a still day, with no tide, there's no rocky waters, there's nothing.

On a really bad day, it's a high tide, all the way up the beach, waves, and seafoam, storm clouds everything. I have to deal with it them days, but by them days it's usually too rough for a lifeboat to reach me, so I should begin to address low tide days, where there's a slight wind, the wind that helps the boat along.

No, Jacob, I don't want everyone to just forget it, but I don't want to be defined by it. Is that how you see me? As depressed?" he asked, I shook my head very slowly.

"Not as depressed." I said, he almost frowned at me, "I remember that night, a lot." I said, Jack sighed.

"I really wish you hadn't found me." he said, I looked down. "Not in a whole, I didn't want to be saved way, but more in the way of I wish it hadn't been you and I'm beyond thankful that you never told Connor." He added,

"But I do think we should be worried that he never... knew." I said squinting at Jack, he almost laughed.

"Your friends?" he asked, I nodded. "They saw you faint, right?"

"Right." I agreed,

"Are they being insufferable? Are they overcompensating, are they parenting you?" he asked, I shook my head almost instantly.

"No."

"Then you're fine. They're not fixating on what happened, they're fixating on Jacob." He said, "and they'll be there for you. The moment you need them." he added, I smiled then jumped as Connor appeared on the step beside me, his own bottle of coke in his hand.

228

"Riley cleaned my car. He's officially my favourite." He stated, Jack laughed.

"I hope you paid him."

"I gave him a fiver." Connor replied,

"Profitable." I said nodding, Connor agreed then turned and looked behind us, so I also looked up.

"BBQ?" Ste asked, Jack hummed.

"Sounds good." Jack said,

"Staying for tea?" he asked, I looked at Connor, he smiled briefly then nodded to me, so I nodded back.

▼▼▼

"Hey." I heard whispered, I tried to ignore it. "Hey." Whispered again, I groaned, rolling myself over and trying to bury my face into my pillow. "Hey don't ignore me." was said, so I laughed turning my head and seeing the faint blurry outline that I presume was Kian.

"What?" I whispered, my voice sounded heavy with sleep, Kian laughed turning on my bedside lamp so I groaned harder.

"Happy birthday." He said, I began to laugh reaching for my glasses and slipping them on. Kian grinned at me once I did and took a seat on the opposite end of my bed.

He held a very well wrapped box on his crossed legs, and a far too smug smile, obviously for waking me up. I fingered my phone lightly, groaning when I read it was just past midnight. He passed me the package.

"I got you something that to a non-ballet dancer would probably come across as weird, or like I didn't try." He said, I laughed as I ran my fingers underneath the join in the paper. "Go on, open it." he said, I smiled as I did, not tearing the paper as I unwrapped it, he laughed the moment I

229

did, which was when I saw the stretching band. "It's blue," he said, "and apparently the best stretch you'll get." He said amused, I nodded.

"I totally appreciate this." I said, Kian nodded raising his hands as if saying *'I told you so'* to no-one in particular.

"Connor and I are taking you out for tea tonight, and he wouldn't let me tell you until your birthday, so this is me telling you." he said amused, I nodded to him. "After of course our day of classes." He said tilting his head at me, so I copied.

"Which was why I was asleep before midnight."

"Fine, fine I'll let you go back to sleep." He said, then stepped off my bed, I grabbed his hand back, pulling him towards me and kissing his cheek.

"Thank you." I said, he grinned as he got back into his own bed, "Although, now you've woke me up. I'm going to pee." I said, he laughed as he lay back in his bed and watched as I got out of mine.

"Grande Pirouette à la seconde." Arlo announced as we stood around him, holding the barre after our warmup. Arlo was stood in the middle of the studio, looking around almost hopeful that someone would come forward and demonstrate it, *so* he didn't have to.

"Large pirouette." The boy directly across from me said, Arlo nodded it almost looked disappointed.

"Yes." He said then sighed, "à la seconde?" he asked,

"In second position." I said, Arlo nodded to me, he gave me a small smile, so I smiled at the ground.

"It refers to a large pirouette in second position. This pirouette is usually performed by male dancers." He said, then waved his hand at us, as if to say '*you guys*'. "It is a series of turns on one foot with the free leg raised to the second position in the air at ninety degrees." He said, it was returned with numerous confused looks, "you will complete a normal pirouette, but instead of keeping it in passe position, you extend your leg out." He said, the room all 'ahed' together. "You will have all seen them before, and I can guarantee you'll have done them." he said, then he looked at Kian,

"No pressure?" Kian asked, Arlo laughed.

"You're our resident competition boy Cunningham, you must be able to do a grande Pirouette à la seconde." He said, Kian looked across to me I began to laugh. "Spread out on the floor." Arlo requested, so we did, then all watched as he pirouetted, I laughed to myself almost instantly as Max had me do them all the time. "Your turn." Arlo stated, I nodded to him as I prepared, then I began to turn, not focusing on anything or anyone as I went around, and around. I could hear Arlo speaking, but not the words, until I began to lose speed.

"Oh we've lost Kian." Arlo said, he sounded amused, as I brought myself to a spectacularly steady spot. "And Jacob." He said, then began to applaud me, "You turned more times than a fidget spinner, kid." He said, I laughed.

"Max likes to do pirouettes." I said, Arlo raised his eyebrow at me.

"Catch your breath, and we'll go again." He ordered, then clapped his hands to start the beats.

"Nineteen then?" Margo said, I nodded to her almost wary as she leant across the canteen table to speak to me, I frowned back at her because she hadn't gone to get any food yet. "What comes with nineteen?"

"Nothing." I said, "literally nothing. I did it all last year." I said, she laughed.

"True. I was devastated Kian wouldn't make tonight a piss up." She said tutting to me,

"Look at us being adults." I said lifting my water bottle up to her, she lifted her own knocking the lids together, as Kian returned to the table, I groaned pretty much the moment he did. "Don't sing." I said more to Margo, "do not begin singing." I said, they both laughed as Kian placed the cake he'd brought over down in front of me.

"I spoke to Ash. He said you can have a piece of cake, so long as he gets one as well." He said, I laughed as Margo lifted a piece off the tray with a knife and slid it onto the napkin which she then put in front of me. I ran my finger down the icing that was in little domes on top of the cake, I looked at it on my finger then ate it. I saw Kian smirk at me when I did, so I grinned back.

I delivered the napkin full of cake to Ash in our free between lunch and Pas De Deux. He didn't seem like he was expecting me but welcomed me in, I took a seat on the couch then held the napkin out to him.

"I was joking." Ash said, I pushed my hand closer to him.

"Come on, take the cake." I said, he laughed as he reached into his drawers. He brought out a little rectangle package.

"Swap?" he asked, I nodded letting him take the napkin, then I took the package. I began to open it when I was holding it, I glanced up seeing him take some icing on

232

his finger and eat it before putting the cake behind him. I frowned at him when I opened the package to find a journal.

"Food diary." Ash said, I glanced at him. "Happy Birthday." He added, so I smiled at him. "Thought I'd replace your notebook for an actual diary." He said, as I turned it over. I ran the palm of my hand over the cover, of the silhouette of the ballerina with the words '*If you stumble, make it part of the dance*', wrote in cursive above her. "You've been doing brilliantly." Ash said, "outstanding in fact. I'm so happy with your progress, but I want you to keep up your food diary." He said, I nodded.

"I'm happy too." I replied then I actually looked at him. "Thank you Ash."

"You're welcome."

Miss Olivia made us take a seat on the floor when we arrived into our Pas De Deux lesson, she told us to stop warming up and to take a seat, as Madame Rose would be in to talk to us soon.

The whispers between ourselves silenced the moment Madame Rose walked into the room, she seemed mildly impressed as she stood before us, because she didn't need to wait for silence.

"Good afternoon first years." She said,

"Good after Madame Rose." We chorused back; Kian smirked at me after we did as Margo laughed behind her hand on the other side of me.

"I have come to talk to you about the scholarship auditions you will all be taking part in, in the next few weeks." She said, then she proceeded to explain the scholarship process to us, much like Frankie and Cory had when I stayed at theirs. I listened to every word she said, trying to figure out if something had changed or if there were any rules, she waited until the end to go through the list of rules.

"You must all wear exam wear. FREED approved, of course. Girls your hair must be in regulated bun, underwear rules apply." She said, I looked at Kian as he raised an amused eyebrow. "And finally," she said, so I looked back at her, she looked straight back at me.

"All boys must start and finish their audition on flat ballet pump." She said, I sighed as she opened the floor to questions.

Chapter 13

I followed the music to discover which studio Kian had taken Elijah too. It appeared to be the last on the corridor, so I let myself in, closing the door quietly as they were already dancing, neither of them noticed when I walked in so instead, I watched them.

They were laughing with each other as they moved through the moves, talking to each other and what Miss Olivia would say was putting each other off, but their steps didn't even falter. They did every step perfectly, as if there wasn't even any thought going into it.

I smiled as Kian caught Elijah's leg when he'd raised it, holding it almost vertical to their bodies, then he slid his hand down Elijah's leg, and picked him up, they spun together whilst Kian held Elijah up with just one hand, until he practically dropped him, *but* caught him, just far enough from the ground for Elijah to go up onto pointe.

They danced alongside each other, in perfect unison *that's* when Elijah spotted me, he grinned at me pulling his tongue at me but continued to dance as I laughed. Kian pulled Elijah towards him, holding Elijah's hand as Elijah pirouetted then stood to Kian's front dancing perfectly with him, they moved as one, until they stopped and just looked at each other as the music ended, they laughed with each other as they took a step away from each other and both bowed, I began to applaud. Kian nodded to me amused, as Elijah walked back towards Kian, then grabbed for his crotch.

"I see you still get hard for me dear Kian." Elijah teased, Kian began to laugh pushing him away and walking towards where I was stood.

"Jacob, meet Elijah." Kian said, Elijah gasped happily,

"Oh. Biblical." He said, Kian almost choked on his sip of water.

"Elijah." He shunned, Elijah laughed, a real musical laugh which made me smile. "We were going to go for a coffee, have a bit of a catch up. Talk about Australia. Want to join us?" Kian asked, I began to nod then I paused.

"Won't I be intruding?" I asked, they both shook their heads, as they began to pick up their clothes. Elijah pulled his tongue at me as he pulled a black and white stripped t-shirt over his leotard.

"No. In fact I'd like to learn as much as I can about you." Elijah said, then fastened the button on the pair of ripped jeans he'd stepped into. He then sat to take off his pointe shoes.

We left the campus to find a coffee shop, which was unsurprisingly easy. We walked through the queue all getting a cold drink then taking a seat on a little round table, so our knees bumped against each other.

"How is it then?" Kian asked as he stirred his frappé with the straw. "Australia?" he added, Elijah smiled as he scooped cream out of his cup with his own straw.

"It's amazing. It's like a completely different world. The ballet is something else, and I'm weirdly good at hip-hop." He said raising his eyebrow, Kian laughed.

"Hot though?"

"Sometimes. I've come to fully appreciate air conditioning. There was only once, it was in February or something stupid like that, it was so hot, something like eighty-six degrees... which is about thirty here. We were all soaked through and not even in the fun way." He said quirking his eyebrow at me, it sent a shiver down my spine.

"How thankful are you to be back?"

"It's freezing." Elijah snapped, it made me laugh, he smiled at me so I took a sip out of my mixed berry cooler.

"Are you going to see…"

"Mr. Nurse Man? I am." Elijah replied, they both laughed so I frowned at him. "My Dad." He said, "my Dad's a nurse. Granted not my nurse because that'd be weird, but, a nurse." He said then nodded to Kian, Kian nodded back.

"Dad didn't know I was coming back until yesterday morning, then he got all annoyed because he'd have paid for the flight and he'd have sorted everything out. I told him I'd see him soon, and hung up on him." He replied as he rolled his eyes.

"And my tutor, my God. Madame Florence was so pissed at me, because our scholarship auditions are literally the week after Spring break, and I decided to come here." he said grinning, it made me laugh so he looked at me. "Enough about me. It's your turn. Jacob, tell me all about you." He said, I stuttered lightly, then looked at Kian for help. He shook his head at me drinking from his frappé, so I looked back at Elijah, as he grinned at me.

I lay looking towards Kian's bed, which I knew would be empty. I hadn't even looked at the time but I knew his bed was going to be empty, I yawned burying my head into my pillow before reaching for my glasses, putting them on then looking down at Elijah as he lay on the floor between our beds. His arms were up above his head as he scrolled through his phone, until he saw me.

"Good morning." He said softly, then he sat up, looking at Kian's bed. "He still goes for his Saturday run." He said as I rolled onto my back, resting my hands on my head.

"I don't know how he does it. I have minimal motivation to get on doing *that*, or anything at this time of morning." I said, he laughed as I closed my eyes.

"I'm sure." He replied, "no problem setting up camp though." He said, I opened my eyes turning my head to frown at him, he grinned at me nodding towards my bed so I looked down. "Unless it's for me of course. Then I am flattered." He said resting his hand on his chest. I sat up, making him laugh almost instantly.

"I just need to pee."

"Bullshit." He said amused, "it's okay, don't be embarrassed." He cooed at me as he looked back down at his phone. "It's why Kian runs. Purely to run off the erection." He said, a little smirk at his phone so I got out of my bed, going into the en-suite, I turned to look at him before closing the door. "I won't tell anyone." He whispered then he winked at me, so I turned away seeing my blush in the mirror above the sink.

"I hear you dance en pointe." Elijah said, as he picked up a tote bag. I nodded back to him almost frowning as he grinned at me. "Want to join me?" He asked, reaching into his tote bag and showing me his pointes, I began to nod, then I stood.

"I just need to get changed." I said, he laughed.

"Don't worry. You don't have to wear your uniform with me. I'm going like this." He said, so I looked down him. He wore joggers and a vest top. "My theory is, if you can lift your leg, you're wearing the right clothes." He said amused, I smiled back at him. "Come on." He added, holding his hand out to me.

I smiled at it, then went under my bed getting the box with my pointes out before taking his hand and letting him lead me to a studio. He let us in, then sat in the middle of the floor, so I went to sit beside him.

"Oh, black pointes, you're a man." He said, I laughed shaking my head at him.

"My Dad brought me them, as a replacement for my practically destroyed ones."

"Practically destroyed." He repeated as he got his own out of his bag. "How many have you destroyed then?" He asked amused as he twirled the ribbon of his pink pointes up his ankles.

"Many." I said amused, "there's my first pair from when I was fourteen, they were worn through, my second pair, they died when I was just sixteen, Connor and I spray painted them, made them a rainbow." I said, he laughed,

"Amazing." He said amused,

"Third, fourth, and the last were my fifth." I said, he laughed.

"I used to wear through a pair at least once every two months." He said laughing, "we'd train every day, and nine times out of ten I was en pointe. It got to a point of being very rare I'd be in flat pump." He shrugged lightly. "But I love it." He said, I nodded.

"I love it." I agree as he stood,

"So, come on, show me what you've got." He said, I stood with him, watching as he searched through his phone, then looked towards the speaker, I laughed when *Faith* began.

"I was not expecting that." I said, he shrugged.

"Good warm up song, good fun." He said, then he walked back to me, he rose onto his pointes, so I rose onto mine. He rose his arms into fifth, I laughed and copied. "Ready?" He whispered, I grinned nodding to him as he lowered himself, and prepared to pirouette,

"So ready." I said, Elijah raised his eyebrow at me then nodded in time to the beats.

"So, how did you and Kian meet?" I asked, as we sat on the floor. He was twirling the ribbons around his fingers, it had started in an effort to take them off, but he seemed to give up with that.

"I was his first Pas De Deux partner." He said then he looked at me and grinned, "and his first girlfriend."

"Really?" I said, almost in a laugh. He nodded back.

"We're friends now because we dated then, we didn't date because we were friends first, and like, I'm pretty happy with it. Considering Kian turned out to be gay." He said grinning, it made me smile.

"Why did you break up?" I asked, Elijah laughed softly.

"We just did. We were thirteen. It wasn't anything serious. We didn't break up because I transitioned, and we didn't break up because Kian came out. It was just, natural. I suppose." He shrugged at me, then he smiled so I smiled back.

"How did you know you where?" I asked, he laughed as he untied his ribbons.

"It was hard, I'm never going to downplay that. I remember being hell-a confused because every aspect of my life was wrong except for ballet.

Ballet was my serene. I was unhappy with everything else, but then I'd get to ballet and I'd love wearing the tutus, I loved the ballet dresses and the costumes, I loved dancing pointe." He said stroking his palm over his pointes. "I didn't get it, I thought I couldn't be Trans, I enjoyed the tutus too much."

"So, what happened?" I asked, he laughed as he took off his shoe then started on the other.

"It was my ballet mistress actually, she was amazing. She sat me down one day because she felt we needed to talk, and of course I did everything she asked. She told me she thought I was unhappy, and before I could protest, she stated she didn't mean in class.

She didn't say that she thought I was Trans, she didn't say anything regarding that, all she said to me was that tutus, ballet dresses and pointe shoes are just objects. They do not determine my gender in anyway shape or form. If I'm comfortable in them it does not change who I am." He said, I smiled into my knees. "Then she said, it might mean that I'm gay though." He added amused, so I laughed.

"She was right. I am gay." He said amused, I looked at him. "And of course, pointes, tutus and ballet dresses ARE just objects. They by no means determine whether I'm a boy, or a girl. She whispered to me when I'd transitioned and I was dancing en pointe, that boys should be terrified of competing against me because I have this amazing talent that none of them have." He said, then he laughed. "Well, none of them but you." He said, so I smiled, "I still dance Pas De Deux with Kian sometimes, he likes to do it with me because I know him, and obviously he knows me. I danced with him this week, I helped him with your Pas De Deux assessment." He said laughing, I grinned. "I am not still his girlfriend." He added then looked up at me and winked.

"You compete?" I asked, he nodded to me it was almost amused.

"I've always competed. I usually compete against Kian. He is a bitter loser." He said laughing, so I also did, "if ever I won, he said it was because the judges knew I was Trans." He said then he grinned at me, so I smiled back. "He of course never meant it vindictively, he's my best friend he was forever taking the piss. We did a Pas De Deux from Dorian Grey in the competition we were in the summer before school. It was amazing."

"But did you win?"

"Of course we won." He replied, I laughed. "You don't compete?"

"No. My Dad did. He adored competing, but because I've always said I wanted to be a ballet dancer, I wanted to dance on stage in productions, he never let me compete."

"Have you performed before?" He asked, I nodded.

"Besides the annual show my dance school put on. I was in a My First Ballet last year which was a lot of fun, and I perform regularly in schools with my Dad and his two best friends. They do a presentation with a dance medley, then a scientific presentation about pointes."

"Cool." He said nodding, I nodded back to him grinning as I did. "So, am I allowed to ask why I've been resigned to the floor?" he said, I laughed as I looked down at my feet.

"I came back."

"Where had you been?"

"Sabbatical." I replied, then glanced up, Elijah frowned back at me, so I frowned at him.

"You don't want to tell me?" he said, then he shrugged, "that's fine." He added.

"I don't know, my brain got a bit confused." I said, then I sighed. "I began to fear that I wasn't tall enough, or thin enough, or that I didn't have a big enough dick." I said, Elijah laughed it almost sounded like a cough.

"I know what it's like to feel like your bodies wrong." He said, I winced. "Are you better now?" he asked, I sighed.

"I'm getting better. I'm riding the tide." I said in a deep breath, Elijah laughed softly.

"I like the sound of that. Right now…" he said, his eyes sparkled when I looked at him. "I'm surfing the waves."

"Kian." I whispered, he hummed at me without turning to look at me, but that was okay as I was watching Elijah, ensuring he was still asleep. "Random question."

"Sure?" He asked, although he sounded tried.

"How likely is it that you might get back with Elijah?" I asked, he laughed it still sounded tried.

"I love Connor, if that's what you're trying to get at." He said, I smiled.

"It wasn't, but nice to know." I said, he looked at me,

"It's extremely unlikely Jacob, we've been there, done that, got the t-shirt, and as I say, I'm happy with Connor. Is it because he's so touchy?"

"A little." I said, he laughed.

"You don't have to worry about your best friend's heart." He said, I looked away from him. "Unless," he said, I remained looking away   "Do you like Elijah?" He asked, I shushed him, he began to laugh, "Fantastic."

▼▼▼

"Come on, come on you need to come out with me. I am not going back to Australia before we have a drink."

"Well good that means you'll have to stay." Kian replied as he sat on his bed, Elijah groaned at him kneeling on the end of his bed then bouncing on his knees, Kian moaned at him making me laugh, they both looked at me.

"You'll come out won't you Jacob?" Elijah cooed at me; I bit my lip so I wouldn't laugh. "And drag this ballet bore out with us too." He added directing his attention to Kian who rolled his eyes.

"Can Connor come?"

"Yes." Elijah stated, then he smirked at me, "I look forward to meeting my best friend's boyfriend." He added, I laughed. "See whether he's any competition to me." He added winking at me, I continued to laugh.

"Do you have to ask Ash if you can come out?" Kian said, my laughter stopped instantly,

"Oh I feel as if I've missed something." Elijah said, we both nodded to him as he frowned,

"I'll ask Ash, but if he says I can go but can't drink, I just..."

"Won't drink." Elijah said, he sounded appalled.

"Elijah likes to get people drunk." Kian announced, "you've never been properly drunk, even if you've been one hundred percent intoxicated. You've never experienced being drunk with Elijah."

244

"It'd seem I've got a reputation." Elijah said to me, I smiled back at him as he grinned.

I got first hug with Connor when we found him in the, what Elijah was calling, pre-drinks bar. Margo had sworn she'd join us later but I didn't hold out hope, instead I just hugged Connor when I saw him.

He laughed into my ear then let go off the hug and went to Kian, he kissed him then turned to look at me as if it had made him shy, I laughed shaking my head at him then I pointed at Elijah,

"How do we begin?" I asked, Elijah grinned,

"Pitches my love. Pitches." He said happily then grabbed my hand and walked me to the bar, we returned back to the table with two pitches of similar colours and four glasses. He poured one of the drinks into two of the glasses, and the other into the rest. "Drink up." He said, Connor and Kian did as ordered,

"So, how does tonight go?" I asked, then laughed and took a sip out go my own glass, "drinks-wise." I added, Elijah smiled.

"I perfected this recently, you know with calorie counting over there." He said, I smirked. "So, pitches, followed by beer and cider round. The main course is your choice of spirit drink, and as many of them as you like, followed by dessert."

"Cocktails." Kian said, it was almost mocking, "which admittedly is my favourite part of the night." He said more to Connor who began to laugh into his glass.

"I never had you as a cocktail guy." Connor said curiously, Kian laughed.

"Probably the most homosexual thing about me." Kian said,

"Hear, hear." Elijah said, I laughed.

"Nee the ballet." Connor said, we all shouted back at him, he laughed.

"Well, I didn't know how much I didn't want to see that." Elijah said, I laughed as we both stood watching as Connor and Kian enjoyed each other's tonsils almost too much. "Let me get this straight." He said, I began to giggle immaturely, maybe the alcohol was going to my head.

"My best friend, Kian, is dating Connor, who is your best friend?" He said, I nodded, "so, if your good self decides to put me out of my misery, your best friend will date my best friend, whilst I date my best friends boyfriends best friend, and you too." He said, I giggled as I nodded.

"That was complicated." I said, Elijah laughed as he looked at me.

"You're drunk."

"I am not." I replied, he shook his head,

"Spell my name." He said, turning to look at me, I laughed covering my mouth as he raised his eyebrow at me, "Go on."

"E..." I said, he nodded "L-I-E-J-A-R." I said, he began to laugh shaking his head at me,

"You're drunk," he accused, "they're horny and I have a full bladder. Let's move and come back for them." He said, then he nodded. "Yeah?" He asked, I nodded to him.

"Yeah." I said as he took my hand, and made me walk. We walked pass numerous clubs that were closing, he had let go of my hand and had linked our arms, so our hips bumped together as we walked. "Oh my god I'm going to explode. Why does everything close at three around here?"

"Because it's a Wednesday." I replied, Elijah growled at me so I laughed burying my head into his shoulder as he changed the direction we were walking in. Until he stopped at a staircase that was hidden behind a little wall, I frowned at him.

"What?" He asked,

"What?" I repeated back, so he laughed. "You needed to pee." I said, he nodded, and waved his hand towards the staircase, so I did the same, he sighed at me and climbed up a few steps until he sat, so I followed sitting beside him,

"Go one up." He said, I didn't question him as I moved up a step, I did however begin to question him as he undid his jeans and pushed them down with his boxers. He just laughed until he touched my knee.

"Shut up or this is never going to happen." He stated, so I zipped my mouth, he sighed, it sounded relieved then he looked at me. "It's perfectly hidden," he said, I frowned at him, "Doesn't put me on view to the entire town." He stated, I laughed, "like you shouldn't stand at the top of a hill and pee, I should seek out somewhere that doesn't require me to flash everyone." He stated, I frowned at him. "Oh and somewhere to sit down." He said grinning lightly, I laughed although I think it sounded drunk.

"Don't you have a thing that you can use to pee with?" I asked, he cocked an eyebrow at me,

"I have perfectly working genitals that does that for me." He said,

"Right." I said, he began to laugh, groaning at me as he stamped his feet against the step they were on. "I meant like..."

"Oh I know what you meant." He said, then he lifted his hips pulling his pants back up, then moving up so he was sat the step above me, I looked up at him. "You're obsessed with finding out if I have a dick, aren't you?" He said, I must've blushed so he laughed. "I know a perfectly good way to let you know." He whispered, I frowned at him, "which I'd most certainly let you do."

"You like me, don't you?"

"Was that not obvious Jacob?" He replied, I laughed, "I've just let you sit next to me as I peed." He added raising his arms up into the air,

"I like you." I agreed, "and sure I might be drunk, but I do, I really like you."

"Good." He whispered, then he kissed me, I gasped into it then began to kiss him back, my hands settling on the back of his neck as he pulled me closer to him.

Then he pushed me up, so I began to stand, although I frowned at him as he stood me up. He pulled me backwards until he was leant against the wall. I frowned at him once we broke the kiss.

"You're not getting anywhere if I'm sat down." He said, my frown became more intense so he laughed then took my hand, running my palm down his chest, then slipping my hand into his jeans, he pulled his tongue at me when I looked at him then he gasped when he pushed against my hand.

We went back to Connor's flat, when we finally picked him and Kian up from where we'd left them. It was almost as if they were significantly drunker than when they left and Elijah and I, significantly more sober.

We helped our own best friend get undressed and ready for bed, then put them both into Connor's bed together. We stood at the end of the bed for a few minutes, once we did.

"I realised something." Elijah whispered, I looked from Connor to him, "like just then, one of those, oh my god yes kind of eureka moments." He said, I laughed quietly,

"What did you realise?"

"You didn't make me come." He said, I coughed as I looked back at him, he silenced me before I could begin to argue. "So, I thought. You could finish off, then I could finish you off." He said, then he grinned, I grinned back although mine was completely surrounded by a blush.

We lay down on the floor between Connor's couch and television, having moved the coffee table and pulled all the cushions and blankets off his couch and surrounding seats so we had something to lie on.

We lay, looking at each other, nose to nose, him stroking his nose against mine, then trying to knock my glasses off as he did. I laughed and laughed, trying to move my head back but he held my hair, so instead I kissed him. Feeling his laugh against me before he began to kiss me back.

We lay with the only sound in the room being our breaths, until I felt Elijah lean his head on my shoulder, so I looked at him.

"You know what you mentioned when we danced?" he whispered, I hummed although I wasn't sure, he lifted his head up to me, still leaning his chin on my shoulder. "About when your head got confused." He added, I nodded whilst looking down at him. "You do not need to worry." He said, as he squeezed my crotch under the blanket, I swallowed down my yelp which made him smile. "For the record." He added, then he pushed himself up, leaning on his elbow, looking down at me. "And I am very impressed by your ability to follow directions also." He said then nodded to me. "Kian was right."

"Right? Right about what?" I asked, Elijah grinned.

"That I'd like you." He whispered, I smiled.

Elijah went to see his Dad during our morning lesson. Leaving us to Pas De Deux, whilst Connor recovered in bed.

Kian, hadn't wanted to leave him, although I think he didn't want to leave Connor's bed more, every time I looked over to him, he was wincing at whatever Miss Olivia was ordering.

"Where did you end up last night?" I whispered to Margo, as she rose into an arabesque, she laughed but her arabesque didn't wobble.

"I went to the first bar you said you'd be at." she said, then stepped into her pirouette. "I didn't find you, but I found a very attractive man, so win, win I suppose." She said, I began to laugh, Kian groaned again, we both looked towards him.

"Why did you let me get drunk?"

"I did not." I replied, as we walked around Margo and Abi, "I was surprised any alcohol actually made it into your mouth, as it was connected to Connor's for most of the night." I said, Kian smirked as if he was proud of himself.

"There will be no talking in your Pas De Deux assessments." Miss Olivia snapped; Kian winced as I looked at Margo who rolled her eyes. "Gentlemen, pay attention to your ladies as you move into the lift." Miss Olivia said, I took a deep breath as I held Margo's waist to lift her, she nodded to me, jumping to help as I lifted her off the floor. Miss Olivia nodded as she passed us.

"So, it'd appear everyone got some action last night then?" Margo said, I shushed her as Kian frowned at us both.

"I know you probably found a willing volunteer, but Jacob?" he asked, I laughed as I moved down onto my knee, my other raised, Margo sat on it.

"Jacob got some love from your best friend." She said, as he ran her fingers through my hair, Kian looked at us

250

as Abi curtseyed like she was supposed to when Kian went onto his knee.

"You slept with Elijah?" he asked, Abi looked at me as I began to shake my head, I redirected it from Kian to her, shaking my head over and over.

"We didn't sleep together." I said, "alright, we kissed a little. There was some fooling around." I added then looked at Margo and sighed. "Thanks."

"No problem sweetheart." Margo replied as she stepped off my knee, Kian began to laugh.

"That's quick. Even for Elijah." He said, he sounded mildly impressed, "where you asking him about his dick? Did you encourage him?" he asked, I laughed as we walked towards the barre and drank from our water bottles. He pulled his phone out of his trainers. "Connor's awake." He said amused, I smiled as I pulled a t-shirt on over my leotard. "So very confused, but awake. I have also been informed that Elijah's done with his Dad."

"No one ever texts me." I said, Margo cooed at me.

"I'll see you two after repertoire." She said, then blew us kisses, Kian looked at me.

"Repertoire." He repeated, I frowned at him as he grinned unlocking his phone again and typing into it.

Arlo seemed pleased that he'd trained us well enough to come into his class and to begin to warm up on the barre without his direction. He didn't even check us, he just stood searching through his folder and the tablet he played his music out of, which was why he didn't notice when Elijah came into our class.

None of our class really noticed, only Kian and I who both grinned at him as he came to stand between us on the barre.

"Hungover?" Kian asked without turning to him, Elijah sighed as he took the baseball jersey he wore, off. He had proper repertoire attire underneath and his flat ballet pumps on.

"Disappointingly not." Elijah tutted, then looked over his shoulder at me. "I remember every detail of last night vividly." He said, I laughed it was quiet as Kian hummed,

"Yeah, you and I need a chat." Kian said, Elijah gasped at me.

"Appears I'm in trouble." He said quietly, I laughed as Arlo clapped his hands, we all moved to the centre.

"Développé." Arlo announced, then looked around us, I looked at Kian he shrugged back at me.

"It means developing movement." Elijah said, Arlo began to nod then frowned.

"You're not one of mine." He said, Elijah grinned at him, "but as you know the answer, you can stay. Please continue?"

"A développé is a movement in which the working leg is drawn up to the knee of the supporting leg and slowly extended." Elijah said, he got a nod.

"Can you demonstrate?" he asked, Elijah hummed.

"Don't pretend you dislike being the centre of attention." Kian said, Elijah grinned at him, then prepared.

He looked around to ensure he wasn't going to kick anyone then brought his leg up to the height of his knee, he looked around again then began to extend his leg, until he was stood his legs creating the perfect right-angle.

"A développé takes a lot of balance and control." Arlo said, as he examined Elijah's position. "The strength in your supporting leg has to be solid." He said then nodded to Elijah. "Thank you. If you don't feel your balance is up for

252

it. Please start on the barre." Arlo said, most went to the barres, I glanced at Kian as he also went. "Jacob?" he asked,

"Jacob will be fine." Elijah said, so I looked at him.

"Oh yeah? Why's that?"

"Jacob can dance on pointe." Elijah replied, then grinned at me, so I smiled back.

"Prepare boys." Arlo said, I turned to look at him as I prepared my arms. "Raise to knee." Arlo said, so I did, I glanced sideways at Elijah who was grinning as he also did. "And take your time as you extend." He said, "do not over extend this can be dangerous and can cause injury. Don't push it further than it can go, this will come with time and practice." He said, as he watched the barres.

"Keep your supporting leg straight." He added, so I straightened myself then began to extend my leg, feeling as my calf and knee quivered like it did when I went into a long arabesque on pointe. "And hold." Arlo said holding his hand up in front of him, I saw as Arlo nodded to the barres, probably an acknowledgement that they could lower their leg, I glanced at Elijah then back at Arlo as he lowered his hand. "Very impressive Jacob." He said, I smiled at him, and I relaxed into first position. "And the boy with no name."

"Elijah." He replied, "Master?" he asked,

"Arlo. Just Arlo."

"Oh I've heard much about you Arlo." Elijah said as he looked towards Kian, so I also did seeing him leant on the barre watching as they spoke. "You're like Jacob's ballet dad. Legendary." He said, I laughed as Arlo did.

"Prepare your other leg." Arlo said, I watched as everyone turned around on the barre.

"Do you guys ever do anything for fun around here?" Elijah said as he walked with me across the field towards where

Kian was sat beside Connor, who'd finally recovered enough in his hangover to come and see him.

"We did that last night." I said, Elijah laughed.

"I mean non-alcoholic." He said happily, "I'm not hungover, but I don't want to get drunk again. Don't you have anything like a basketball court, a swimming pool?"

"Do you?" I asked, he nodded.

"They allow us to have fun in Australia." He replied, I laughed. "Just no skating on the school grounds." He said as he shrugged over dramatically. "Don't you even have a ball?" he asked, I laughed as we reached Connor and Kian. "Do either of you have a ball?" Elijah stated, they both frowned up at him.

"Why? Are you looking for one?"

"Two actually." Elijah replied, then kicked Kian's leg. "A football." He stated, Connor began to nod as he went into his backpack, he revealed an almost new football.

"Do you just carry that around?" I asked, Connor nodded to me as he rolled it towards Elijah.

"You don't know when an opportunity for football may come up." He replied as he stood, Elijah moved backwards with the football so Connor followed him.

"I know you'll play." Elijah said to Kian, who sighed.

"The last time I played football with you, we both ended up in A&E." Kian replied, I frowned at him, "strained wrist." Kian said, I looked at Elijah,

"Dislocated shoulder." He said, Connor laughed.

"Are you sure you two were playing football, right?" he asked, they both laughed.

"How did that effect ballet?" I asked, they both shook their heads.

"It didn't." Kian said, "I could still dance." He said in a shrug,

"And I went on holiday about two days after I did it." Elijah said amused, so I laughed. "Come play." He said, I saw as Connor shook his head.

"He won't." he teased, I scowled him as Elijah turned to look at him. "Jacob hates football. Always has. I'd beg him to play it with me in the home but no…" he said, Elijah turned back to me,

"In the home?" he repeated, I shrugged.

"Jack came along sooner rather than later." I replied, Connor laughed.

"Come play Jacob." Elijah said, so I nodded to him, he grinned as I heard Kian sigh behind me, "two on two." He added, then pointed at Connor. "You're so on my team." He added, Kian laughed as I did.

"Yep. He is." We agreed as Elijah ran off with the ball.

"You so like him." Connor said as we stood side by side watching as Kian and Elijah fought for control over the ball. Connor and I had given up a good while ago.

"Why?" I asked, Connor laughed.

"You can tell. You're smitten." He said happily, "oh and he managed to persuade you to play football. I tried for fourteen years and got squat." He stated, I groaned. "I knew it." he whispered.

"He likes me back." I said nodding, "but he lives in Australia."

"Long distance." Connor said, I shook my head.

"No, no way not after how Cory and Frankie talk about their time apart. I am not strong enough for that."

"You are." He said softly, I looked at him. "But equally," he said as he looked at Kian, "I wouldn't do it."

"Because of the sex?" I asked, he laughed.

"Because of the sex." He agreed then he grinned at me, "and because he's so gorgeous I'd be worried about being on the other side of the world. I mean, what if I forget what he looks like."

"Disaster." I said, he nodded.

"It would be a tragedy." He replied,

"Are you guys going to help, or what?" Elijah shouted towards us, we both laughed as we ran towards the ball, joining in on the fight for control.

Chapter 14

I had been lying in my bed for what felt like hours, but it was still dark out. The room around me was quiet. I figured both Elijah and Kian were well asleep, but for some reason I couldn't let myself fall asleep.

I'd spent the last part of an hour trying to make out the blurred shapes that I couldn't define because I wasn't wearing my glasses, *and* because it was dark, until the bathroom light flicked on. I winced against the light trying to figure out who it was that had gone into the bathroom.

"Elijah?" Kian whispered when the bathroom light flicked back off, I heard a hum as a reply, then movement, I tried to watch it but couldn't. I figured Elijah had gotten into Kian's bed.

"How was your Dad?" Kian whispered; Elijah laughed softly.

"He was fine, happy even. He was made up I was home and had made me a proper breakfast. He asked what I was thinking, whether I'd stay in Australia or not. I told him it depended if I got a job there or not."

"What did he say?" Kian asked, Elijah laughed again.

"If I stayed, he'd move over there as quick as he physically could."

"With Josh?"

"Oh of course, Josh in tow, he's only ten, he can't abandon him yet." He said amused, it made me smile. "I like your boyfriend."

"I quite like my boyfriend too." Kian replied, I rolled onto my side to look at them.

"I can fully see why you're attracted to him, as well. Have you guys slept together?" he asked, I presume Kian nodded, there was silence for a little while.

"What did you do with Jacob?" Kian asked, Elijah sighed.

"I only jerked him off." He said, I rolled my eyes. "He also jerked me off. *Well*."

"Because you wanted to?"

"Have I ever done something I didn't want to?" Elijah replied, Kian hummed.

"Did he make you come?" Kian whispered just that little quieter, I had it had completely surprised me because I didn't know that the genitals Elijah had could do that – to that extent.

"Yeah…" Elijah said, "but only because you taught me how." He added, in the quieter voice like Kian had spoken in. "You were the one who taught me how to soak the sheets." Elijah whispered; I felt my cheeks burn red. I imagined it was extremely obvious and was thankful it was dark.

"But why Jacob?"

"Because I like him." Elijah replied. "Honestly. Hand on heart, I really, really like him. Which is shit because I go back to Australia in two days. Kian, two and I probably won't actually see him again until what? Christmas, spring break next year?"

"So, you wanted to touch him as soon as possible."

"Yeah." Elijah replied, "and you were all up on Connor's tonsils and I didn't want to see that."

"I love Connor."

"I know." Elijah replied, "I know you do, and I am so happy for you Kian. But it still hurts."

"You cannot be jealous?" Kian replied, Elijah laughed.

"Since we were thirteen, I have been jealous if someone so much as thinks in your direction, and I can make you jealous. I really can, without even being cruel, I can make you jealous, but I won't."

"Elijah." Kian said softly, they both sighed together. "If you were to get with anyone, anyone at all, I'd be glad if it was Jacob." He said, I hid my face into my pillow. "And I know I have no say in who you sleep with, who you like, whatever, but I wanted you to know that."

"Thank you." Elijah whispered back, "and I very much approve of Connor, like to the extent of if he was available, he would be mine." He said, they both laughed, their laughs were cut off, and I could only imagine that they'd kissed. "I love you." Elijah whispered; I rose my head just slightly.

"I love you too. I always will and nothing, or no-one is going to change that." Kian whispered back. "But I know I love Connor, with all of my heart. It was proven I suppose when you came back, because I do love you.

I have, and I will always but it's more like you'll always have a piece of my heart, you'll always be there." He said, "but I think you're going to have to share it."

"Gladly." Elijah replied, "I better be fucking best man." He said, they both began to laugh.

I woke up confused, as I definitely couldn't remember when I had eventually fell asleep. I sat up, reaching for my glasses then looking around the room. My gaze focused on Elijah as he was facing me, but still asleep in Kian's bed. I was still looking at him when Kian came out the en-suite. I turned to look at him, he raised his eyebrows back at me.

"Kick you out?" I asked, Kian laughed then shook his head.

"No, we were just talking. It got late; we fell asleep." He shrugged as he examined his bed, he obviously decided there was no way he was getting back into it, he came to sit on the end of mine.

"What?" I began then I paused, he frowned at me.

"What?" he repeated, so I shook my head,

"I mean, how important was your relationship with Elijah?" I asked, Kian sighed and looked back at me.

"He was my first partner." He said, then laughed. "We were thirteen, at the time I suppose he was my first, and last girlfriend."

"And that's it?" I asked, he shook his head.

"We took each other's virginities." He said softly, "we were Pas De Deux partners, we sometimes still are Pas De Deux partners. We just ended up sleeping together. Frequently."

"Why did it stop?" I asked, Kian laughed softly.

260

"Australia." He said,

"That recent?" I asked, he nodded.

"The day we submitted our ballet school applications was the last time we slept together because it was apparent that we were not going to be with each other for school.

We weren't together. I mean, I slept with a handful of guys when I was still sleeping with Elijah, we weren't exclusive, or committed or anything like that but…"

"You loved him." I said, he looked straight at me. "Right?"

"Right." He said, "Jacob?" he asked, his forehead creasing as if he was thinking, so I waited. "Do you like him?" he asked, I looked at Elijah then I began to nod.

"Yeah." I said, I ensure it sounded confident, "I mean, yeah I do. He's special."

"He's definitely special." He replied, it made me smile, then Kian laughed so I looked towards his bed as Elijah sat up, he frowned at both of us.

"You guys talking about me?" Elijah asked, I smiled as Kian almost scoffed.

"Always." He replied.

I followed the music through the corridors until I found the studio it was coming out of. Elijah had booked out one of the studios during our class with Madame Rose, he'd decided it was in his best interest not to crash Madame Rose's class, as we were all pretty certain she would be far less inviting than Arlo was.

I went to find him once it had finished, whilst Kian disappeared off somewhere. I stood in the doorway, watching as Elijah danced.

"I know you're there." He said, without turning to me, I lifted my eyes from his pointes to his face he smiled at me through the mirror.

"What are you doing?" I asked as I walked in, I let my shoe bag fall off my shoulder and onto the floor beside the door, then I walked around him, so I could lean on the barre he was facing.

"Scholarship." He replied, I frowned. "What? I don't want to pay for my second year." He said simply, I laughed.

"You're dancing en pointe." I said, he nodded,

"There are no rules for scholarship auditions." He said, I frowned. "Well, besides the clothes, the hair and the underwear rules, but they're pretty standard."

"Madame Rose told us boys had to start, and finish in flat ballet pump." I said, he frowned then stopped dancing.

"What?" he said simply, I shrugged.

"She didn't like it when I danced en pointe for my Christmas ballet audition. She believes pointe is for girls, and girls only." I said, he tutted.

"Madame Florence actually told me that she recommended I danced en pointe for the scholarship audition. She told me to use my strengths, and that's one of them." he shrugged then looked towards the stereo system as the song finished, it restarted a beat later.

"Why did you choose this song?" I asked, Elijah smiled, I saw it in the opposite mirror.

"Because it's appropriate." He said nodding, I frowned back at him. "I have no tears left to cry." He said as he turned to me, "I have figured it all out, I am in the right place, in my mind, in my body." He said,

"But you haven't had the surgery." I said, he laughed.

262

"Oh god I love you." He said, I felt my eyes widen, as he continued to laugh and laugh. "Jacob, firstly there is not just one bulk surgery. If there was, trans guys would be humping it like a dog on heat." He said, I frowned.

"Secondly, you don't have to have any of the surgeries to be happy." He added, "or at least. I don't." he said, then he sat on the floor, so I sat opposite him. "I'm not dysphoric, not really. I would like to have a dick, I'm not going to lie the thought of having a penis is something else, but the need isn't there, not really.

Sometimes I yearn it, sometimes it hurts, other times I'm pretty chill about the whole thing. My transition was seamless, my Dad practically changed pronouns overnight, he took me to the barbers for a haircut, he worked through changing my name with me. It was exactly what I wanted, I wanted to be identified as a boy, and I was. I don't need top surgery; I have nothing there for them to operate on. Bottom surgery will happen as and when, I think I'm going to wait until it's more advanced, and I don't take T, but I'm happy. I'm so happy it's unbelievable."

"That's good." I said nodding, he nodded back to me.

"Madame Florence would have actually murdered me, if I hadn't practiced it at least once this week." He said amused, I smiled.

"Can I see it?" I asked, he began to nod then stood, so I moved back until I was sitting against the mirror, I watched as he rose onto and off pointe then looked at the stereo system as the song finish, he turned away from me, and stood his hands on his hips, his right foot raised onto pointe.

I watched him take a deep breath, as the music began then he raised himself completely onto pointe, his arms rose above his head into fifth and then he went into développé, I smiled as he outstretched his leg, his frame not quivering at all, then he flawlessly moved into a pirouette section.

The ending of his dance was the beginning in reverse, it made me smile as he came out of the pirouette section, and into développé, before lowering himself from fifth, into the position he started in, he turned his head to look at me, then he began to laugh as I just looked back at him.

"Well?"

"I would not want to compete against you." I said, he laughed happily as he leant his head back, his chest raising and falling as he breathed deeply. "That was actually amazing." I said, he grinned at me, then leant down in front of me, he lifted my chin and kissed me so I began to laugh.

"You know." he said, I nodded as he ran his fingers down my cheeks. "She only said you had to start and end on flat ballet pump." He said, I met his eyes as he grinned at me. "She said nothing about the middle bit."

▾▾▾

"I need your help." I said, Max frowned at me as he turned to look at me.

"Anything." Max said nodding to me, so I nodded back as I walked into his studio.

"We have this scholarship audition coming up." I said, he continued to nod, "and we need to prepare our own piece for it. Madame Rose has stated that all boys must start, and end on ballet pump, but…" I said then tilted my head, "I, no, Elijah pointed out that she said nothing about the middle bit. I want you to choreograph a dance for me, that starts and ends on ballet pump, and is pointe in the middle."

264

"Whose Elijah?" he asked, I laughed.

"Priorities Max." I said, he smiled,

"I think I can do that."

"Will it work?" I asked, he nodded thoughtfully,

"If it was anyone else, I'd say no, but I think you can make it work." He said, I grinned at him, he grinned back.

Elijah hugged Kian tight, rocking him from side to side as they spoke into each other's ears. The hug had gone on for quite a while, and I couldn't imagine it'd end any time soon. Their rocking began to slower and then, they finally let go each other, kissing each other's cheeks then, he hugged me. He squeezed me as tight.

"Now, you better stay in touch." He said, I nodded into his shoulder. "And I want your scholarship audition sent to me, so I can watch it, I am not missing the perfected version of that dance." He said, I laughed into his ear. "And I'd love to introduce you to this amazing thing called phone sex." He whispered into my ear, I laughed out loud shaking my head at him, he grinned winking at me, then he kissed me. "Break a leg, both of you with your Pas De Deux assessments, and of course your scholarship auditions."

"You too." I said, he smiled at me, "you'll own it." I added,

"Thank you. Now I better go, get in my taxi before I miss my flight. I'll let you know when I stop in Dubai, then of course when I get back home." He said, hugging us both again. I glanced at Kian as he left, Kian sighed.

"He's in for a long flight." He said, then looked back at me. "I'm going to get a shower, get ready for Pas De Deux. Okay?" he asked, I nodded to him

"Going to touch yourself?" I asked, he laughed then began to nod in a sigh,

"Yep." He replied, then closed the door of the ensuite as I went to sit back on my bed.

"How do you feel? Are you anxious about your assessment?" Ash asked, I shook my head slowly.

"No, I'm okay with my Pas De Deux assessment, Margo's an amazing partner, we both know the sequence it should be fine."

"But?" Ash asked, I looked at him and shrugged.

"I'm wary of my scholarship audition."

"Nervous?" he asked, I nodded.

"Very. I'm not even thinking about if I get it, it's just the initial doing it."

"You know Jacob, this audition does not determent anything. You will get onto second year regardless."

"Yes." I said nodding, he nodded back. "I am aware. I'm just nervous, I suppose."

"Which is completely natural." He replied, I hummed at him. "Jacob, I want you to make sure you have breakfast on the day of your scholarship audition."

"Of course." I said nodding,

"And, if you need to take time out for any reason, whether it is to drink water, to eat a protein bar, to even go the toilet. You take it. Your teachers are well aware and will allow this. Auditioning can be a lot of pressure, a lot of stress so make sure you look after yourself the next two weeks. Okay?"

"Okay." I said nodding,

"Can you tell me about last week?"

"Last week?" I repeated, he nodded as he clicked off his pen.

"You had a visitor, didn't you?" he asked, I smiled.

"Elijah."

266

"Tell me about Elijah."

"I'm going to miss him." Margo said, as we stood on the other side of the studio, looking through the window as Kian and Abi completed their Pas De Deux assessment.

"Who?" I asked as I watched Abi go into her arabesque, because apparently, I missed her, I missed dancing Pas De Deux with her, I just, missed her.

"Elijah." She said, so I looked at her. "He brought some life into this place." She said amused, I smiled at her. "And you liked him." She added, I sighed. "Can I ask you something?"

"You already did." I replied, she elbowed me in the ribs.

"I know I probably shouldn't ask this literally minutes before an assessment, but why did you stop liking me?"

"I didn't."

"Sexually Jacob." She said, so I pointed through the window. "Abi?"

"Yeah. I slept with her. I couldn't like you anymore, not really. I mean you're hot, there is no denying that but after that… we're friends." I said warily, she nodded then she laughed.

"You just friend zoned me."

"Hard." I agreed nodding she smiled,

"You actually liked Abi?" she asked, I nodded.

"I guess so, but I fucked that up."

"And Elijah?" she asked, I stuttered. "Oh, I see, so your dick liked me, your head liked Abi, and your heart likes Elijah." She said, I frowned at her because that *didn't* sound right.

"Jacob and Margo." Arlo requested, so I looked in his direction. "Come on through." he said, Margo looked at me almost warily, then she kissed my cheek.

"Come on love. Let's Pas De Deux the shit out of this." She said, as she took my hand and walked me into the studio, we both stood in the centre, our feet in third, our arms relaxed. Madame Rose nodded to us, then to the music, I looked briefly at Margo when it began.

▾▾▾

I felt sick as I sat with the number eight pinned to my leotard. Kian was sat beside me, number six on his as we watched number one audition. The room was silent except for the extremely well-known piece of music from Swan Lake that was blasting around the room.

Number one danced it well, she didn't go a foot wrong, her pointe work was strong, I couldn't falter her but I didn't feel anything. Not until Kian knocked his knee against mine.

"Okay?" he whispered, I nodded to him as I opened my legs so I could lift the water bottle I'd set between them up to show him, he smiled at me as I took a sip out of it.

"I'm good." I said quietly,

"Do you promise?" he asked, I nodded as number one sat down, and number two took her place. He was dancing to Bluebird from Sleeping Beauty. "Elijah made me promise that I'd record your dance." He said, I smiled, "so, you have to promise to hide my phone during my audition."

"Deal." I said nodding, he nodded back to me. "I do feel slightly sick." I said, I saw worry flicker across his expression.

"Like you used to?" he asked, I shook my head.

"No, like butterflies in my stomach kind of sick. What if she stops me halfway and tells me I can't dance?"

"She can't." he whispered back, I frowned as he looked towards the table where the ballet school people were sat. "She's not in charge." He added, I nodded.

"Number three please." I heard, so I leant forward looking towards the girl's row as Margo stood up. She wore a tutu, white with black ribbons around the hem. Her pointes were tied the neatest I'd yet seen, her bun the same,

"Wow." Kian murmured,

"Wow." I agreed. We both jumped when the music began.

"Thank you number seven." They said, Abi nodded to them then curtseyed before retaking her seat. I felt as Kian squeezed my knee. "Number eight." They requested, I took a deep breath, a long swig of water then I stood. I placed my pointes down in front of their table then stood in my place, every person on the table looked up at me exactly at the same time.

"Jacob Kennedy." I said, there were a few hums as they nodded to me.

"When you're ready Jacob." The man with the American accent said, I nodded to him, bowed then walked into my position.

I swallowed hard as my music began, Max had chosen *Beautiful Trauma*, and we had lay our heads alongside each other on his studio floor listening to it on repeat.

Around the fourth time, I got it, and like Elijah had said, it felt insanely appropriately, after the fifth time we began to dance. Max had started it simple, and had told me to go through from first to fifth position with my arms,

269

whilst remaining in first position with my feet. I looked up towards were my hands met, then I dropped them down, and walked towards my pointes, lowering myself to the floor and taking off my pumps, replacing them with my pointes, I wound the ribbons up my ankles, then I spun, so quick that I could stand up and I began to dance.

Max had put a lot of extension into the dance, as that was my greatest attribute and we'd have had to have been mad not to include it, he'd stated I'd extend a lot, I'd show off my balance, and the length of my legs, and then, I'd kill with the pirouette section.

Which, I believed I did, I closed my eyes as I turned, around and around, going from a pirouette into a grande pirouette à la seconde, lowering my body, until the floor was what brought me to a stop. I stayed there for a beat or two, looking around the room as I did, until I looked directly at Kian who held his phone at chest height, he wasn't watching me dance through the phone, so I smiled at him then I stood, took a run and jumped into a jeté, I took a deep breath in when I landed, *because* I'd landed it and I continued around, until I was stood before them again.

I rose up onto my pointes and I ran my arms through first to fifth position again, then lowered myself to sit on the floor. I rose my right onto pointe, unwinding the ribbon from around my ankle, then taking the shoe off, before raising my left, I did the same then put my pumps back on, standing myself back up, raising onto my toe then into an arabesque. I held it until the music had officially finished, then I lowered my leg, walked forward, picked up my pointes and held them to my chest as I took my bow.

"Jacob." Madame Rose said, I whipped my head in the direction of her voice, "what did I tell you?" she added in the annoyed voice you do when you have company and you're trying to pretend that you're not pissed to the high heavens.

"You told me, all boys must start and end in their ballet pump." I said, "which I did." I added, the table conferred in front of me

"Jacob." She repeated, a little angrier.

"He is correct." The man with the French accent said, so I looked towards him. "He did in fact start, and end in his ballet pump, and although this is obviously a bylaw, he did not break it."

"Thank you Jacob." The woman in the Australian accent said, I nodded to her. "Please take your seat." She continued, I bowed to her again, then took my seat back beside Kian. I felt as my racing heart began to slower, as I let a long breath out. Kian began to rub my back.

"That was awesome." He whispered, I smiled then leant my head on his shoulder.

Max, Cameron, Frankie and Cory all stood huddled around me at the kitchen table, watching the video Kian had taken on my phone, they hadn't uttered a word since I'd pressed play, they simply watched, and bit their tongue if there were any critiques.

I looked up at them when it finished, rolling my neck looking at each of them in turn, I landed on Cameron.

"I am not the ballet genius here." he said, they all laughed as they retook their seats around the kitchen table.

"You can say that again." Max said, as he went back to making his burrito that he'd abandoned when I stated I had a video of my audition.

"Your choreography?" Frankie asked, Max nodded. "Can tell." He said more to Cory, "développé, arabesques and a pirouette section in the bridge. Yeah, that's Maxwell Whelan's choreography."

"Predictable apparently." Max said, I smirked at him.

"Have you thought about what school you'll go to?" Cory asked, then waved his fork at me, "if you get it. I mean?"

"There were a few." I said, they all began to nod.

"I always dreamed of going to Paris." Max said, Frankie and Cory sighed in agreement.

"Or New York. The New York ballet would've been something else." Frankie said, they all nodded as one, I looked at Cameron as he rolled his eyes,

"Where would you like to go Jacob?" he asked,

"Australia." I said, then turned to look at Cory. "Would you recommend?" I added, Cory nodded, it looked like he didn't even need to think.

"Jacob it is an experience of a lifetime." He said, then looked around the table, because he needed to gain permission from my parents.

"I wouldn't go without you guys." I said to Cameron, then Max. "There would be no way I would move to Australia without you both."

"You danced amazingly Jacob. The choreography merely complimented you." Max said, I smiled at him, he smiled right back.

"Oh, not to take the spotlight or anything…" Cory said, then looked at Frankie as he began to nod.

"We've been approved to adopt." Frankie finished with, we gasped as one.

"We're going to meet her next week, then hopefully we'll get the ball rolling."

"Her?" Cameron asked, they both nodded.

272

"A little girl. You know her actually," Cory said to Max, he managed to look extremely confused back to him. "She's in your beginner's ballet."

"Melody?" I said, Cory smiled at me as he nodded.

"Melody." He repeated, I saw as Max began to nod because he remembered her.

"That's great news." Cameron said, "I'm so happy for everyone at this table tonight." He said,

"Why are you happy for Max?" I asked, Cameron threw some cheese at me, I began to laugh as he did.

I sat up late with Cameron after Cory and Frankie had left, and Max had gone to bed. I had originally planned to go back to the boarding house but it had turned ten, then eleven and by then it was practically midnight and I'd missed curfew.

"I have one question." Cameron said, I looked at him across the couch as he nursed a can of coke.

"Okay?" I replied,

"Do you want to go to Australia because that boy you like is there?" he asked, then turned to look at me. I shook my head as he met my eyes.

"No, that'd totally just be a plus point." I said, Cameron smiled.

"Like heated seats in a car?" he asked, I laughed but nodded.

"Like heated seats in a car." I agreed, "how did you know I liked Elijah?" I asked, he laughed so much he almost choked on the sip of coke he took.

"Max mentioned that all you could talk about in your rehearsals was Elijah. Dead give-away son." He said, I sighed as he laughed. "Tell me why you want to go to Australia." He said, I frowned lightly. "Persuade me that I

273

also want to go." he said then turned on the seat, sitting cross-legged and facing me, I copied.

"May I start with the weather...?"

▾▾▾

"Ront de jambe." Madame Rose snapped, whilst twirling her wrist to indict the speed we should be going at. "Keep it up." She ordered, "ront de jambe en l'air." She ordered, I sighed as I overly leant against the barre, Kian was stood beside me, also overly using the barre.

"Stand up straight." Madame Rose snapped, we both did, "do not become lazy just because the term is coming to an end." She said, I sighed as Kian did, then we began to laugh. "Girls, Relevé on the barre, boys centre floor." She said, so we moved, I caught Margo's smirk as I found my place and listened to the sequence of instructions Madame Rose was giving us.

Margo always began to giggle as we stepped as one bowing and curtseying respectfully, at the end of Madame Rose's lesson. She for some reason always lost it, and today was no different, although she was silenced pretty quickly by Madame Rose's hand.

"First years." She said, we all waited nervously for what she was possibly going to say, "I would like to make you aware that your Pas De Deux results have been listed, alongside the recipients of the Scholarship." She said. "I do not want to see you rushing to read it. I want the corridors to remain as orderly as normal." She said, then she dismissed us.

I looked at Kian, seeing his nod, as he looked across to Margo who almost nodded. We walked out of the studio, got out of view of the door then we began to run.

274

We dodged second years as they came back the other way, and avoided Arlo narrowly, we heard his half attempt of telling us to slow down but he either gave up, or we were too far away to hear it. Kian reached the board first, he ran his finger down the Pas De Deux results, he tapped it then nodded.

"Acceptable." He said, Margo and I looked over his shoulders,

"I can live with that." Margo said nodding, I began to nod with her,

"That is quite good." I said, as Kian moved along the wall,

"Jacob?" he said, so I turned to look at him, he nodded his head towards the wall so I went to him, reading what he was.

First Year Scholarship is awarded to;
JACOB KENNEDY

Chapter 15

Cameron was the only other person awake when I finally got around to waking up. I'd manoeuvred the maze of people sleeping on my bedroom floor and managed to not step on, or wake any of them up as I went to the bathroom.

I decided to then go downstairs, as I didn't want to have to fight my way back into bed. Cameron was walking around with a bin bag when I reached the living room, the doors to the other half of the room were still closed as he picked up cans and other debris that had been left around the place.

"Quite a party." Cameron said, I looked towards him, he smiled. "Hung over?"

"Probably." I said, he laughed.

"Your father is." He said simply, I smiled as I leant back against the computer desk. "He woke up. Swore at me and went back to sleep."

"Yeah. That sounds like Max." I said, he nodded smiling at me, so I smiled back,

"Are you ready for this Jacob?" he asked. I shrugged lightly.

"Connor said he'd stay today. Pack with me. Whether he still will in his state is debatable, but..." I said, then took a deep breath in, "yeah, yeah I'm ready for this." I said, he nodded to me then hugged my shoulder, kissing the side of my head.

"Either pick up a bin bag, or get a shower." He said, I laughed.

"That bad?"

"You smell of ale." He said, then he smirked at me. "Funny really as I'm sure you were drinking spirits. I'm going to make a killer fry up. Which I know will kill off my twin brother, but remedy my husband." He said raising his eyebrow at me, I laughed.

"Well, I guess I'll go and get a shower then."

I could smell bacon when I got out the shower, it grew stronger as I got closer and closer to my room. I opened the door to my bedroom then sighed, as I had definitely forgotten about the maze of people on my floor. Although, now Connor had woken up. He was sat, his back against my bed rubbing his eyes as Kian remained asleep, his head now on Connor's lap.

"Morning." I whispered, he looked at me, it took a moment for his eyes to adjust.

"I think I drank your house." He said, I laughed, stepping into a t-shirt and a pair of joggers then sitting beside him.

277

"I think you had help." I said, looking towards Margo who slept at the foot of my bed.

"Was a good party." He said, I laughed. "I'm going to fucking miss you." He said, so I looked at him.

"Yeah, I'm going to fucking miss you too." I said, he sighed then kissed my shoulder, so I lifted his head and kissed his lips lightly.

"If he woke up now, he'd be so confused."

"He'd think you went poly on him." I said, looking down at Kian as he continued to sleep.

"God I need to pee." Connor said as we both looked down at Kian, I laughed.

"Wake him up then." I said, Connor groaned, I grinned at him as he sighed.

I went downstairs again, once Connor had gotten enough will to move Kian and go the toilet. I waited for him at the top of the stairs, then went down with him, watching his confusion as he saw Caspar, then Cameron.

"I must've drank far more than I thought." Connor said as Caspar continued to moan at Cameron for making food.

"Come grab something Jacob." Cameron said, "and Connor, meet my twin brother Caspar."

"Twin?" Connor repeated, I nodded to him as he frowned then came to sit beside me at the kitchen table. "Did I meet you last night?"

"You did." Caspar said amused, "you asked me if I smoked weed because I looked like the kind of guy that would." He said, Connor looked at me mildly alarmed.

"You were pretty drunk by the time the adults arrived." I said, he whimpered lightly then began to eat the bacon sandwich Cameron had offered up to him. Frankie and

Cory were the next to appear, both looking far too fresh as they'd obviously slept on our couch.

"You're a good wife Cameron." Cory said as he took his own bacon sandwich and took a seat.

"Thank you. I pride myself on my housewifery." Cameron replied, then placed a variety of different strength coffees on the table. Kian appeared once we'd moved to sit on the couches, he looked pretty unhappy with the idea of being awake, as he sat beside Connor, leaning his head on Connor's shoulder. They whispered to each other until Connor laughed and threw the blanket that was at our feet over Kian's raised knees.

"Food?" Cameron asked, Kian shook his head as he groaned burying his head further into Connor's shoulder.

"So, when do you go then?" Cory asked, I looked at Cameron as he blew on his coffee cup.

"We leave the day after next." He said nodding to me, "layover in Singapore, then onto Australia." He said,

"Classes start after the summer?" Frankie asked, I shook my head.

"Classes start in July." I said, Cory laughed.

"Oh yeah, school terms are completely different." He said then looked at Frankie. "The start of the year, is the start of their school year. You'll be going in on term three? Right?" he asked, I nodded.

"Still in your first year?" Kian asked, I smirked at him slightly but nodded all the same.

"I won't do my end of term assessments until December now." I said, he tutted as he raised his head so he could lean his chin on Connor's shoulder.

"Mines in like two weeks." He said, Connor smiled.

"And will you have sobered up by then?" he asked, Kian pulled his tongue as Max appeared.

"Oh sleeping beauty." Frankie said, Max raised his middle finger to him. It made me laugh.

"Do you want food?" Cameron asked, Max began to nod. "Bacon?" he added, Max hummed then went and took Cameron's seat once he'd stood to go into the kitchen.

"Do you know where you're going to live yet?" Cory asked, as Cameron came back, he passed a plate to Max, who sat up better on the chair to let Cameron sit on his knee.

"Sam's house." Cameron said as he looked at Max, Max nodded.

"Sam's letting us live there whilst he studies then we'll figure everything else out."

"Any jobs?" Frankie asked, Max smiled as he picked at the bacon. "You've got a job?"

"I have. Sam's starting up his company and has asked me to dance in it."

"You've never been a part of a company." Frankie said, he sounded mildly surprised, as Max nodded to him.

"I know. I'm pretty excited for it."

"And yourself?" Cory asked, Cameron laughed.

"I won't be working for the first few months, a bit of a holiday, but I'm going to be in a revival of The Boy from Oz come November." He said, then smiled at Max as he continued to pick through the sandwich.

"I'm devastated though." Max said, we all frowned at him, especially me, as we'd had multiple conversations in the last few weeks that stated that moving to Australia was the best-*fucking*-thing that could have happened to all of us, with Max's company place, Cameron's almost instant casting in a musical and my schooling. "I won't get to watch you two attempt at being parents." he said, Frankie and Cory both gasped at him.

"Actually, yeah. I'm pretty devastated about that too." Cameron said thoughtfully, I smiled at him as he winked at me.

Frankie and Cory, drove Kian and Margo back to the boarding house when they both felt as if they'd sobered up enough to face the world. Max went for a shower, whilst Cameron continued to tidy up with the help of Caspar, and then progressed to moving things we were taking into boxes, whilst Connor and I stood in my room, packing away all my things, whether I was taking them or not.

"Oh my god. We were little." Connor said, I turned my head to look in the direction he was stood, he held my framed picture of us, the bubble wrap poised in his other hand. "Pride?" he asked, I nodded.

"We were sixteen." I said, then sat on my bed, he sat next to me,

"This is my second favourite picture." He said, I frowned at him,

"What's your first?" I asked, he laughed as he took his phone off my bedside table, he scrolled through it, then turned it to me. "Oh my god." I said laughing as I took his phone.

We were nine, definitely nine because we were at the holiday camp, the home had taken us to when it was being renovated. We were on the beach, both in just our trunks. I still had my thin wired glasses that I wore for too long during childhood. I had loved them because they had little cartoon characters over the arms, and I wouldn't change them, not until I was eleven and Ste advised it'd be wise too.

Connor had his cap on sideways, the peak to the left, he had a spade in his left hand, holding it up as if to show it off, whilst I had the bucket, it was full of sand, and you could see the sand falling out of it in the photograph. I remembered it was Adam who had taken the picture, he'd have been thirteen, maybe fourteen and he had been put in charge of the little digital camera for that holiday.

"That's definitely my favourite picture."

"We'll definitely be recreating it in Australia." I said, Connor raised his eyebrow,

"You think I'll be able to get to Australia?" he asked, I nodded to him.

"Definitely, I will be paying for you to come and see me, at least twice a year, and with your boyfriend, I'm sure he'd not miss the chance to watch the Sydney ballet."

"True. He hasn't shut up about it, since you announced your choice." He said amused, I laughed quietly, then I hugged him tight, and he hugged me back.

▾▾▾

"Welcome to my humble adobe." Sam said as he turned the key in the large door that appeared to be just made out of windows.

In fact, the entire house appeared to be made out of windows but there was no way you could see in, that intrigued me as I walked into the house, then I lost my breath.

"Obviously, this house isn't lived in. Live in it for me, put pictures up, make it a mess." Sam said amused to Max and Cameron as I walked into the kitchen.

There were no walls, no doors everything was open, you could walk from the living room to the kitchen with ease, the whole house had wooden floors and white walls, with the occasional exposed brick pillars to separate the rooms.

"Oh he's found the pool." Sam said, so I turned from looking at the fridge, to looking out of the big glass windows that lead to the pool. I walked towards them, pushing the doors open and standing outside. "It's heated." Sam said as he came to stand beside me, I moaned.

"I want to make as much money as you do. Some day." I said, Sam laughed so I looked at him. "Where are you going to live?" I asked, he smiled.

"I have a flat."

"A flat?" I repeated, "that doesn't sound right."

"A condo." He said amused, I laughed. "I prefer it there, it's smaller, a better size for just me." he said, I nodded to him as Max and Cameron came out onto the patio.

Sam began to tell them important things about the house, and apparently on how to manage the pool, so I walked away from them. Walking around the pool and leaning on the fence, looking out of Australia.

Frankie and Cory had dropped us at the airport. Cory telling us everything, and anything he could remember about being in Australia, places to go, to eat, to see. The ballets, the beach.

Everything, he'd spoken for the entire journey then he let Frankie say his piece at the airport. Where he stood, hugging Max tight, and talking quietly to him for the good part of ten minutes. Caspar had followed behind, with Connor in his car, and had almost not let Cameron go as they hugged themselves.

I had squeezed Connor to every inch of his life, as I'd already said my goodbyes to Kian and Margo the night before in the boarding house. I'd had a session with Ash, more of a social call than a therapy session, where we just spoke for the hour and he wished me well. Arlo had been outside the therapy room when I left, he hugged me tight, as had Miss Olivia.

Madame Rose wished me luck and gave me an affectionate pat on the shoulder. I'd spent the night in the room I shared with Kian, we ordered pizza and drank sugary drinks. He made me promise I'd tell him when I arrived, and if I didn't, he'd be on the phone to Elijah to make sure I had in fact arrived.

"I'm going to go call Frankie, let him and the rest of them know we're here." Max said, I turned to nod to him.

"Want something to eat?" Cameron asked, Sam laughed.

"Give over sweetheart, first lunch here is definitely on me." he said, Cameron smiled at him. "Besides we need to talk in depth about your new role, no?" he said, Cameron nodded then pointed towards the house. I shook my head, so he left me on the patio. I looked out over Australia and took a big deep breath in. Then, I let it out.

▼▼▼

I watched as the little loading circle went around, and around, I begged it to connect as I looked between that and the clock on the wall.

I could hear the noise of Cameron and Max making breakfast, and knew they'd be calling me down pretty soon, I looked back at my computer, it connected.

It had connected to Connor's flat. It was pretty dark, but I'd figured out it was at least eleven back home, Connor was sat in the middle of the screen, he seemed as happy to see me, as I was to see him. Kian was sat to his left, Margo to his right. They all waved together as if they'd been practicing it.

284

"Is that a tan Jacob?" Margo teased, I laughed, stretching my arms out in front of me as I did.

"Oh. I think it is." I said nodding, "we have a pool. I have been using it." I said simply, they all laughed. "Although I heard a suspicious splash a few nights ago, and don't know how much I want to use the pool now." I said, then smiled at them, they all smiled back.

"Max and Cameron are like my relationship goals." Kian said, I saw Connor's eyes widen, "just so you know." he added, Connor appeared to panic.

"Is it the first day of school?" Connor asked, as if to change the subject, I nodded.

"How could you tell?"

"The leotard." Connor replied, I smiled.

"You wear black, that's exciting." Kian added, I laughed as I looked down myself.

"Only for repertoire." I said, Kian nodded to me.

"Jacob breakfast." Cameron shouted, I sighed towards the door.

"Don't worry. We better go. Curfew is calling." Margo said, "and I'm sure these two want to get into each other's pants. I miss you Jacob, just so you know." she said, I laughed.

"I miss you too." I said, then blew a kiss to the screen.

"Break a leg Jacob." Kian said, then blew a kiss back, then moved out of the screen. Margo followed.

"How is it?" Connor asked, he was looking over his shoulder, but turned back to me as he finished the question.

"It's amazing." I said nodding, "honestly. it's always so warm though, and that I don't know if I can deal with." I said, he laughed. "How's Cory and Frankie?" I asked, "and Melody?"

"Not too bad actually. She's a great kid, Frankie's teaching Max's classes, you know that so she goes to that, and they're quite a nice little family. No squabbles yet." He said amused, I laughed.

"How are you?" I asked, he nodded to me.

"I'm okay." He said, then he smiled. "I'm good."

"Yeah." I agreed, "So am I."

Max drove me to school, as we'd all agreed that I wouldn't board, especially with a house like we had, it wouldn't be necessary to board. We'd figured out how I got from the house to the school, but they'd both insisted they drove me on my first day, and I had no complaints.

"Ready?" Max asked, I nodded as I took a deep breath in, "it won't be that different from London."

"Just warmer." Cameron replied, "are you aware it's winter right now? We're in Australian winter. I'm wearing a t-shirt." He said, I smiled at him as Max rolled his eyes.

"What are you two doing today?" I asked,

"I have rehearsal." Max replied turning to look at me, "Sam wants me to take my pointes, so it could be exciting." He said, I nodded then looked at Cameron.

"I'm going shopping, for food mostly but you never know." he said, I nodded again.

"I have repertoire, and this afternoon I believe is the mixed class. I will start Pas De Deux next week, after my new teachers have assessed me enough to give me a partner." I said, then took a deep breath. "Right. I'm going to go." I said, "Definitely." I added then opened the door.

I stepped out of the car, then waved to them both, they waved back and waited until I'd walked into the building to drive away. I had met with the Principal earlier in the week, he had seemed very nice, and had sat and spoke through everything with me.

He answered all my many questions and talked about the records that had come from the National Ballet School. We talked for hours, and I had felt much better following it.

I however, still didn't actually know my way around the school, so I walked aimlessly looking into different studios until I found First Year repertoire. I let myself in, taking a place on the barre, removing my joggers and putting on my pumps then I began to warm up. Working through the barre exercises without looking at anyone else.

I kept my eyes focused forwards, so I didn't think too hard about Kian not being on the barre in front of me, then I met eyes with the teacher. He came in looking happy, in his own black leotard and grey shorts. He ran his hand through his hair as he took off his bracelets that filled his arm, and his watch. He put them into a mug then began to scroll through his music.

"Morning boys." He called, he didn't get a response so I looked around the room, then back at him as he rolled his eyes. "G'day." He said, they all replied. "Welcome back, let's get straight to work." He said, then pressed play on the music. An average warm up track came on, then he came over to me.

"Jacob?" he asked, then smiled. "I presume." He added, I nodded to him. "Master Chase." He said, then held his hand out to me, so I shook it. "But these guys just tend to call me Chase." He said, I nodded to him. "I've heard a lot about you from Arlo. He spoke really highly of you." He said, I smiled. "Right, onto the floor boys." Chase called then went to stand at the front of the class, I took a deep breath then moved to the floor, watching Chase as he demonstrated what he wanted us to do.

I looked to my left, then sighed because Kian was *not* going to be there, like Arlo wasn't teaching the class. I opened my arms into second like Chase had done, then prepared my feet. My arm was knocked down just before I went into the sequence, so I turned then I laughed happily.

"Elijah." I said, he grinned at me, wrapping his arms around my waist and hugging me, so I hugged him back.

"How are you doing?" Elijah asked, I nodded to him.

"Just getting used to Kian not being around." I said, he nodded as he stood beside me.

"It's okay." He said, then he winked, "because you've got me, and I'm better." He said, I grinned at him, as he opened his arms into second, so I also did, he knocked his fingers against mine then went into the sequence, so I did too.

EPILOGUE

I watched Max as he ran on to take his bow, he rose up onto his pointes as he did, then smiled at the applause as he ran to his final place. I could see Elijah stood in the opposite wing, he was pulling faces at me, and I was doing it back, trying to keep our laughter quiet, as we'd been told off many times for our laughing in the wings.

He looked surprised when the technician told him it was his turn to bow, I smiled as I watched him run on, he rose onto his pointes at the back of the stage then pirouetted down the centre, until he reached the front and he bowed. The audience cheered loudly for him, like every night so he bowed again, then ran to his side.

"Ready Jacob?" the technician on my side asked, I nodded to him, then prepared myself to run on, I counted a few beats then ran to the centre of the stage.

I stood for a few moments just letting the applause set in, then I continued down to the front, and took my bow, once, twice then a third time. I stood up straight, looking around the audience even though they were completely blacked out.

Cameron was definitely in there, somewhere. As his The Boy from Oz contract had ended last month, and we'd finally managed to persuade him to come and see our ballet.

Sam was also in there, but by now he was probably at the side of the stage. He hadn't missed a performance yet, not since he started his company four years ago, he was at every company performance without fail.

Connor and Kian would be in the audience next week. Connor had sent me his flight confirmation last week, informing me that he was coming to see me, Kian had done exactly the same with Elijah.

Frankie and Cory had been to see us a few months ago, on opening week, they'd brought Melody along with them, she'd begged Max, Elijah and I to sign her first pointe shoes that she would need to replace soon anyway, so we did. She had said she loved Sam's version of Cinderella, and Elijah's portrayal of Cinders had received numerous compliments from her.

I reached down to pick a rose off the stage in front of me, I held it in my hands smiling at it, as the rest of the company joined me at the front of the stage, Max on my right, Elijah on my left. Max squeezed my hand, smiling at me, so I smiled back, because even though I'd taken his principal role in Sam's company two years ago when I'd finished school, he still loved to dance in his ballets, and to

290

dance with me on stage, although he sometimes bantered for the lead roles with me.

I turned from Max, to Elijah he'd joined the company when I had, Sam declaring that Elijah was the only person who could dance his Cinderella, his Romeo and Juliet, and his Peter Pan. Sam loved Elijah almost as much as I did *even* now that our relationship had met its natural end. Elijah lifted my hand and kissed the back of it, winking at me, so I squeezed tight.

He was the only person who knew that I was proposing tonight, to the girl, *now* woman who sat beside Cameron in the stalls.

After the National Ballet School's company auditions Abi had been offered practically the entire world. She had messaged me asking what I thought of Australia and I told her that it was an opportunity of a lifetime

She flew out within the month, started in the Australian company whilst I finished my second year. We met up for a milkshake, then a meal, then to watch a ballet – *which* was totally a date.

And now, it was three years later and I was going to propose to her tonight, on the beach because according to Elijah that was romantic *af*.

I squeezed Max and Elijah's hands at the same time, then lifted them up between us.

I wear a waist coat, royal blue, six buttons, a glittered collar but not in a stupid way in a totally cool, and one hundred percent manly way. They're accompanied by tights, which by the way are totally not stuffed and on my feet are peach strong pointe ballet shoes, they shine when the lights hit them, the ribbons perfectly tied around my ankles, the shoes immaculate.

I take another bow.